Readers love
TA MOORE

Bone to Pick

"TA Moore brings readers a solid, well written, suspenseful mystery in *Bone to Pick*. The plot is multi-layered and peppered with suspicious characters who had me fooled almost to the very end."

—The Novel Approach

"*Bone to Pick* is a great mystery that is sure to pull readers in from the beginning."

—Top 2 Bottom Reviews

Liar, Liar

"*Liar, Liar* is a great suspense with some twisty moments and really fun characters. I can definitely recommend this one, particularly if you are a fan of romantic suspense and like your heroes a little bit outside the box."

—Joyfully Jay

"I highly recommend this story to everyone in the mood for something tense, action packed, and oddly romantic."

—Love Bytes

Dog Days

"Wow. *Dog Days* turned out to be even more than I expected… Trust me when I say you won't regret reading this… not if you love twists, turns, and horror."

—Rainbow Book Reviews

"I was completely sucked into this story right from the beginning. I couldn't put the book down. I was completely fascinated with the lore and how the world is set up and the background for each character."

—Molly Lolly Reviews

By TA Moore

Bone to Pick
Every Other Weekend
Liar, Liar
Wanted – Bad Boyfriend

WOLF WINTER
Dog Days
Stone the Crows

Published by Dreamspinner Press
www.dreamspinnerpress.com

TA MOORE

EVERY OTHER WEEKEND

DREAMSPINNER PRESS

Published by

DREAMSPINNER PRESS

5032 Capital Circle SW, Suite 2, PMB# 279, Tallahassee, FL 32305-7886 USA
www.dreamspinnerpress.com

Every Other Weekend
© 2018 TA Moore.

Cover Art
© 2018 Bree Archer.
http://www.breearcher.com
Cover content is for illustrative purposes only and any person depicted on the cover is a model.

Trade Paperback ISBN: 978-1-64080-751-8
Digital ISBN: 978-1-64080-750-1
Library of Congress Control Number: 2018934251
Trade Paperback published October 2018
v. 1.0

Printed in the United States of America
∞
This paper meets the requirements of
ANSI/NISO Z39.48-1992 (Permanence of Paper).

I'd like to thank my mum, who is my faithful reader,
and the Five who've always had my back.
Also Penny, who knew it had to be a parrot!

CHAPTER ONE

THE SOUND of his phone as it rattled to life... somewhere... jolted Clayton awake. He rolled over, silk sheets cold as they tangled around his legs, and stretched the full length of himself in his bed. A glance at the clock showed the minute hand just shy of five o'clock.

"Hell," he muttered. No one ever called about anything good at five in the morning.

He kicked the sheets off his legs and scrambled out of bed. His phone was still in his jeans where he'd dropped them the night before. It buzzed resentfully as he fished it out and thumbed Accept on the call.

"Yeah?" he said.

When he turned back to the bed, he saw last night starfished over the mattress in the sleep of the... well, not innocent, but responsibility-free. Last night snored gently into the pillow. Clayton grimaced and padded quietly to the bedroom door as Maureen's rasp sighed in his ear.

"It's too early," she acknowledged. It wasn't easy to tell if she meant that as an apology or a judgment.

"I'm up," Clayton said. He tucked the phone under his ear as he headed into the kitchen. "If this is about Jane's case, I told her going in that we'd have to commit for the long haul. On paper—"

"Not Jane," Maureen said. He heard the suck and exhale as she drew on a cigarette. "New case."

Aw shit.

Clayton pulled the fridge open. The backdraft of cold that flowed out of the white box made his balls squeeze up tight to his body and chased the last dregs of sleep out of his head. He shivered and grabbed the carafe of cold-brew coffee so he could bump the door shut again.

"I already told you I can't take on any more pro bono cases," he said. "I'm sorry, but they don't pay—literally."

She snorted harshly. "I've seen your car, Clayton. It's not like you're hurting."

"No, I'm not." Clayton poured out a mug of coffee and took a swig. It was strong enough to make him grimace. He carried it over to the long glass windows that dominated one wall of the apartment and looked down at the traffic that flowed like water in the street below. "I don't intend to start either. No more cases."

"One more."

Clayton frowned. His reflection mugged the expression back at him, all sharp bones and carved hollows. "I'm not haggling."

"She's got a busted arm, a five-year-old, and no place to go," Maureen rhymed off. For a woman with a forty-a-day habit and an asthma inhaler, she could talk quickly enough when she wanted to. "If we don't give her something she can use, I don't know what she's going to do. So one more case."

Just say no. You have billable hours to make. With the topic at hand, Clayton wasn't sure if he should call the voice on his shoulder an angel or a demon. It definitely had the pointed tones of the firm's senior partner and Clayton's mentor, Daniel Baker.

"She asked for you," Maureen said, as though she could hear his internal debate.

"Me?"

"By name," Maureen said. "Clayton, she thinks you can help her."

"One meeting," Clayton conceded. He always made billable hours. Real estate ebbed and flowed, crime stats rose and fell, but love always died. "I'll give her advice, get her a plan, and you get her a lawyer who has time for her case."

Maureen made a noise that could, optimistically, pass for agreement and hung up before he could hedge any more. It was hard to hold it against her. After nearly twenty years at the head of a battered women's shelter, she made the most of what she got.

The day's schedule ran through Clayton's head as he drained the cold coffee and headed back into the bedroom. His afternoon meetings were set in stone, but the morning was more modular. Skip lunch, push back a meeting with a junior associate, relocate his coffee with Baker to the office instead of the ridiculously pretentious tearoom that Baker liked, and his day should fall back into place without a wrinkle.

If he skipped the gym that night, he might even be able to have a life.

The self-pity dropped into his mind just as he opened the bedroom door and got an eyeful of last night's bare ass and long legs.

He snorted at himself as his cock decided it had warmed up enough to twitch with interest.

No time for that.

"I've been called in to work." He gave last night's ass a slap on the way past the bed to make the man groan and stretch and scratch. "So you need to shift."

Last night—God, he had to have had a name, but Clayton realized it was gone from his head—rolled over and rubbed his hands over his pillow-creased face. "What time is it?"

"There's coffee in the kitchen." Clayton hooked a mesh shirt from the back of a chair and tossed it at the bed. Last night batted it clumsily out of the air and tangled it around his fingers. "Sorry. Duty calls."

He left the guy to get dressed while he went into the bathroom and let the shower's heavy jets pummel the night before out of him. Glitter, sweat, and the stickiness of come washed down the drain, and the hot water sucked the tiredness out of his muscles and shoulders.

By the time he got out of the shower and got dressed, the rangy young man who'd been a shot of seduction in tight leather pants had turned into a chatty art student from Wisconsin in gym clothes. He'd helped himself to coffee and toast.

"I had a good time last night," he said through a mouthful of bread and marmalade. He grinned cockily and pointed at a bit of paper on the table. A string of numbers was scrawled across the back of a Chinese menu. "I figured if you wanted to do it again some time, you could call me?"

"I might just do that."

He wouldn't. He never did. It wouldn't be a one-night stand if they met again. But that seemed a bit harsh to point out before the sun was up. So he stuck the menu on the fridge instead. "I've got to deal with work first, though."

There was something about the way last night looked at him that suggested he had a good idea of what Clayton wasn't saying. But he didn't push it. It wasn't as though Clayton had made any promises he hadn't kept.

Instead he just brushed a goodbye kiss over Clayton's mouth and let himself out. Clayton licked the taste of orange and second thoughts off his lips as he listened for the click of the front door. Then he checked his watch and made a face at the time. If he wanted to pull this off, he needed to get going.

NADINE GRAHAM was a short, not-quite-young woman who came with lots of boobs, blonde hair, and blue denim. Her clothes were expensive, with painted-on jeans and cut-down-to-there T-shirts, and her jewelry was all clunky pretty plastic and cheap metal—except her wedding ring, a white-gold band with diamonds that didn't need a fancy cut to make them look bigger or a magnifying glass to see. Something to make it clear she was taken.

There was a tight look around her eyes that hinted Clayton wasn't the only one who had second thoughts about his morning's choices.

Sure enough she gave him a quick, uncomfortable smile as he folded his long body into a chair meant for someone smaller and set his briefcase down next to him.

"I… I think I made a mistake," Nadine said. Her eyes flickered around the room, at the chipped walls and "This is Consent" posters. "I shouldn't be here."

"No one should be here," Clayton said. He glanced at the plastered arm she held balanced awkwardly in her lap as though she weren't quite used to the bulk of it. The cast had a bit of wear to it, so it wasn't new, but no one had written on it yet. Clayton filed that away. Most people had at least a few friends with Sharpies who'd insist on scrawling something—a heart, a "Get Well Soon," or, if you were a guy, a cock and balls. "Sometimes it's just the safest place they have."

Nadine folded her arms as though she could hide the cast and picked at it absently with her candy-pink nails. "I'm not… I'm sure it is," she said. "It's just not… you wouldn't understand."

Clayton shifted back in the too-small, understuffed chair. It still felt odd to consult with a client while wearing jeans and his old college sweater, but a suit and tie just made people at the shelter uncomfortable.

"I'm not the police, and I'm not Child Services," he said. "I'm just a lawyer. If you don't want to do something, I can't make you do it. All I'm here to do today is give you information on your options. If you want me to."

She gave him a sharp look out of ridiculously blue eyes. The flicker of shrewdness belonged to a woman who looked less worn down. "And then?"

"Up to you."

She folded her lip between her teeth and finally she nodded. "Okay."

Clayton ran through a quick and dirty short list for her—the top ten things to do if you're leaving an abusive husband. He also outlined her legal recourse under the law regarding her marital status and custody arrangements. Laid out bare, no padding to cushion the blow, it sounded brutally unencouraging. But it was still better than a lie.

Nadine listened in silence until he got to the end, and then she choked out a wholly unconvincing laugh.

"I'm sorry," she said quickly, one hand cupped over her mouth. "I didn't mean to... this just isn't me. It isn't us. We're not, we're not like people like that. He's not a monster. I'm not a victim."

It wasn't Clayton's job to push her into anything. God knew, it wouldn't work. He still had to fill the silence.

"I'm a divorce lawyer, Mrs. Graham," he said finally. "I deal with a lot of broken marriages. Mostly they aren't monsters or victims, just people who can't do it anymore."

Through her fingers, he caught the edges of a bitter smile. "How many of them are in a—Jesus Christ—women's shelter?"

"Some."

Nadine looked away from him and gnawed her lower lip until the lipstick came off and he could see the puffy bruise underneath. Her eyes kept flicking around the space as though the doors were locked and she needed a way out.

"You think I should leave him, right?" she said. "I don't blame you. I think I should leave him. Except, what if I can't do that? What would I do? He's... he takes care of me and Harry. I'm useless on my own, always have been."

She said that as though it were a fact, rhymed it off like a date learned in history.

A pointedly loud voice interrupted the conversation as, from the other side of the door, Maureen rambled on about the many good, imaginary qualities of one of her dogs. The one she had with her fought nightmares, apparently, ate them like cotton candy.

"Dogs don't like cotton candy." The voice was young and dubious but intrigued.

"Bacon cotton candy," Maureen countered promptly. "Dogs love it."

Nadine unfolded herself—Clayton hadn't realized how much she had hunched in on herself until then—and quickly flicked the damp from her fake lashes with her fingertips. She was ready with a smile as Maureen, demon-eating dog tucked under her arm, scooted a stocky little boy into the room.

"Sorry to interrupt," Maureen said in her raspy voice. She sounded like a big woman, the sort Clayton remembered from his childhood who all had tits like shelves and flat feet in worn flip-flops. They were unimpressed women who he'd thought were the source of the phrase "keep your feet on the ground." And although he had never seen her impressed by anyone, she was a small, gently-worn, half-Korean force of nature. "Harry just wondered where you were."

Nadine's smile was genuine for the first time as she held her hand out and wriggled her bubble-gum pink fingers at her son. "Right here," she said. "Did you miss me?"

"No," he said with offended little-boy pride. When Nadine mock-pouted at him, he relented. "Maybe. Are you okay, Mom?"

"Of course," Nadine said.

It wasn't a bad lie, but Harry didn't look like he bought it. He gave Clayton a suspicious look and put himself in front of his mom. His face was round and freckled, wholesome as a kid on an old adventure novel, but he had the jaded, tired eyes of a disappointed middle-aged man.

Clayton had seen those eyes before.

"Who are you?" Harry demanded. "Were you mean to my mom?"

"No, he was not," Nadine blurted out, clearly embarrassed. She caught Harry's arm and tugged him back to her side. "That was rude, Harry. Mr. Reynolds is a friend of Mrs. Park, and we're talking. Okay?"

She waited. Harry twisted around to frown at Clayton, who sat back and tried to look as harmless as possible.

"Daddy said men and ladies can't be friends," Harry said.

The answer creased Nadine's face with a slap of misery, and she had to struggle to keep her voice from cracking as she went on. "That's enough, Harry. Your daddy says lots of silly things. Okay?"

Harry shuffled his feet on the ground and scowled. "Okay," he finally muttered.

Nadine wiped her face again, so he saw a smile when he looked back at her. "Why don't you go with Mrs. Park and play with the puppy. Okay?"

"He doesn't just eat bad dreams," Maureen coaxed. "He does tricks too."

Harry was obviously torn as he glanced over at the magical, bad-dream-eating fluff ball that wriggled in Maureen's arms. He squirmed in place.

"You sure you're okay?" he asked.

Nadine rolled her eyes and gave him a gentle shove toward the door. "I'm so fine," she said. "Go on."

With a last glare in Clayton's direction, Harry slouched away toward Maureen, who crouched down and leaned in to ask, "Would you like to carry him?"

Harry's unhappily slouched back straightened as he blurted out, "Yes, please." She suppressed a smile and passed the fluff ball to him, and the dog promptly licked his face in the hope of stickiness. Maureen nodded reassurance to Nadine and then led them out of the room.

"He... James and I had an argument, and I hurt myself," she said. "He didn't think I needed to go to the hospital, and when I insisted, he locked me out. Harry snuck down and let me back in after it got dark. I mean, James didn't think I'd stay there all night, but Harry was...."

She took a deep breath and pressed, her fingertips against her eyelids as she tried to hold the tears back.

"He isn't like this. It's not his fault," she said. "He's just... he's trying to change things—for us—and that's... it's a lot of stress. People put a lot of stress on him. It's not like he hit me."

Clayton pulled a tissue out of his pocket and leaned forward to offer it to her. "I can help if you want me to," he said. "Now. Later. It doesn't matter."

She took the tissue and twisted it between her hands instead of using it.

"I can't leave him," she said. "I wouldn't be able to take care of myself, never mind Harry. I haven't worked in five years, and when I did, I was a waitress—a... topless waitress. That's going to impress the judge, isn't it?"

"It's my job to get you what you're due. Both of you."

Nadine popped her jaw sharply and pugnaciously to the side and snorted. She pushed a sweep of pale hair behind her ear. "No one gets what they're due from James," she said. "He doesn't like to lose. What if I leave him and I don't get custody of Harry? James loves him. I know he does. But he's not… patient. I can't risk that, can I?"

Clayton wanted to tell her. It wouldn't do any good; it had to be her decision. But he still wanted to.

"With divorce there's always a risk that you won't get the outcome you want, that *I'd* like," he said. "Sometimes nobody's happy at the end."

She took a deep breath and twisted the tissue between her fingers until it tore. "Can I think about it?"

"Of course," he said. "You have to be sure."

Nadine nodded and got gingerly to her feet. The habit of courtesy made Clayton's muscles twitch to offer her a hand, but like his suit, that just made people here feel uncomfortable sometimes. He waited until she was on her feet and then followed suit.

"Before you go," he said. She paused and looked at him warily. "Maureen said you asked for me by name. I don't think we've met before, so I wondered how you'd heard of me?"

"From James," Nadine said. A quick smile twitched over her face when Clayton raised his eyebrows. "Sort of. This guy Davy, someone he worked with, was gloating at a party that he had this shit-hot divorce lawyer and all his wife had was this pro-bono schmuck Reynolds from a shelter. Her name was Mia? Mia Avagyon?"

The name sounded vaguely familiar, but not enough to pull up a face and a marital history from Clayton's memory. That didn't mean anything. Clayton had been a lawyer long enough that only the very rich and the very terrible cases stood out to him without the prompt of a case file. but he nodded as though he remembered Mia.

"James laughed at him, right in the middle of the party. He said that Mia wasn't just going to get the girls, she'd get Davy's ball sac too. That you worked for this fancy firm that kept the best private investigators in the state on retainer, and they'd find out if Davy had ever even cursed at a kid before. These days Davy can't see his children unsupervised anymore. So last night, after I left, I called Mia and she told me to come here. I thought she'd ask questions, but she didn't."

It was the first time that an abusive husband had ever referred anyone to Clayton. He wasn't sure how he felt about it, but that was hardly Nadine's fault.

"If you decide to go ahead with this, Nadine," he said, "I will do my best for you and Harry."

She nodded and didn't move, as though her feet were glued to the floor.

"The thing is, I do love him," Nadine said, her voice hopeless. She glanced around at the room again, at the walls in need of paint and the duct tape patches on the carpet hidden under carefully placed chairs and cheap rugs. Her throat worked as she swallowed. "I suppose you hear that all the time."

Clayton thought about those dark, old-man eyes in a wary kid's face—not Harry's, a skinnier face and dirtier, usually, but the eyes were the same.

"Every day of my life," he said.

"YOU'RE LATE," Heather, his assistant, chided him as he jogged past her and into his office. Her wig was black today, a severe bob around her peaches-and-cream pretty, round face. "You have a meeting with Mr. Baker in five minutes."

Clayton snorted and set his briefcase on top of the desk. The oxblood leather of the briefcase was almost exactly the same color as the dark walnut wood it sat on.

"It's coffee," he said as he pulled the sweatshirt over his head. "Spare suit?"

She tutted at him and then clicked off to fetch the dry-cleaned Richard Bennett suit he kept in the office. One cup of piss thrown at you as you left court and you learned to be prepared. Clayton toed his sneakers off and then shoved them and the sweatshirt into a drawer.

"Here." Heather passed the suit bag backward into the office through the door without looking. "And do you know what would happen if I turned around and saw you in your boxers?"

"I would wonder when I started wearing boxers." Clayton took the bag off her and unzipped it. "Or underwear."

Heather snorted and closed the door behind her, and Clayton skinned his jeans off down long legs and stepped into the suit pants. The gunmetal-gray fabric and narrow leg struck the careful balance between severe and stylish, although the gray shirt probably veered more to severe.

"Heather, I need you to run a request for a background check down to the PIs." He shrugged the shirt on and let it hang unbuttoned as he reached to pop his briefcase open. It wasn't hard to find Nadine's file mixed in with the Redwelds the firm used for paying clients. "As a favor."

Heather came back into the office to pluck the file out of his hands. She eyed it unhappily. "Any chance she's just a 'down on her luck' lady who needs help to find her husband and hit him with divorce papers?"

"No."

"They never are," she sighed. "All right. I'll get in touch with Larry and see what they can do."

She turned to go and nearly walked face-first into Daniel Baker, as the senior partner of Talley, Baker, and Jenks let himself into the office.

"Sir," she squeaked as she tucked the folder behind her back. "Sorry. I didn't see you there."

Baker raised a sandy eyebrow at her. "That's because the door was closed, Ms. Finnegan."

With her back to him, Clayton couldn't see her face, but on past performance, he knew her complexion had gone strawberry. Heather was unflappable 90 percent of the time—an ex-cop and weekend punk, two years part-time education away from a master's degree—but 10 percent of the time there was Daniel.

That was pretty much how she described her sexuality too—90 percent pretty ladies and 10 percent inexplicable crushes.

"Yes, sir. Of course, sir," she squeaked out. "Let me get out of your way."

She edged around him, back into the main office. Daniel let her get halfway back to her desk, and then he cleared his throat. "Oh, and Ms. Finnegan?"

"Sir?"

"Don't think I didn't see that." He held his hand out and waited. When nothing immediately happened, he sighed. "Ms. Finnegan, hand it over."

Clayton buttoned his cuffs and sighed. "That's fine, Heather. I'll talk to the investigators later."

The file dropped into Daniel's hands, and he gave it back to Clayton. "No, you won't," he said. "You've billed your full quota of pro bono hours this year. If you want to volunteer more, that's up to you, but no using company resources. Agreed?"

It was hard to argue with the man you owed 40 percent of your career to. Clayton nodded. "Of course," he said. "I just wanted to chase up background details."

Daniel sat down and flicked a bit of lint off his immaculately tailored knee. He'd been the one who told Clayton to spend his first paycheck on a good suit. "If you wear a $30 suit, your client will assume that's what you'll get them." Of course he eschewed severe and just went with expensively stylish, from the dachshund-print lining to the cameo cufflinks.

"Make partner when it comes up," he said. "Then you can do what you want."

"Maybe I don't want to." Clayton caught Heather's eye—she'd just cooled back down to flustered pink—and mouthed "Tea" at her. He straightened his collar and stepped behind the desk to sit down. "I have enough of a reputation now. I could start my own firm."

Daniel looked amused but didn't challenge the assertion. He just laced his fingers together and, as Heather put the order in with the coffee shop downstairs, changed the subject back to business.

"Justin Harris is getting married."

"Again?"

"Again. I'm already working harder than I care for, so I want you to handle his prenuptial agreement. It's straightforward. Same as the others."

At the end of the meeting, one-third of Clayton's month was blocked off, he'd agreed to a dinner party with Daniel and his latest protégé, and he'd dodged an attempt to set him up with someone Daniel's ex had dated. He finished his second cup of tea and got up to show Daniel out.

They paused at the door as Daniel picked an imaginary crumb from his tie.

"Of course," Daniel said. "I can hardly stop you asking someone a favor."

It took a second for Clayton to realize what Daniel was referring to. The pro bono case had been filed away in his brain for later, and it took a second to unearth it.

"I don't think Larry Jenkins likes me enough to do me favors."

Daniel chuckled. "No, she does not," he said. "However, Kelly would, and Larry mentioned her partner has finally taken a leave of absence and is driving everyone mad by not actually absenting. So."

"He's an idiot," Clayton protested.

Daniel rolled his eyes. He always seemed to enjoy Kelly, disasters and all. "He's a romantic."

"Same thing." They both knew that. Clayton had just learned it earlier than Daniel.

"He's at loose ends, is the point," Daniel said. "Call him or not. It's up to you."

Not, then, Clayton thought pettily.

IT WAS seven o'clock in the evening before Clayton's conscience wore his irritation down.

Kelly—he presumably had another name, but no one would admit to knowing it—was the bane of Clayton's existence. The fact that he was completely unaware of that and would think it was a joke if he found out only made him more annoying. The man was always in a good mood, believed wholeheartedly in love—despite the fact he was about as good at picking a partner as Clayton's mother—and genuinely believed that "things can only get better." He was probably a perfectly fine idiot, but as December bore down on him, everything about Kelly made Clayton feel like the Grinch.

He was also, whatever mess he regularly made out of his personal life, good at his job, otherwise he wouldn't be the firm's go-to investigator. Under the circumstances he was Clayton's best option, but he had taken some time off.

By the time Clayton came to that realization, it was too late to get Kelly's personal number. All he had was the invitation to a housewarming party that he hadn't attended earlier in the year. He preferred his socializing drunk, in the dark, and preferably debauched, but he'd accept polite, work-based, and shallow. A midsummer barbecue where the world's most wholesome man held court with his newest ex-to-be was his idea of hell.

The house was an hour's drive from the office, out in Santa Monica, where the housewives and children ran free.

Clayton parked his bike behind an old, beat-up Chevy and tugged his helmet off. He didn't need to check the house numbers. The invitation claimed "you can't miss it," and the only house that fit that description was the old sunshine-yellow Victorian-style townhouse. It had a garden and a baseball hoop mounted over the garage.

Across the street, a door creaked open and an old woman peered out suspiciously. She probably kept an eye on Kelly's place for him, probably made him cookies and tried to set him up with her nephew. Kelly was the sort of man people did that for.

Bile bubbled nicely in Clayton's stomach as he stalked up to the sky-blue front door and pressed the doorbell. When no one answered, he clenched his jaw and pressed it again. He could hear the *bing-bong* of it echo through the house, and a cat howled.

Fine. He had a cat instead of a dog. Close enough.

Clayton was just about to press the bell again when Kelly finally jerked the door open. He was bare-chested and half-asleep, with a baby cradled against one broad, tattooed shoulder as it cat-wailed and fussed.

Lust caught in the back of Clayton's throat and dried his mouth out. But then, that was the thing that irritated Clayton most about Kelly. He wasn't Clayton's type—too short, too muscular, too cheerful, and currently too holding a baby—but he was still the hottest fucking man Clayton had ever seen. It was as though he did it on purpose. He wasn't even *that* short, just close enough to average to make his self-deprecating short jokes funny instead of self-hating.

"I need a favor," Clayton said through the sticky hunger on his tongue.

There was a pause as Kelly distractedly bounced the grizzling baby on his shoulder and looked baffled. If Kelly had turned up on Clayton's doorstep at that time of night, Clayton would have told him to fuck off. So of course Kelly scratched his head, shrugged, and stepped back to wave Clayton into the hall.

"Sure," he said as he patted the baby's back. "Come in. Sorry about the mess."

Asshole.

CHAPTER TWO

INSIDE, KELLY'S house was all bright colors and clutter that covered scuffed-up wooden floors. One wall in the living room was half-painted, and a can of paint and a well-dried brush were left on a square of newspaper to wait for the next burst of enthusiasm.

It was a lived-in house, the sort of house a child could grow up happily in.

Clayton felt a sting of "dog in the manger" bitterness at the thought. He wasn't father material, but his contrary strain of covetousness resented anyone who had something he didn't have, want it or not.

"Did you adopt?" he asked stiffly.

"Huh?" Kelly padded back into the room, bare feet half-hidden under the frayed cuffs of his jeans. A sports bottle dangled from his fingers, and the baby was still screeching on his shoulder, its little body tight and pink with misery. "I'd made coffee, but it's gone cold."

"That's fine," Clayton said. He hadn't come for hospitality, just for business... sort of. Despite himself, he repeated his question with a nod at the baby. "Did you adopt?"

It was hard to imagine Kelly doing undercover work. Every emotion spread over his face like a flag. Right then he looked confused, and then he glanced down at the baby, and realization flashed over his expression.

"Oh, Maxie?" he said. He patted the back again. "No, he's my nephew."

Covetousness couldn't explain the relief that slipped through Clayton's gut at that news. So he ignored it and took the sports bottle of vivid green liquid from Kelly.

"So you're babysitting," Clayton stated the obvious.

Kelly tilted his head and stared at him for a moment, then visibly shrugged off the banality of the comment. "Yes," he agreed.

That said, Kelly sat down on the couch and folded one leg up under him. His jeans pulled tautly over his crotch, where the denim was faded down to white along the seam. The baby hiccuped and finally stopped the thin, miserable yowl it had been making. It still fussed miserably to itself as Kelly rubbed his hand over its back in slow petting motions.

Clayton was fairly sure there was something perverse in how distracted he was by that hand.

"You said you need a favor?" Kelly said. He braced his elbow against the back of the couch and propped his head on his fist. His eyes were pale blue, almost gray, and he watched Clayton curiously as he waited for an answer.

"I need a background check run on someone." Clayton sat down on a battered old leather chair and twisted the top of the sports bottle. He took a drink that tasted like lime and flat water. "Just the basics."

Kelly raised his eyebrow. A narrow scar bisected the straight bar just at the edge of his brow bone. Clayton had always wondered what caused it but never quite unbent enough to ask.

"Boyfriend?" Kelly asked with a crooked smirk that carved long lines into his cheeks.

Clayton gave him a flat, unamused look. "No."

This time Kelly raised both eyebrows. "Girlfriend?"

"Fuck off."

Kelly laughed—a low, rough purr of humor that made Clayton want to lean into it as though it were actual warmth. It was this open *happy* sound, with no edge or agenda, just amusement and an invitation to join in. Clayton first heard that laugh at the office, and his type or not, he'd planned to have the scruffy, dark-haired man under him if he was even *slightly* inclined that way.

But Kelly didn't do casual, and Clayton didn't do anything else. He still resented the universe for giving a laugh like that to someone he couldn't have.

"It's a client's husband," he said.

Kelly's face settled into a curious expression. "Why are you here, then?" he asked. "If it's work, you don't need to ask for a favor. Just run it down to Larry and invoice it to the firm. You prefer to work with her anyhow."

That was true, and under normal circumstances, Clayton would claim that preference with no shame. He had a good working relationship with Larry, who was a to-the-point, sharply suited lesbian who had only a bit more faith in matrimony than Clayton did.

"It's a pro bono job," he said. "Nothing to do with the firm. I'll cover your fee personally."

Kelly studied him thoughtfully over the baby's crop of wispy brown hair. Finally, he gave a brisk nod and pushed himself up off the couch.

"Right, well, if this is work instead of a booty call, you'll need to give me a minute." He shoved his free hand through his hair and scratched the nape of his neck. "And a coffee. Would you...."

He made a move as though he were going to pass the baby to Clayton, and Clayton recoiled as far as the back of the chair would let him and warded the offer off with one hand. "I don't do babies."

Cradled in the crook of Kelly's arm, Maxie squawked and thrashed his tiny red fists in the air as though to say he didn't do Claytons either.

Kelly sighed. "Fine."

He hooked a baby... thing... out from under the coffee table with one bare foot and crouched down to put Maxie in it. There were more straps involved than seemed necessary to Clayton. The child couldn't even hold its own head up yet. Did it really need to be buckled in like a fighter pilot?

Still, it gave Clayton a chance to indulge his curiosity and discreetly study Kelly's tattoo. It was the first time he'd seen it. The splash of bright colors were usually hidden under T-shirts and sweaters. If he had to guess what sort of tattoo Kelly would have, Clayton would have said something more stereotypically masculine—a dragon or wolf. Instead a stylized parrot draped over the shoulder, and the spray of blue and red feathers fluttered as heavy muscle moved and flexed under his skin.

"Can you at least watch the baby while I go clean up?" Kelly asked as he secured the last strap and sat back on his heels. "Make sure a wild dog doesn't burst in and carry Maxie off?"

"Why?" Clayton asked as he shifted his attention away from the spread of Kelly's shoulders. "Do you have many feral, baby-stealing dog packs roaming the neighborhood?"

Kelly gave him a lazy grin. "One would be enough, wouldn't it?" He gave the baby seat a tap to set it rocking and pushed himself to his feet. "Give me ten minutes."

He hitched his jeans up over his lean hips and headed out of the room. Clayton watched him go and then looked down at the baby.

"If a feral dog breaks in here, you're on your own," he said dryly.

The baby stared up at him with huge unfocused blue eyes and screwed its face up, ready to scream again, all red folds and pink gums. Clayton gingerly reached out and rocked the padded chair slightly.

"Fine," he said. "I'll give you a head start."

Either the motion or the promise satisfied Maxie. He went back to relatively quiet fussing as he bounced.

It only took Kelly five minutes to come back downstairs, his damp hair finger-combed back from his face and jeans swapped out for a different pair. The laces on his battered old combat boots trailed behind him as he came in. He took a quick look at Maxie and gave Clayton a thumbs-up.

"I guess he likes you," he said. "Okay. Where were we? Pro bono client, background check, want me to work for free. Did I miss anything?"

"I said I'd pay your fee."

"Sure. I'm going to gouge you for a couple of hours' work for some woman with a sad enough story to pull *your* heartstrings?" The emphasis on *your* wasn't entirely flattering. Kelly shrugged a pale blue shirt on over his shoulders and buttoned it as he talked. If Clayton expected that to be less distracting, he'd have been wrong. The crisp cotton exaggerated the inverted triangle of Kelly's torso, from the heavy breadth of his shoulders to the tight tuck of his waist. "Cover any outsize expenses, and we'll call it square."

That was generous. Clayton knew what Kelly usually got paid. He approved the invoices when they came over his desk. It still rubbed him the wrong way. Couldn't Kelly just play along and have one repulsive flaw?

"Aren't you saving up to take your boyfriend to Acapulco or something?" he asked. That wasn't something he should care enough to remember, but everyone needed a hobby. Clayton kept track of Kelly's boyfriends in the hope that one day he'd realize it was easier to give up. "He'll be thrilled you turned down money."

"It was Bali, for the surfing," Kelly corrected easily. "And he went back to Donegal."

"Was it health-and-safety mandated?" Clayton asked, mostly as a joke and a bit of a jibe. More than a bit, maybe. "The two of you in the same zip code just too *much* Irish."

Kelly narrowed his eyes for a second and then shook his head. "No, his whole family died in a freak accident," he said. For a second

Clayton's stomach dropped, because even he had a limit to his pettiness, apparently. He opened his mouth to apologize, but before he could get the words out, Kelly blithely finished the story. "Got sucked down in a potato bog. The whole clan. Tragic."

The *sorry* caught behind Clayton's teeth. He gave Kelly a thin, severe smile. "Ah, the vaunted Kelly humor."

Kelly snorted. The genial smile faded down to a grim ghost of itself, and something colder showed through Kelly's pale eyes. "Least I crack a smile, Claymore." The use of the sobriquet made Clayton's jaw clench in annoyance. It was better than a lot of nicknames he'd had, but what "Baker's Claymore" lacked in alliteration, it made up for in ridiculousness. He wasn't even Scottish. The Reynolds were, if drunk old men with big stories could be believed, as Irish as Kelly. But he'd earned it, so he held his tongue as Kelly continued sharply. "Liam's none of your business. My personal life is none of your business. So if you can't mind your manners, you can find another investigator willing to do you a favor."

Annoyance clenched Clayton's jaw, and he had to swallow the hot bubble of harsh words that stirred in the back of his throat. It wasn't that people didn't talk to Clayton that way. Lots of people did. Even if he did still resent it, he frequently deserved it or had at least earned it somehow. What pricked him on the raw was that, like the shirt, the fact Mr. Nice had a temper, just made him more attractive—like a dash of salt to season all that caramel-tanned skin.

He could still say sorry. He probably should. But the closest he could manage was a stilted "Fair enough" as he fished an envelope out of his pocket and held it out. "This is all we have for now. I just want to know what he's worth, if he has a police record, and what sort of asshole he is."

"Maybe he's not an asshole?" Kelly leaned forward to take the envelope. His fingers were long and elegantly shaped, but old scars and calluses roughed up the skin over his knuckles. Clayton had grown up around men who had hands like that. He'd put a lot of distance and hand cream between him and them. Kelly tore off the end of the envelope. "Maybe the relationship just ran its course."

"He broke her arm."

Distaste twitched the corners of Kelly's mouth. "So, this asshole? What's his name?"

"James Graham." Clayton felt a nip of guilt and added, "Nadine seemed to think he was dangerous to more than just women and children. This isn't part of your job. If you don't want to take it on...."

"I said I would."

Apparently that was enough as far as Kelly was concerned. It left Clayton wrong-footed, with nothing to do with the well-reasoned arguments he'd come prepared with.

"My contact details are in there too." He motioned to the envelope. "If you find anything out or need something from me, you can call me at any time."

Kelly looked amused. "Thanks for the permission." He showed Clayton back to the sky-blue door and, as he opened it, admitted, "Let's be honest. You're doing me a favor too. When I arranged this break, I had a boyfriend and the delusion that I was a lot more interesting than I actually am. Now I'm single, and I did all the things I had planned in the first two days."

He leaned against the doorframe and folded his arms, and his shirt pulled tightly across his heavy shoulders. Clayton resisted the urge to make a list of all the things he could do with Kelly. It would fill more than a day. The tug of lust in his gut made him ache, and he wondered dourly if he should have taken last night's number after all.

"Glad to be of service," he said. "Once Maxie's mother picks him up, you can get to work on this."

Kelly gave him an odd look.

"What?" Clayton asked.

"My sister-in-law died," Kelly said. "Three months ago. I already had time off booked anyhow, for the holiday with Liam, so I could pitch in with Maxie since my brother isn't... coping."

He said *coping* in a careful, measured way that made it obvious it was a make-do word and what he wanted to say was that his brother wasn't sober, around, or able to understand the situation. He settled for *coping*, or he would have if Clayton believed a word of it.

"Very funny."

Kelly folded his arm behind his head and scratched the nape of his neck as he pulled a dubious face. "I suppose, if you have a really dark sense of humor."

Clayton waited for the mask to slip and Kelly to let him in on the joke with a smirk. It didn't. Then he remembered that he never had asked *why* Kelly had taken time off.

"I didn't realize," he said. The words sounded stiffer than he meant them to be, with a sharp edge to them that sounded unkind, for some reason. "I'm so sorry."

The corner of Kelly's twisted up in something like a smile. "No reason you should know," he said. "Besides, I kind of asked for it with the whole Liam gag. Don't worry about it."

"Still," Clayton said. He shifted on the doorstep and sweltered under his suit in the muggy evening heat. Sometimes he forgot how hot LA could be. He spent his life in courtrooms and offices, air-conditioned for the comfort of men in suits, or nightclubs where the sweat was part of the charm. He resisted the urge to tug at his collar. "If I knew, I wouldn't have asked. I can find someone else."

Kelly looked away down the street. His eyes flicked over the row of cars parked along the curb, from the rusty Mustang propped on blocks to the glossy yellow Hummer parked half up in someone's yard.

"I didn't really know her that well," Kelly admitted. It sounded like a confession, something to be ashamed of. "My brother's been... away."

"Jail?" Clayton asked.

That snapped Kelly's attention back on him. A startled frown pulled his eyebrows down toward his nose. "What? No. His work just takes him away a lot."

The question had startled Clayton nearly as much as it had Kelly. Too many ghosts today. They made him fall back into old habits. Back when jail or jailbait were the most common reasons for someone's family member "going... away".

"If you're sure."

Back in the other room, Maxie sneezed, hiccuped, and started to cry again. Kelly closed his eyes for a second and thumped his head gently against the doorframe.

"Trust me," he said. "A reason to squeeze their share of this out of my brothers is just what I need."

A good man would probably have argued or rolled up his sleeves and sacrificed a very expensive suit to baby spit. But Clayton was under no illusions about who he was, so he could just leave.

Of course, so did most people eventually, once the congratulatory glow of being a good person wore off. If you were lucky, they left.

"Let me know if you need anything," Clayton said. "If I can't get back to you, Heather will."

He strode back down to the road, threw his leg over the bike, and braced one foot on the pavement as he pushed it upright. A husky laugh chased him, and he glanced back at Kelly with a coolly raised brow.

"Always figured you were more the convertible type." Kelly pushed himself off the doorjamb. The light was starting to dim toward dusk, and it cast shadows over his face. "Like the bike, though. You look more...."

Before he could finish the thought, Maxie belted out a wail that made both men flinch. It was a big noise from a small body.

"Better go," Kelly said as he motioned over his shoulder. "I'll update you tomorrow."

He ducked back into the house, the door closed behind him, and Clayton was left to wonder what the bike made him look more of.

Not that it mattered—Clayton yanked his helmet down over his ears and started the bike—but he still wanted to know.

CHAPTER THREE

"OH LOOK at the wee mite," Kathleen fussed as she took her grandson from her son. She *mwah*'d against his rash-pink cheek and picked at the grubby onesie that Kelly had wrestled the baby into before he left the house. It had been clean then. "What happened to the lovely outfits I brought over for him?"

Kathleen Kelly was five foot nothing of condensed first-generation Irish immigrant. Forty years on—first in New York and then city-hopping around Nevada and California—and she hadn't lost the accent. Kelly always figured it was a silent protest of how aggressively his dad had embraced America and everything about it.

"He barfed on them, Mom," Kelly said as he shrugged the baby bag off his shoulder and set it on the table. "Any coffee?"

She *tch*ed at him. "You know I won't have artificial stimulants in my house," she said as she chucked Maxie under his chin. The baby stared at her with suspicion. "They're no good for you. I don't care what the doctors said, Byron stopped acting out once we cut out all the caffeine from his diet."

Kelly scratched the old scar in his eyebrow. "Or he stopped getting caught."

"Now don't start." Kathleen lifted a finger—the warning finger, they called it as children—and wagged it at him over Maxie. "You've stepped up for your brother, helped to take care of Maxie. Don't ruin it now by dragging up old fights you two had when you were boys. Byron could be a handful, with his... attention problems, but you were a little snitch. As bad as each other, in the end."

Some moms said they loved all their kids equally. Kathleen was more "I managed to love you all the same, despite everything." It drove Kelly mad as a kid, when he was sure of the injustice of it, but there was no point arguing now. Kathleen's image of their childhoods had calcified into scab-knees and mischief.

"So no coffee?" Kelly asked again.

It was the secret code. All the family knew it. It used to get them a candy or a can of soda from Mom's secret stash. Now it was a coffee or a beer. Not every time. Sometimes you struck out. Kathleen gave him a look, took in the bags under his eyes, and softened.

"There might be a jar under the sink," she said. Then to cover her own backside, she added, "Mrs. Lowry brought it over. Couldn't exactly throw it back at her, could I?"

She picked up the baby bag from the table and dangled it from the crook of her elbow as she headed for the stairs. Maxie squirmed and fussed in her arms, and Kelly had to resist the urge to say the baby didn't like to be held like that, that he liked to wriggle.

It wasn't as though he really knew anything about babies. Until Marie died, his only experience had been the fat, placid cocoons that his sisters-in-law shoved at him "for a hold." They'd all been quiet and genial, weighed down by breast milk and baby fat—unlike Maxie, who was made of wire, wind, and spite.

Kathleen baby-talk narrated her way upstairs. "We're going to find you a lovely wee outfit, aren't we? You're going to be the best-dressed bab in the country. And get you a blankie so you don't get cold. We don't want grandma's precious bab to get cold."

"It's California, Mom," Kelly yelled up.

"And how many children have you raised?"

Kelly supposed he had to give her that. He crouched down to hunt for coffee in the cupboard under the sink, amid the bottles of bleach and antibacterial soap. Kathleen might feed the family on organic produce, but she never met a chemical cleaning product she didn't like. The stronger the better. It probably wasn't the best place to keep coffee, but there the dusty jar of instant was, right at the back, under an old wax-stained polishing rag.

He boiled the kettle and got a mug out of the cupboard. It was strange. He was nearly thirty years old, and his childhood seemed a long way away, but nothing had changed here. The kettle was still slotted into the same plug, the mugs still in the same cupboard, and the mugs were still the same LAPD-branded ones he drank out of as a kid.

Even the family photo on the fridge was still there when he went to get the milk, held up by the faded "Happy Mother's Day" magnet that one of them got her when they were kids. All six of the Kelly boys crouched on the grass in their LAPD baseball jerseys, while Dad grinned over them in the background.

The seventh Kelly boy poured an overdose of flavored creamer into his coffee and shoved the fridge shut. Look at that. Even his old childhood resentments were just where he left them, not quite brushed under the rug.

He turned his back on the fridge and dragged a chair out from the kitchen table just as someone rapped on the front door.

"Sweetheart, will you get that?" Kathleen yelled from upstairs.

He grabbed a swig of coffee and grimaced at the taste—too much sweetener—and yelled up, "Sure."

It wasn't family. They always used the back door. Kelly gave his hair a quick rake through with his fingers on his way down the hall and checked the front of his shirt for stains before he opened the door. A vaguely familiar woman stood on the doorstep with an armful of casserole dish, the gunmetal navy of her uniform somehow starker than usual in the sun and on the porch.

"Oh," she said, and her voice lilted with surprise. She tried to free one hand from the dish to push the aviator sunglasses up onto her forehead. Big green eyes blinked at him out of a freckled face. "Hi. I'm Officer Andrews. I work with your brother?"

"Which one?"

She dimpled at him. "Good point. You must be—"

"The one who's not a cop?" Kelly finished for her. "Yeah, that's me. Is that for Mom?"

Andrews glanced down at the casserole as though she'd forgotten it was there, and color pinked up her face. "Oh, um, yeah. She said she really liked it at the last barbecue, and I know… what with everything that happened…."

Kelly stepped back and waved her in through the front door. Once she was inside, he relieved her of the casserole and yelled upstairs.

"Mom, Officer Andrews—"

"Claire," she muttered to him.

"Claire has dropped by."

The speed at which Kathleen made it back down the stairs with Maxie squawking from a pale blue cocoon of angora in her arms betrayed that she had designs on poor Claire. She still had, at last count, two unmarried sons. That counted.

Kelly snorted at that bit of self-pity while Kathleen hugged Claire and fussed over how pretty her hair was now that she'd cut it. He was a grown man. He didn't need to be his mom's favorite. Besides, Mom might be okay with him being gay, but that didn't mean he trusted her taste in men.

She'd probably pick out some nice Irish lad like Liam for him—all brogue and the ability to bake, someone the rest of the family could view as unthreatening. And she could correspond with his family back home. As opposed to what, Kelly asked himself wryly, a tall, flatly American divorce lawyer with razor-sharp cheekbones and even sharper fashion?

His libido, as always, chimed in with an enthusiastic yes. The tug of sticky interest in that idea spread like warm honey through his groin. His cock twitched, and he set his jaw. Now was hardly the time to start fantasizing about the unattainable Clayton Reynolds.

That had been last night, all tangled sheets, his own impatient hand and weird adolescent guilt about doing it with a baby in the house.

Enough. He pulled his brain back from the sweaty precipice of his... what? Not a crush. He didn't want to peel back Clayton's prickly exterior and find the nicer person inside. He just—every now and again—wanted the asshole to pin him down and be clever at him while they fucked. So maybe an issue, but not a crush. Whatever it was, he shoved it to the back of his head the same way he shoved the casserole into the fridge.

Talley, Baker, and Jenks were his firm's best clients. A one-night stand with Clayton—no matter how hot he looked in that stupid suit on that bike—was not worth the risk of losing that account.

Probably.

He closed the fridge and, because he was a well-trained Kelly boy, stuck the kettle on and quickly rinsed the betraying cup of coffee under the tap.

"See?" Kathleen said as she pulled Claire with her into the kitchen. "I told you, if you have time, it would be no trouble to make you a cup of tea. Sit. Sit."

With a helpless laugh, Claire gave in and sat down at the table. She checked her watch.

"I have about half an hour," she admitted. "So, how's Bry doing? I haven't seen him since he went back to work. I know he and Marie were...."

"Separated," Kathleen said. She bounced Maxie in her arms as she talked. "Nearly a year now. I always knew it wouldn't end well. Poor

Marie could never deal with him being undercover, not coming home every night. Still, I didn't think it would end like this. It was such a tragic accident, but she shouldn't have been out driving that late."

Or that drunk, but that wasn't part of Kathleen's narrative. Just like their childhoods, she had her own way of seeing things.

"Mom, I have to go," Kelly said. "You sure you're okay taking care of Maxie today?"

"Of course," Kathleen said. She looked down and beamed at Maxie as though he were the cutest thing in the world. "Me and Maxie can have a lovely visit with Claire, can't we?"

"Okay. I'll come and grab him this evening," Kelly said. "Nice to meet you, Claire."

"You too, ummm—" She stalled on his name. Kathleen took advantage of her distraction to shove an armful of baby at her. Claire blanched and held her arms stiffly as Maxie did his aggressive squirm-and-arch reaction to a new person. "Oh no, Kathleen. I don't—"

"Just for a second, dear. I just need a quick word."

Kelly headed out into the garden. Gone-to-wood herbs grew in two long planters along the path that were decorated with the stubs of his dad's old cigars.

The sun had crawled high enough in the sky to burn off the last drizzle of morning mist, and the sky was a flat, unrelenting blue. "Claire's a lovely girl, isn't she?" Kathleen said as she pulled the back door shut behind her. "I've heard that robbery-homicide already have their eye on her after she worked with them on a few cases."

"Mom…."

"She's a friend. Byron can have friends, can't he?" she challenged.

"Since when has Byron ever been friends with a woman?"

Kathleen couldn't disagree with that. Since he hit puberty, it had been Byron's motto that men and women couldn't be friends, so she just *tch*ed and batted the topic of conversation out of the air with one hand.

"Your dad really appreciates you stepping up like this to help Byron," she said. "You know he'd never tell you that himself, but he does."

Kelly nodded. He kind of hated that secondhand, halfhearted praise from his dad still made him feel like a little kid who just got a slap on the back. "How is he?"

"Oh, he's fine," Kathleen said. "Sick of desk duty. I might finally convince him to retire. Really, sweetheart, he's doing much better. He's even stuck to his diet this time."

"Good," Kelly said.

"We're going to have a barbecue in a few weeks. We'd love all you boys to come," she said. "It's just going to be family, a few friends, some of your dad's old friends from work."

She stopped and waited hopefully.

Dad's friends from work. That was another family code, a newer one. It meant, "You're going to come on your own, right?" and "We don't care if you're gay, but… not everyone understands," and "We love you, so won't you lie for us?"

Kelly swallowed the bitter taste on his tongue, because what was the point.

"'Course," he said. "It's been a while since we all got together."

Kathleen laughed, relieved that he wasn't going to make a scene, and squeezed his arm. "Christmas," she said. "Can you believe it? All my boys in one city at least, and we still hardly ever see each other."

Yeah, well, there were a lot of reasons for that.

"I know, Mom," he said as he kissed her cheek. "Hard to believe. I'll see you later."

IF KELLY *had* planned to take Clayton's money, he'd have felt bad about it after he finished the background check. There was easy money, and then there was James "Jimmy" Graham. The guy wore who he was on his skin.

Since it would get back to Larry if he turned up at the law firm with a report in hand, he told Clayton to meet him at the food van down the street—kind of like a date, a sly little voice in his head insinuated. He ignored it and grabbed his burger from the bright-eyed, wide-smiled kid behind the hot plate. The food was hot through the cardboard against his fingers.

"Hope you don't enjoy your Angry Burger, sir," the girl rhymed off gleefully. She saluted him crisply. "Choke on it!"

Kelly stuck money in the tip jar anyhow. It was the schtick. Miss Ann Thropy's Burgers—service with a scowl. It was hard to get used to for a Californian, but the burgers were worth it. He left the confused customer in line behind him to weather the prickly menu and retreated to one of the folding tables set up along the wide curve of the sidewalk dining court. The tall mirrored buildings glittered with the bright blue reflection of the sky, and a homeless guy slouched under a tree provided a droned music soundtrack.

Kelly unpacked the burger. It was already cut in half, juice and hot sauce slippery under his fingers as he picked it up. The bun was black—charcoal or octopus ink; there were options, but Kelly hadn't really cared—and the two patties had been marinated in coffee before they were slapped on the grill. Kelly took a bite. He wasn't sure it tasted good, exactly, but he wanted another bite.

"That looks disgusting," Clayton said at his shoulder.

Kelly jerked with surprise and nearly choked on a mouthful of half-chewed coffee meat. Hot sauce burned more than usual when it went down the wrong way. He coughed and grabbed his bottle of water as he twisted around to bring Clayton into view.

"It's delicious," he said from behind his hand. Once he swallowed, he gave Clayton a wry grin. "Better when you don't choke on it."

"I hope you pay more attention to your surroundings when we pay you to do surveillance." Clayton sat down opposite him. He tilted his head back to the sun for a second, eyes closed and hair tipped with gold. Then he scooched his chair sideways into a bar of cast shade. "That didn't take long."

Kelly put the envelope on the table between them. "I've never been burned on surveillance," he said. It was a lie. Everyone got burned. Murphy's Law saw to that. There'd be construction, some angry woman would mistake your car for her cheating ex's, or something would just put the target's nerves on end. Kelly placated his conscience, which always sounded like his dad, with a silent "Well, lately." "And your client married a dirtbag. Hell, the dirt was easier to find than the bag."

While Clayton flicked through the report and a frown pleated between his straight, sandy eyebrows, Kelly watched him. One day he was going to work out *exactly* what it was about Clayton Reynolds that he couldn't just ignore.

Obviously Clayton was handsome. He had the sort of stern, sharp-boned face that belonged in a European castle or a silver-screen Western—all harsh angles and intensity. His shoulders were broad, his hips lean, and his legs looked a mile long in his tailored dark blue suit.

All of that explained why he made Kelly's mouth dry and his mind dirty, but not the way he stuck in Kelly's head.

He worked with plenty of attractive men, people he gave a solid second look to, but they didn't crawl into his fantasies or take up space in his brain while he went about his day. It wasn't as though there was even anything to it other than an itch to be scratched. Clayton was probably a catch for someone, but not for Kelly.

He didn't do intense, reserved men who wore their feelings on the insides of their bones where no one could see them. His lovers were good-natured and easygoing, the sort of men who didn't need anything from you but still wanted to be with you.

Until they didn't. Even then, there were no hard feelings.

So one day he'd work out why long, lanky, and knife-sharp— not what he wanted, not what he needed—had worked his way under Kelly's skin. Probably not today, though. Kelly took a bite of his burger. He'd just started to chew when Clayton looked up from the timeline of Jimmy's douchebaggery.

"What do you think of him?"

Kelly swallowed hard and wiped hot sauce off his mouth with a napkin. The heat lingered on his tongue, and he took another swig of water while he dragged his thoughts out of the gutter.

"On paper it looks like she's in a good position," Kelly said. "Even without her broken arm, she has plenty of reasons to leave him. I can't see custody being an issue if he gets to court."

"If?" Clayton said. "You think she's in danger?"

"He already broke her arm. And he's got more than just pride on the line." Kelly wiped his hands on his jeans and leaned over to flick back pages. "Look. The house is in her name. No bank accounts or credit cards, so he's probably fed all his finances back through her accounts, even if she doesn't know about it. If she leaves him, he stands to lose a lot. That's just his own finances. His associates are… unpleasant people, and if any of their business interests are entwined with his, then it could involve them."

Clayton looked sour but not surprised. He knew what the facts meant better than Kelly did.

"Damn it." He pushed the file back into the envelope and sat back. His jaw was set so tightly it looked as though the sharp hinges were going to slice through the skin. "I had hoped she was just afraid of him."

Kelly didn't need to state the obvious, that other people were afraid of Jimmy Graham. It was laid out in the stark black and white of his record, the red hidden under the dry terms of the charges—assault and battery, false imprisonment, possession with intent, criminal threat. He wasn't a nice man. If a broken arm was all she got from him, she was luckier than most of the people in his orbit.

He shoved the carton with the uneaten half of his burger across the table like a greasy protein consolation prize.

"If you want lunch."

Clayton gave it an unimpressed look and pushed it back to Kelly. "I'm a vegetarian."

Kelly flipped the carton shut and pulled it back to his side of the table. Yeah, it was just like a date. Awkward. A middle-aged man in a pair of tie-dyed shorts that he really didn't have the body for skated past them. The wheels rattled over the concrete.

"Do you want me to chase up more details on Mr. Graham?" he asked.

"Did you miss something?" Clayton asked as he picked up the envelope. He pulled an apologetic face a second later. "Sorry. Not yet. There's no point putting more man hours into this until Nadine decides whether to go forward or not."

"If you're sure."

"Thank you for this, though," Clayton said. He held up the envelope. "I appreciate it."

"Well, let me know if you need anything else," Kelly said. He grinned. "Same deal."

Clayton gave him a tight shadow of a smile. "I probably won't," he admitted as he stood up. "Not this time. Probably not the next. Maybe never."

There was a raw scrape in his voice that cut through his usual service. Something too honest to hide? It wasn't any of Kelly's business, but he asked anyhow.

"This case, this client, has really gotten under your skin. Why?"

Clayton stood in the sunshine, the scrappy black-and-silver food truck behind him, and adjusted the cuffs of his expensive suit. It looked like a photo shoot for some glossy magazine profile. Turn the page and there'd be a picture of him with his sleeves rolled up to drink a mug of artisanal coffee.

The rawness lingered in his voice, something real under the polish.

"Children should be scared of the dark and monsters under the bed, if they're scared of anything. Not their parents." He paused and twisted his thin mouth into a smirk as he slapped the envelope against his leg. "That and I don't like to lose, Kelly."

He gave one last salute with the envelope and left. Kelly watched him go and wondered what else Clayton kept tightly folded down under his pressed shirts and excellent suits.

CHAPTER FOUR

IT DIDN'T matter how much bleach was slopped around the floor at the end of the day, the gym always smelled like old socks, sweat, and ass. Kelly figured that most of the fighters had broken their noses often enough that they didn't care.

Kelly danced backward over the canvas, his gloves tucked up to his chin as Cole bounced back off the ropes. There was blood on Cole's mouth. He wiped it off on his arm, grinned with bloody teeth, and came after Kelly.

The gym rats on the sidelines jeered good-naturedly—"stand and fight" and "let's see that pretty face"—as Kelly cautiously retreated. Sweat stung in his eye as it dripped down behind his goggles, and he blinked it away.

He blocked a hard left with his forearm, and the rattle of it jarred up into his shoulder. He jabbed a punch into Cole's stomach, and that earned him a grunt of pain, a short-lived feeling of smugness, and a haymaker that came out of nowhere and knocked him on his ass.

"Sonov—"

Cole tapped him in the ribs with his toe. "Mind your manners."

Cole pinned his glove between his ribs and elbow to yank it off. Then he held out his hand to Kelly and wriggled his fingers. Kelly grunted and took the offered help to get up. His ears were ringing, and the abrupt transition from prone to upright made his stomach twist. For a second, he felt like he might do a Maxie and just barf on his own feet.

Cole slapped that out of him with a tap to the cheek to get his attention. He held up his middle finger in front of Kelly's nose.

"How many fingers am I holding up?" he asked.

Idiot. Kelly gave him a shove to get the sweaty bulk of him out of his space.

"You know, they have a Boxercize class at my gym," he muttered as he rubbed his jaw. "I could just go there."

Cole laughed and grabbed him by the shoulder to steer him out of the ring.

"Boxercise won't teach you to avoid a punch to the face." He casually slapped the back of Kelly's head. "And your mug just begs to be punched."

Kelly ducked away from him and crawled under the ropes. He dragged his gloves off and grabbed a bottle of chilled water from one of the loitering gym rats. It was unlabeled and tasted like tap. He drank half of it down in one go. That would replenish about a third of the hydration he'd sweated out letting Cole beat him up.

He doubled over and braced his hands against his knees as he caught his breath. His ribs hurt, his jaw ached, and it felt like he'd gone ten rounds with Conor McGregor instead of sparred for twenty minutes with a forty-year-old. Maybe—not that he'd admit it aloud—he'd gotten a bit out of shape.

"You're one to talk." He pushed himself upright and looked up to where Cole dangled his long, lean body over the ropes. "That pretty face of yours is held together by staples."

Anyone else would get laid out for that—if not because they'd brought up the surgery, then because they'd called him pretty. Since his little brother had said it, Cole just grinned and wiped blood off his chin.

"The curse of the men in our family," he said easily as he ducked under the ropes and jumped down. He hooked a long arm around Kelly's throat and planted a noisy kiss on his temple. "Why d'ya think Da had to leave Ireland? His face needed the break. Come on. Take those stupid goggles off, and I'll take you for a beer."

"How you coping?" Cole asked as he slid a pint of Guinness across the table. Froth dribbled down the sides of the glass and soaked into the coaster. Cole spun a chair around and straddled it as he took an appreciative drink of his own beer. "With Maxie and, you know, Liam."

Kelly ran his thumb up the side of the glass to gather a rime of foam. He didn't actually like Guinness—he preferred a beer that he didn't have to chew—but to come out with that would cause more arguments than him being gay.

Okay. Maybe not. It was his and Cole's thing, though. They sparred. They went for beer. Back when they started, when Cole had been twenty and Kelly ten, it was ginger ale. Kelly figured it was the same thing back then. He hadn't been a smart kid. Now it was beer, and Cole asked about stuff that he'd probably rather not.

"Liam asked me to go back with him," he said. "To Ireland. I thought about it."

"Jaysus," Cole said. The Irish in his voice thickened. He'd never been there, but he'd picked it up from Mom and Dad before years of America had rubbed the burr off. "Mom would have killed herself."

Kelly flinched. "Not funny." He took a draught of the thick, yeasty beer and set the pint glass back down carefully in the ring it had left on the coaster. "It should have made sense to go. I did like him."

"You don't move to another country because you like someone," Cole said. "You move because you can't live where you are without them."

"Well, fuck," Kelly said. He slouched back in his chair and nursed his Guinness. "That's beautiful."

Cole flashed a wide, white grin that crinkled the corners of his eyes. He looked like their dad. He had the same pale gray eyes and red-fair hair that faded to gilt instead of gray, but he smiled more than Dad ever did.

"It's not bad," he acknowledged. "What did you say?"

Kelly puffed his cheeks out with a sigh. "Waited until he noticed that I hadn't booked my ticket and pointed out I didn't want to go?"

Cole pulled a face that tried not to be horrified but didn't quite make it. "That's an approach."

"Yeah. I could have handled it better."

"You could have talked to me about it." Cole folded his arms over the back of the chair. He cracked a sly grin. "I've got good lines, if nothing else."

Kelly shrugged. "You'd have told me not to go."

"I'd have been right," Cole said. "You didn't go."

That wasn't entirely the point. Kelly let it go anyway. Some things weren't worth the argument.

"So Maxie's with his dad tonight, right?" Cole asked. "How's that going?"

"Great. Byron said he'd spend the night with him at Wil and Molly's. I left Maxie there earlier." Kelly pulled his phone out to check for any updates from his second-oldest brother and his second wife. "Yeah, he ghosted. Molly says she'll drop him back at mine tomorrow."

"It's his job," Cole said with a sigh. "It's hard enough being a cop. Being undercover is twice as bad. Byron can't always just take a night off, not if it would jeopardize his cover or lose him a lead. You know that."

"It's his son." Kelly took a swig of Guinness to try and wash the words out of his throat. It didn't work. "He could take one night off. The department could pull him out if he wanted."

That was off script. They both knew it.

"Mom said you dropped Maxie off with them for the day last week," Cole said to change the subject. "She said you had a job? I thought you'd taken time off."

"I didn't think Mom minded."

"She didn't," Cole insisted. "But you know she can't take Maxie for long. With Dad's health, he can't cope with a baby in the house."

"Dad was at work."

"I know, but you know that Dad can't cope with Maxie right now. It just ends up in a row with Mom about Byron and… everything, and he doesn't need the stress. We don't want him back in the hospital, do we?"

"No."

Cole reached over the table and scruffed the back of Kelly's neck with casual affection. "I know it's not fair. Okay? Byron will sort himself out, Mom will hook him up with someone who can be a new mom to Maxie, and then it will calm down. If you need a break, call me or Wilde and tell your work to go to hell. Not like the world is going to end if some cheating husband gets his end away, right?"

"You know that's not all I do, right?" Kelly asked.

Cole laughed and let go. "I know, I know how hard you work, kid," he said. "But it's not like you're stopping murderers, is it? You can take a vacation."

"Yeah, well, Clayton's a… friend."

"A… friend?" Cole asked. He grimaced. "You're fooling nobody, kid. Last Thanksgiving you talked about this Clayton guy—what a great lawyer he is, how he does all this pro bono work with battered women, the nice suits he wears—more than you did Liam. A crush is one thing, though, but you're not dating one of that turncoat Baker's boy toys. You can do better than that. Look. New guy at the precinct's supposed to, you know, swing your way sometimes. He's Catholic and all, so Mom will be happy. You want me to put a good word in? Talk you up a bit? Leave out the shit stuff?"

There were probably worse things, but Kelly couldn't think of any. "No."

"It's no trouble," Cole said cheerfully. "He's probably coming to the next barbecue at Mom and Dad's. You know how Dad is about making the new guys feel welcome. I'll introduce you."

Kelly shook his head and sucked down a gulp of Guinness. "I can find my own boyfriends."

Before Cole could press his case, the first notes of "Mack the Knife" trilled from Kelly's pocket as his phone jittered against his hip.

"I gotta take this," Kelly said. "Then I'd better head out."

He drained the rest of the pint and stood up. Cole followed suit and dragged him into a rough hug, complete with backslap.

"Let me know if you need any help." Cole stepped back and mock-slapped his face again. "And don't block with your face."

"Asshole."

"Jerk."

Kelly left Cole to finish his pint as he wove through the customers between him and the door. The bar had been empty, or near enough, when they limped it, but the clock had ticked past seven, and ESPN's pregame coverage of a hockey match was up on screens behind the bar.

He dodged around a tired woman in a suit. His shoulder hit a man in his blind spot by the bar, and he twisted around to bring him into view. "Sorry!" he said and held up his phone. The dial tone had gone dead, and the red Missed Call hung on the screen. "I have to make a call."

The guy wiped liquor off his mustache with finger and thumb. "You made me spill my fucking drink."

He wasn't drunk enough—yet—to hit aggressive without a run-up. Kelly clapped him on the shoulder.

"Sorry, man. I didn't see you," he said. A wave of his free hand caught the bartender's attention. "Get the guy a refill would you, Mike? On my brother."

Behind the bar, Mike shrugged and did as he was told. The shouldered man looked a bit put out that it had been settled so quickly, but his friends dragged him to the bar to mumble sourly over his fresh drink.

Kelly pushed through the line at the door and out onto the pavement. Hot night. The temperature hung in the air like moisture, sticky in his mouth as he breathed. Sweat broke on the back of his neck as he walked away from the clatter and chatter of the bar to dial Clayton back.

Cars growled by along the road. Locals went past at high speed in desert dust as they raced the lights home or to the pub while fresh tourists crawled nervously along from the rental place in SUVs with maps plastered up against windshields.

A couple of loitering kids, poser toughs in new Converse and custom-made skull-grin bandanas, gave him a sidelong look as he stopped. After a quick assessment of him—old phone, older jeans, the newest things about him the bruises on his knuckles and jaw—they decided he didn't have anything worth the hassle of running away afterward.

Clayton picked up the phone after two rings.

"Hey," Kelly said. "What you need?"

"I will owe you for this," Clayton said grimly.

"For what?"

There was a pause. Kelly couldn't see it, but he'd watched Clayton in enough meetings to imagine the way he pinched his nose.

"Apparently there's been some developments in the Graham case. Can you meet me at the Saint Bernard's Shelter?"

It begged for a joke—something about dogs and commitment that invited flirty banter. But there was something in Clayton's voice that sounded almost brittle, somewhere between angry and frustrated. It felt like intimacy, and even though Kelly knew it wasn't, he couldn't quite convince himself to shatter the illusion.

"Where?" he asked.

"Why do we pay you again?"

"I can find out, but it will be quicker if you tell me," Kelly said. He'd already turned and had his hand out to hail a passing taxi. The driver gave him the same assessment as the wannabe toughs and came to the same conclusion. Behind the dirty windshield, the red-faced man glanced away and kept going. "Fucker."

"What?"

"Not you."

The next taxi had nowhere better to be. He pulled in, and Kelly climbed in as Clayton clipped the address off in his ear.

THE LITTLE boy wasn't crying.

Kelly would have been, at that age, maybe even now. He stalled in the doorway as Mrs. Park, the small, tight-mouthed woman who'd let him into the building, pushed past him with the first-aid kit.

The boy's mother—Nadine, Kelly recalled from the background check, a dropout from a place more trailer park than town out in the desert—sat on the sagging old plaid couch and bled apologetically into a wadded-up tie as Clayton crouched next to her and held it to her face. She looked like she'd been tossed through a car window, with bloody scrapes on her face and arms. Someone had torn the earrings out of her ears and left the lobes split and raw, and from the amount of blood on the blue cotton jacket, she had a broken nose under the crumpled folds of patterned silk.

"I'm sorry," she muttered through the cloth. It was a monotone litany of self-blame that shortcut its way around anyone else yelling at her. "I shouldn't have come. I know I didn't listen to you. I brought this on myself. I know I did. I know. I just didn't have anywhere else to go."

"That doesn't matter now," Clayton told her. He gratefully surrendered his position at Nadine's side to Mrs. Park and her first-aid kit. A glance and a nod acknowledged Kelly's arrival and told him to wait a minute. Kelly couldn't help the distracted flicker of interest at Clayton with his collar undone and his sleeves rolled back from his wrists. It was the closest to casual Kelly had seen on him. He pushed that aside for later and focused his attention back on the room. "Just let Maureen clean you up. Okay? Then we'll decide what to do."

Kelly winced as Mrs. Park carefully peeled the makeshift bandage off Nadine's face. Fresh blood poured out of a nose that hadn't so much been broken as crushed. It was swollen and canted toward her cheek, with shades of bruise pooled under the skin and around her eyes.

She flinched as the wet cotton wool touched her lip and clenched her hands into fists on her knees. A whine worked its way out of her throat.

"We'll need to get—" Clayton started.

"Can't it wait? She's—" Mrs. Park interrupted as Nadine ducked the wad of cotton wool again.

The "Sorry. I'm sorry" plaint of Nadine's raw apologies cut under both of them.

It was the kid who shut them all up. "Are you a cop?" he asked abruptly as he stared at Kelly with his jaw set. "Dad says we shouldn't talk to cops."

Nadine tried to bolt up off the couch. "No. I told you." She couldn't quite make it to her feet and sank back into the cushions. Color flushed up her cheekbones and into her temples as she tried to bat away Mrs.

Park's hands. Her voice cracked and spiraled up toward panic. "I told you and told you. I can't talk to the police, and I can't go to the hospital. I can't. For Harry's sake."

"I'm not a cop." Kelly stepped forward and held his hands up. He cracked a grin that hurt the bruise on his jaw. "I'm way too short," he joked.

Nadine nearly choked on a startled laugh. She pressed the back of her hand to her bruised lips. The white cast that ran from thumb to elbow was grubby and badly cracked. She studied him with bloodshot blue eyes full of watery suspicion.

"Really?"

"I'm a private investigator," he said calmly. "I work for Mr. Reynolds. He asked me to come and help."

She blinked hard and took a deep, shuddery breath and then nodded sharply. "Okay. Okay. I'm sorry. I just can't go to the police. I need help, that's all. I'm sorry."

"Don't be," Kelly said. "We all need help sometimes."

"Not like this." Nadine wiped her nose on her fingers. "People don't let their lives get out of hand like this. Not good people."

"You'd be surprised. I see a lot of good people in bad places," Clayton said. "Will you be okay with Maureen for a minute? I need to talk to Kelly."

Nadine gave a very small nod but kept her trembling lips pressed together. Mrs. Park squeezed her knee gently. "She'll be fine," she said.

The kid crawled up on the couch and fiercely hugged Nadine's good arm. "It's all right, Mom," he said. "It's all right. We did the right thing."

She leaned into him and rested her cheek on the top of his head. Blood dripped onto him, but neither of them seemed to notice. "I'm sorry, baby. I should have done better."

Clayton scrubbed his forearm roughly over his face and then jerked his chin for Kelly to follow him into the hall. There was a dog barking somewhere in the building, a persistent *yip* that echoed off the high ceilings.

"Did her husband do that to her?" Kelly asked after he pulled the door shut behind him.

"She says no." Clayton frowned at his bloody hands as though he weren't sure what to do with them. He spread his fingers, grimaced, and then rubbed them roughly against each other. It smeared the blood into thinner patches, and dry scabs of it worked into the skin of his knuckles. When they were as clean as he could get them, he crossed his arms. Lean muscle corded tightly in his forearms. "That might be a lie. She's definitely scared that he'll find her."

Kelly rubbed his thumb along his jaw, where a day's worth of stubble was rough as his thumb raked through it. He assumed that last part was why he was there.

"Not here?" he asked as he glanced around. The industrial beige walls were shabby with age and dented old damage—most of it the sharp-edged chips and scrapes of general wear, but a few deep and fist shaped.

"Apparently he knows she was here."

"Tracker on her phone," Kelly said immediately. He pulled a rueful face as he added, "Or she just didn't think to turn off location services. People don't."

"If I'm going to be her lawyer, I can't afford to have the appearance of impropriety. I know this isn't part of your usual—"

"It has been," Kelly said. He grinned when Clayton gave him a dubious look. "We don't always do family law. Baker's clients tend to be a bit more... precarious."

The spare room at Kelly's was empty. Clients had crashed there before, when something had gone unexpectedly and sharply south with their litigations. But he couldn't justify that with Maxie in the house. Even if Nadine and her son were harmless, the ex clearly wasn't.

"There's a secure house we use sometimes," Kelly said. "My brother's ex is a Realtor. She sorted it out for us. It's mostly just for people to sit in before we drive them to court, and there's not much in there, but it would do for a couple of days until you sort something out. I can get Larry to change the alarm remotely so we can get in."

Some of the wire-strung tension went out of Clayton once he had a solution in hand. Not all of it, but enough to drop his shoulders slightly. "That works," he said. "I would have put her in a hotel but...."

"You don't have the firm for a buffer," Kelly said. "It would look more suspicious than her taking your couch."

Clayton smiled grimly. "Even though the last time I was a danger to a woman's virtue was when I tried to convince my foster sister to steal a soy sauce pot as a souvenir from our favorite Chinese restaurant."

"Clayton Reynolds breaking the rules?" Kelly asked with dry skepticism. "I find that hard to believe."

The smile on Clayton's face flared into a grin, just for a second, and then faded into something thoughtful. He skimmed his pale gray eyes over Kelly in a once-over so quick it could have been Kelly's imagination. Or, Kelly supposed, his height might mean it didn't take that long to get from his head to his crotch.

"Sometimes you stick to the rules because you know how good it feels when you break them," Clayton said roughly, "and how bad it turns out."

It sounded more like a warning than a come-on. If it was, it didn't work. Kelly didn't think he'd ever been anyone's bad decision, but he wouldn't mind finding out what it would be like. Before he could put that tug of want into words, Clayton shrugged the moment off.

"We should go," he said. "I want to get Nadine and Harry settled. Then, if you have time, we can discuss what else I can wring out of that favor."

The thought of Nadine's battered face—the broken nose and tear-raw cheeks—was better than a bucket of cold water. His dad always said domestic violence calls were the hardest. Not the worst—he'd seen worse things in his career—but hard because you knew that the black eye and the broken arm or the bloody legs and bruised face were only about halfway to how bad things would get. They were also dangerous—for the cop and the victim.

When Kelly did the background check, he found that the broken arm was Nadine's first "walked into a door" hospital visit. It obviously wouldn't be her last if she went back again.

"Don't worry about it," Kelly said. "Whatever you need to get her safe."

CHAPTER FIVE

CHILDREN LEARNED by example. Look at Kelly, who'd probably learned to be a Boy Scout, to make friends, to do the right thing, to help people, all at his dad's knee. He probably had heartwarming stories about it.

Other kids only had bad examples. Baker had learned from his mom that brandy was dandy but liquor was quicker. Harry knew that, despite everything that the TV, his teachers, and his books wanted to tell him, not every kid got "The World's Best Dad."

Clayton had learned early on that when something in your life wasn't going how you wanted, the only appropriate reaction was to fuck someone else over. It didn't help, but at least *someone* was worse off than you, and that was something.

That impulse—kicked off by frustration and familiarity—wasn't why he wanted to shove Kelly against a wall and kiss the earnest off that full, ridiculously *un*kissed mouth. It was just more ammunition for his cock.

He did best to ignore the temptation as they got Nadine cleaned up and ready to go.

"But I need my phone," Nadine protested when Kelly asked for it. She squeezed her fingers around the narrow square of plastic and glass. Her voice was clogged and nasally as it wriggled through the puffy mess of her nose. "What if there's an emergency? If Harry gets sick?"

Clayton picked up his ruined tie from the arm of the couch. Blood, snot, and tears had crusted into the thin ribbon of fabric and dried stiff.

"I can wash that for you," Maureen offered.

The skin on Clayton's shoulders crawled with the memory of rough old T-shirts, scrubbed until they were patchy and threadbare but still never quite clean. There'd always been a bit of a whiff around him as a kid—not dirt, just that musty smell of neglect that unloved cars and unloved children got.

"Don't worry about it. Just a tie." He tossed the tie into a trash can, and the end of it flopped limply over the side. He looked back at Nadine. "You said you didn't want James to find you."

"I don't," she said in a small voice as she hooked her arm around Harry's narrow shoulders.

"You said he knew you'd been here."

She pinched her lips together in acknowledgment of that, but her fingers still clutched the phone. Her grip was tight enough that it had split the scabs over her knuckles so they oozed.

"What if my mom calls?" she asked. "What if something happens to her?"

Harry tugged at her elbow. "Gran never calls, Mom. Please."

From the way Nadine's face twisted, that was a painful truth. She looked down at her hands, took a snotty breath, and finally handed over the phone to Kelly. He powered it down with capable, tanned fingers and dropped it in his pocket.

"I'll get you a burner," he promised. "You can't tell anyone where you are, though, not even your best friend or your—"

"I don't have any friends," Nadine said. She flicked a tear off her bruised cheek with her fingers, and a tight, bitter little smile settled on her mouth. "They didn't like James."

If they'd been any sort of friends, Clayton didn't expect they'd feel great about being proved right. He glanced at Maureen and tilted his head to the door. She rolled her eyes at him but patted Nadine on the knee and excused herself to go and get a smoke.

"Before we go, Nadine, we need to talk about what happened," Clayton said. "Do you want Kelly to leave?"

She shook her head before he finished what he had to say. "I can't tell you anything. Please. If I do…."

The words ran out, and she pulled Harry into a bone-squashing hug.

The boy protested with a little-kid's bluntness. "Mom, I can't breathe." He tried to squirm under her arm and nearly slid off the couch.

There was a harsh, unkind part of Clayton that wanted to snap at her to pull herself together. It wouldn't be fair, or do any good, and he knew that, but the situation was bringing out all his worst traits.

He volunteered pro bono hours, but the work was usually clean, at the remove of a legal document and a consultation, not blood on his hands—he'd forgotten how it got under your nails—and the cloying smell of tears and fear on the back of his tongue.

It had been over twenty years since he'd been that sour-smelling, little boy, angry at the world, or at least his part of it. Yet here he stood in clothes that cost more than his old house, and all those bitter, impatient words clawed at the inside of his throat.

Except Nadine wasn't his mom. She loved her son. She had a chance. They both did.

"Nadine, if your husband did this—"

She shook her head. "He didn't," she said. "I promise. Okay? Please. Just don't ask—"

"It was the men," Harry piped up abruptly as he scrambled away from his mom. "They came to the house to see Dad, but he wasn't there and—"

"Harry!"

"I don't care! Dad's a... Dad's a dick," Harry blurted out with a brittle mixture of defiance and fear. It was obviously the worst thing he could think of to say. Tears welled in his eyes, and he scrubbed his sleeve across his face. Nadine reached for him. "I don't care if he gets in trouble. I don't. I hope he... he... goes to jail forever!"

"Stop that. Harry, you don't mean that," Nadine said. "Your dad loves you, no matter what happens between him and me. He loves you."

Harry looked very old for a minute. Maybe that was the first thing he'd ever known as an absolute in his life.

"No," he said firmly. "He doesn't."

There weren't many tears left in Nadine. She covered her mouth with her cupped hand and stared at her son through a film of what she had left. Her two attempts to say something died on her parted lips before she could make a syllable. In the end she just shook her head and slumped defeatedly back into the couch.

"Then you're right, kid. He's a dick," Kelly said. The sound of the word in someone else's mouth made Harry giggle nervously, a shy hiccup of sound. Kelly leaned down and put his hand on Harry's narrow shoulder. "Look, we need to talk to your mom. Could you go find Mrs. Park and tell her that *I* told her you deserve a bar of chocolate?"

Harry glared dubiously at him. "I'm not three."

"If you don't want it, I'll have it," Kelly said.

Harry snorted at that suggestion. He twisted his fingers in the stretched fabric of his T-shirt as he tried to decide what to do. "You'll be nice to my mom?" he asked.

"Hey, *my* mom would blister my ears for me if I weren't," Kelly said. "We're going to be friends."

Harry sighed pointedly. "You can't be friends with a girl," he said. "You're a boy. You can only be friends with boys. Dad says that girls are only good to have around when you're a grown-up."

"Harry!" Nadine blurted, mortification taking precedence over shock and pain. "I've told you, don't repeat everything your dad says. Go with Mrs. Park!"

After a moment Harry looked to Clayton for the final assurance. Clayton nodded at the door. "Go on." He waited for the scuff of Harry's feet to fade away and looked at Nadine.

"I'm your lawyer. I'm not going to make you go to the police if you don't want to," he said. "But if I'm going to represent you, I need to know what's going on."

Kelly perched on the duct-taped-on arm of the couch. It managed not to fall off, and he crossed his arms. His soft, faded gray shirt clung to the solid planes of his body. "We're going to try and find out anyhow," he admitted. "Better you tell us now than we go and whack a hornet's nest."

It took a minute.

Nadine stared down at her knees for a tight resentful second before she finally broke and started to speak. It came out like a confession, in a low, bitter voice that cracked whenever she blamed herself.

"I didn't know who they were. Just two men I've seen with James sometimes, outside in the car with him or at the bar. But he doesn't introduce me to his friends. I shouldn't have let them in, when they knocked on the door, but I thought they were there to see James. He's been okay lately. He hasn't lost his temper in ages, not since I came here, so I didn't want to…." Her composure and her voice cracked at the same time. She finally looked up and admitted wearily, "I didn't want to go back to normal. When did being scared of him become normal?"

It sounded like a genuine question, like she'd appreciate an answer. Clayton wished he could help her with that. He was surprised when Kelly had one.

"When you needed it to be," he said. "People are afraid of being randomly mugged or in a car accident, but they plan for the unleashed, aggressive dog they pass every day and the bully that's always at the school gates. It's not any nicer, but it's easier. It's safer."

Nadine touched her nose with tentative fingers and winced.

"Not today."

Kelly gave her a slow, warm smile. "Can't plan for everything."

She nodded, grabbed for his hand, and hung on to it, her fingers white and bony as she squeezed tightly and took a deep breath. Kelly gave Clayton a quick, startled look, although if he'd ever taken out that smile and that voice before—a hint of learned Irish caught around his *t*'s and *r*'s—he should be used to people getting attached to him. Clayton gestured at him to be patient, at least long enough for Nadine to finish her story.

"I shouldn't have let them in," she said. "James had had a falling out with them over… something. I don't know. I didn't understand what they were talking about. Something about money, I think? He owed them it, or he said he'd get it for them and he hadn't? They wanted to talk, but James doesn't like it… he doesn't like being told what to do. They should have known that. He was…. He does this *thing* where he just yells at you? You're trying to be calm, to talk it out, but he's just screaming in your face until you get mad. Then he's so calm."

Kelly clenched his jaw at the description, a grimace of understanding that Nadine missed and Clayton filed away to think about later.

"And these friends?" Clayton asked. "They got mad?"

Nadine finally let go of Kelly's hand and went to touch her nose again, but she caught herself at the last minute. Instead she pushed her arm out in an abrupt gesture, her fingers spread wide and stiff.

"They pushed me into a wall. My face. They pushed my face into a wall. I think that's when I broke my nose. I didn't really feel anything, but I heard a pop, and one of them ripped out my earrings. They were just cheap, but he did it anyhow. He called it a down payment, and then he… he said he'd be back."

"Was Harry there?" Clayton asked.

Nadine dropped her gaze to her knees and shook her head. "He was outside," she said. "I told him what happened. That's all. He didn't see anything."

As lies went, it was halfhearted. Clayton considered calling her on it, but it didn't seem worth it yet. He needed the rest of the story, and then he could pick at the untruths and fabrications. All of his clients lied to him eventually, but at least Nadine wanted to protect some*one* and not some stocks she'd hidden offshore.

"What about James?" he asked instead.

"He didn't touch me."

"What did he do?"

Nadine looked up at him from under her lashes. "Nothing," she said. "He was... he didn't seem to realize what had happened... until I tried to call the police."

She cuddled her cast to her chest and picked at the cracks in the plaster with broken nails.

"Did he do that?"

She lifted her shoulders slightly. "I wouldn't let go of the phone," she said. "It was stupid. If I'd just listened to—Jesus. Do you hear me?"

"I've heard worse," Clayton said. Nadine looked at him dubiously. "When the violent partner says 'if only they'd just listen.'"

Nadine didn't smile, but something tight and painful loosened around the corners of her mouth.

"Easier said than done, though. He didn't touch me. I think if he had I wouldn't be here. I'd have made excuses for him if he'd lost his temper. Except he didn't. I fell. I was dizzy, and I couldn't... I couldn't see." She gestured at the raw spot of scalp at her temple. It would have bled a lot, a sheet of blood down over her eye. Nadine lifted her broken arm and stared at the cast that was meant to protect it. There was a bitter sort of depth in that. "He stood on my arm until I let go of the phone and then told me he knew I'd been here, but he wasn't worried. That if I left, he'd get Harry. That I'd never see him again."

"I won't let that happen," Clayton said confidently.

"He seemed really sure."

"So am I," Clayton said. "And people pay me a lot of money to be sure about these things."

Nadine stared at him uncertainly, and then, in a mirror of her son, turned to Kelly.

He stood up off the arm of the couch. It listed a bit more than when he'd sat down. He hooked his thumbs in the pockets of his jeans.

"I get paid all right money to find out stuff he can be sure about," he cracked with a flash of that careless, sweet smile. It faded into an earnest expression. "You can trust him. He's a good lawyer, and he's a good man."

It was that kind of sunny optimism that made Clayton want to drag Kelly into his world and his bed until he saw the error of his ways. Clayton was an excellent lawyer, but he wasn't a good man. He wasn't a bad one—Kelly had seen enough of those—but he had flaws.

But it convinced Nadine to finally nod her head and mouth "Okay," so Clayton let it go.

"Good," he said. "Tonight we'll get you and Harry somewhere safe, get a doctor out—"

She flinched. "I can't go to the hospital. He'll know. He knew last time."

"I can get a doctor to do a house call," Clayton promised. He ignored the twitch of dismay from his greedier side. There had been too many empty pockets in his past for generosity to come naturally. He always had to work at it. "There's no way that James will know, but we need to have a medical record of this. We might need it later. Tomorrow we can discuss what your strategy is going to be and what you can expect."

"That it will be hard," Nadine said. "You already told me that."

Kelly gave her a hand up off the couch. "Call it a recap."

Clayton gave him a sharp look. Sometimes Kelly's easy charm wasn't appropriate. "It's important you understand that, just because we can win, doesn't mean this will be easy," he said. "If your husband is going to fight us, he can drag the process out to cause you as much pain as possible."

"I don't think he could hurt me any more than he already has," Nadine said quietly.

That was a failure of imagination on her part, but it could be part of tomorrow's discussion. In the meantime Clayton called a car to get them to Kelly's safe house.

NADINE TRIED not to look dismayed as she climbed out of the glossy black sedan and stared at the small gray house on the handkerchief of dead grass and sand. A heavy strip of chain link fenced it from the street, but that hadn't stopped something from taking a crap right in the middle of the dead little garden. It had *probably* been an animal.

"You sure you're okay?" The cab driver dropped the passenger-side window to check on Nadine. Behind her glasses, Clayton caught the unfriendly flick of her eyes toward him. "If you want, I can take you somewhere else. The hospital?"

For a second he thought a daunted Nadine might actually take her up on the offer. Then she straightened her shoulders and shook her head.

"Thank you, but this is where I need to be," she said.

Clayton handed the driver two fifties. She folded them in her fingers, seemingly caught between temptation and the dark suspicion that it was hush money.

"If someone comes looking for her," he said, "don't tell them where she is. For her sake. Can you wait? We won't be long."

She took the money. He didn't know if that meant she'd bought the story. Either way, she waved goodbye to Nadine, rolled the windows up, and killed the engine. It was the nicest car on the street. Clayton looked around at houses with peeling paint and sagging eaves, all of it starkly lit by the incandescent glare of the LED streetlights. It wasn't rough—no tags on the buildings, no soldiers loitering on the front porch to remind people they were there—just tired. Broken swings dangled from rusted chains in weed-thick gardens, and a scavenger's junk heap of broken fridges and old cars were stacked up around the sides of the houses. In one of them, out of view in the back, a dog barked a monotonous, baritone objection to... something. Maybe them. Maybe a bird.

It was familiar, the sort of neighborhood where people fostered kids like Clayton. Cute toddlers got the well-meaning, college-educated, middle-class families with rooms decorated just for them and weekly appointments for their separation anxiety. Foul-mouthed, angry preteens got a spare bed in a room that smelled of other children and tired foster parents who didn't want to add another kid to their clan but needed the state check. Some of them had been kind. Some hadn't been. Most had been indifferent.

"Not sure this is the ambience our clients would expect when they hear 'safe house,'" Clayton noted as he joined Kelly on the cracked pavement. "In case we ever need one for the firm's clients."

Kelly shrugged. "It's safe and it's a house." He hitched the bag of scavenged clothes Maureen had pressed on them up onto his shoulder. A stuffed panda stuck its head out of the zipper. A torn ear and missing eye made it look a bit piratical. Clayton made a mental note to donate an appropriate check to the shelter in return and to attempt not to let his personal feelings leak out onto other people.

"I didn't mean to criticize," Clayton said.

Kelly gave a quick, slanted grin in profile. "Liar."

"Frequently," Clayton admitted. "Not right now. This neighborhood is just...."

"Depressing?" Kelly offered when Clayton paused. That wasn't the word Clayton wanted to avoid—that it was familiar, resented, too close to the bones he'd layered education and nice suits over—but it wasn't wrong.

"Close enough." He watched as Nadine tried to corral Harry with one arm, half mom and half climbing frame as the exhausted boy whined and hung off her. "Can you look into her husband some more tomorrow? Find me assets to free. Canvass the neighbors—"

"Teach a grandmother to suck eggs?" Kelly suggested. His grin stole any bite from the words, and he started across the pavement toward Nadine. "Don't worry. I'll get you what you need."

Kelly swaggered, all loose-hipped confidence and wide shoulders. He moved like he was at ease in his own skin, and Clayton couldn't help but wonder what he'd be like in bed.

See? Sometimes he lied. Clayton could have helped it. He just didn't want to.

He watched Kelly juggle the gate latch, the backpack, and Nadine's second thoughts. His mind was caught between how he'd slot Nadine's divorce into his caseload and the things he wanted, not needed, from Kelly.

He didn't *need* anyone.

There was quite a list. Somewhere in the middle was that Kelly should buy jeans that showed his ass off better. Clayton was confident he'd like it. He had yet to meet a man with abs and no ass, but it would be nice to be sure.

Clayton shook the thought away and went to help get Harry and Nadine into the house. It was more depressing inside than outside, with stained yellow walls, a few old chairs, and a hoarder's stack of takeout cartons in the corner of the room. If there was any air-conditioning, it hadn't been on in a while, and the house was muggy and sour-smelling.

"The code for the security system is 2785kc," Kelly said over the slow drone of the alarm. He tapped the keypad and hit Enter, and it went quiet, except for the metronome-steady bark of the dog outside. "If someone makes you disable it, leave off the last two letters. The alarm will cut out, but we'll still get an alert at the office and know to get out here."

Nadine nodded and looked around the joyless place they'd brought her to live. Her jaw was clenched against any reaction. It was the face of someone who had to weigh her broken nose against a house in Glendale and a good school district for her son.

"It won't be for long," Clayton promised her.

Kelly glanced at him and then at the shabby room as though he'd just seen it for the first time. "I'll send someone over tomorrow," he promised. "Get it cleaned up. I've got a sister-in-law who runs a cleaning business—crime scenes usually—so she can get this place cleaned up in no time."

Nadine took a shallow breath. "I thought you said it wouldn't be for long."

"It won't be," Clayton said. "But not long in legal terms is still more than a few nights."

It wasn't what he wanted to say, and it definitely wasn't what she wanted to hear. She needed to know the truth, though. If she wasn't going to see it through to the end, it would be safer for her to go back to James now. Once she'd served her husband notice of divorce, she would put herself in a whole new category of risk.

"More than a week?" she asked. Her expression flickered toward desperation as she looked around. "A month?"

"I hope not, but be very sure this is what you want to do," Clayton told her. "I think it's the right thing, but I'm not you. It's your life. Once we start this—"

"I can't change my mind," she said. "I get it."

"You can change your mind," Clayton corrected her. "You just can't take it back."

She looked thoughtful. And afraid.

CHAPTER SIX

"Do YOU think she'll go through with it?"

Clayton leaned against the doorframe and stared at the long-dried swatch of colors on the wall. They had left Nadine—sheets on the beds and the fridge half-stocked with pizza pockets and frozen dinners from the gas station—an hour ago. Clayton could have been back at his apartment by then.

Instead here he was, cold beer in hand as he tried to guess what color Kelly was going to paint his house.

He'd forgotten how good it felt to just give in to the bad idea and see where it took you. Or he'd tried to anyway.

"Do you know what the best bit of legal education I ever got was?" Clayton asked.

It didn't sound like an answer to the question, not yet, and Kelly came in from the kitchen to give him a curious look.

"That no crime-scene tech will ever be that helpful?" he suggested.

"Divorce lawyer," Clayton reminded him. "I've only had to deal with crime-scene techs a couple of times, and we paid them well enough that they were very helpful. No. Baker told it to me after I lost my first case—to him. He took me to Santa Monica Pier for a cheap beer and a carton of pickled mussels."

The advice, Clayton remembered, had stayed with him longer than the seafood had. But he thought he could leave that out.

Kelly laughed, "Sounds like Baker," and took a swig of beer. Since Clayton had already committed to the bad idea, he didn't even bother to pretend not to notice the way Kelly's mouth wrapped around the mouth of the bottle. The image of what Kelly would look like with his mouth on Clayton's cock flashed through his head—full lips slick and stretched, his hands rough on Clayton's hips, Clayton's hand twisted in Kelly's short, messy hair.

The quick, brutal punch of lust that hit Clayton, hot in his throat and balls, caught him by surprise. It wasn't like he was unaware that he wanted to fuck Kelly, but apparently the decision to actually do it made it more immediate.

He glanced down at his hands and tried to dredge up the thread of the story he was halfway through. Just because he'd decided to let the bad idea play out didn't mean Kelly was interested, not without some work on Clayton's part anyway.

"So, Baker told me that the three most important things I needed to know as a divorce lawyer were that the rich settle, the poor fight it out, and the crazy just want to fuck someone over," he said. "The first two aren't always true, but I've never seen the third disproved. It won't be easy, but she's got me. I'm very good."

"Modest too."

"I've never seen the point." Clayton looked back at the stripes of paint on the wall and changed the subject. "Have you decided what color you're going to paint in here?"

Kelly turned to study the wall. There were three different shades of beige, a yellow, an offensively bright blue, and a purple.

"I don't know," he said. "Everyone likes a different color. What do you think?"

"None of them," Clayton said. "But it's not my wall."

"Tell my family next time you see them," Kelly said dryly, and then he handed him his beer. "Hold this for a minute."

Clayton took it, and Kelly kissed him. He cupped Clayton's face in both hands, his fingers rough with calluses, and his mouth was hard and eager as he leaned into Clayton's body. It was a confident kiss, all stubble and soft lips. But more than that, it was wholehearted. Kelly kissed like he held nothing back to save face if he were rejected.

Hunger parched Clayton's throat and slid under his skin until it itched to be touched. His cock thickened under his trousers, and the pulse of *want* settled dully just back from his taint.

Clayton kissed back once, a rough slash of his lips across Kelly's, and then he pulled away. He took a swig of beer and tilted his head back against the wall.

"I would have gotten around to that," he said.

"I know," Kelly said. His smile was slow and full of lazy mockery. It creased the corners of his eyes and carved the not-quite-deep-yet lines around his mouth. It was the sort of smile that looked like you should be able to taste something on it, like honey or sunshine. "I just thought you might take all night to get there."

"I was being charming."

Kelly nodded thoughtfully. "Ah. Well, it worked."

"Seductive."

Kelly hooked his fingers in the waistband of Clayton's trousers and tugged him off the wall. Their bodies pressed together, and the nudge of Kelly's erection pressed against Clayton's thigh. He was all heavy muscle and bone, solidly physical in a way that was somehow more... immediate than the gym-honed bodies Clayton usually took to bed.

"I'm seduced," Kelly promised, and something dark and hungry laced through that lazy, easygoing drawl of his. "Can we get on with it?"

A snort of laughter startled Clayton as it escaped him. It wasn't actually part of his usual pickup technique, not that he'd ever really had to try in the clubs where one-night stands lived.

"Nobody has ever accused me of moving slow before."

"Maybe you didn't spend so much time talking about paint with them?"

Clayton twisted around and set the two beers on a shelf, between a framed photo of Liam and a Captain Sparrow action figure in a Perspex box. Because of course there was. Kelly probably had sports memorabilia in his bedroom too—high school glory days preserved forever.

Kelly wasn't Clayton's type. He wasn't even in the same Venn diagram. Apparently it didn't matter. Clayton didn't want to know why. He just wanted to shove Kelly against a wall and show him you didn't need to be in love to have a good time.

He turned back and cupped a glass-cold hand around the back of Kelly's neck. It was damp with sweat, and Clayton could feel the itch of close-cropped hair under his palm. He grazed his thumb along the heavy line of Kelly's jaw, across the scruff of his stubble, and leaned down to slant a rough, hungry kiss over his mouth.

"Now see, I thought you romantic types liked that," he rasped between kisses as he slid his free hand down Kelly's stomach to the bulge of his cock under his jeans. "All soft words and flowers, moonlight kisses and getting to know you."

He could feel Kelly's grin curve under his mouth. There was something ridiculously, specifically hot about that.

"I do," he said. "On a date. You asking me on a date, Clayton?"

Clayton snorted and pushed himself off the wall. He walked Kelly backward until his thighs bumped into the arm of the couch.

"I'm not even staying the night."

Kelly shrugged and sat down on the edge of the couch to strip off his T-shirt. The bright spray of inked colors on his shoulders slid over the heavy bulk of his muscle as he moved, as though the parrot had fluffed its feathers. Clayton did what he'd wanted to do since he saw it for the first time and ran his fingers over the bright shades. It wasn't some drunken, "spur of the moment" bit of flash. Someone had taken a long time to fit the shape of the bird to Kelly's body, to create the smeared, watercolor stain where the blue and red bled into each other.

"Why a parrot?" he asked.

Kelly balled up his T-shirt and tossed it away. He hesitated for a second and then shrugged easily as he started to unbutton Clayton's shirt. "I've always really liked pirates."

That was such an essentially Kelly reason that Clayton ignored the itch in his hindbrain that thought it wasn't the whole truth. It wasn't a lie either, and besides, Clayton had better things to do right then than play the third degree.

Kelly pushed his hands up under the loose shirt and ran his fingers over the lean slopes of muscle. He pressed a wet, openmouthed kiss against Clayton's chest.

"I like your body," he said. "You're like a knife in a suit."

"Is that good?" Clayton asked.

Kelly glanced up at him from under short, thick lashes. He smiled with lazy appreciation.

"You make it work."

He brushed his thumb over Clayton's nipple with a rough stroke that made Clayton hiss at the sharp prickle of pleasure. Kelly bit his lip in satisfaction at the reaction and did it again on the other side. The pluck of callused fingers made the nipple darken and swell.

Clayton twisted his fingers in the short crop of Kelly's brown hair and tugged his head back until he could see clear, gray blue eyes look up at him. He watched as Kelly ran his tongue over his lower lip to leave it slick and wet.

"I like your mouth. You have a beautiful mouth." Clayton ran the pad of his thumb over the wet curve of it, and the honesty slipped over his tongue before he could catch it. "I like how much you smile."

Kelly laughed. It made Clayton flinch. Offense caught in his jaw like a goad, and the prickly, throwaway kid he'd been was still close enough to his skin to get hurt. He started to draw his hand back.

"See, I kinda like that you don't. Smile much, I mean," Kelly said as he dropped his hands to Clayton's narrow hips. "It makes it a challenge to see if I can get one out of you."

It should have made it better. Clayton wished it were that easy. He'd be a lot less screwed up if it were.

"You think you can make me smile?" he asked as he gave a tug to his handful of Kelly's dark, dense hair. It pulled Kelly's head a bit farther and pulled the line of his throat tight and vulnerable. "You're not that charming, Kelly."

"Wanna bet?"

Mischief sparkled in Kelly's eyes, and he flicked the button out on Clayton's trousers. He dipped his hand into the waistband, his fingers warm as they brushed across his lower stomach toward his groin.

A groan caught in Clayton's throat as he imagined Kelly on his knees again, mouth wet and willing around him. Except he wanted to be the one who made Kelly moan.

"Later," he rasped out of a dry throat and pushed Kelly back onto the couch in a graceless sprawl of inked skin and laughter.

Clayton stepped out of his trousers. The black cotton of his boxers outlined the thick shaft of his erect cock where it lifted up against his stomach.

On the couch, Kelly, his legs still hung over the arm, lifted his hips as he shoved his worn jeans and bright-pink briefs down toward his knees at the same time. "If you need lube, it's behind Captain Sparrow."

Of course it was, Clayton thought wryly. He shoved the box aside and grabbed the lube.

"I've been tested," he said as he rested his hand on the box of condoms. "I've got a clean bill of health. You?"

"Yeah," Kelly said raggedly.

Clayton left the condoms and squeezed lube into his palm. It was slick and cool against his fingers, cold as he reached into his boxers and dragged it along his cock. He admired Kelly, sprawled out naked and hard on the rich, brown leather, as he rubbed the lube from balls to tip. Clayton let his eyes slide over the heavy shoulders down to the narrow hips, before he finally took a good look at the hard curve of cock between Kelly's thighs. It was a nice cock, heavy and tight with a wet, slick head.

Arousal tugged at his muscles, a wire from his balls to his ass and heavy cables of it in his thighs.

"Get up on your knees," he said.

Kelly did as he was told and stretched, all that muscle hard and fluid under tanned skin.

"I thought the Irish were pale," he said.

"Black Irish," Kelly told him with a grin. "And the yard's really private."

The thought of fucking Kelly on the grass, sweaty and sun-warmed and nowhere else to be, sideswiped Clayton on its way to his go-to fantasy bank. He swallowed hard and spun his finger to get Kelly to turn around.

Kelly visibly thought about it for a second, one hand around his cock as he looked Clayton over.

"Maybe I want to fuck you," Kelly said, a hint of challenge in his voice.

Clayton's ass clenched at the suggestion, and he felt the throb of pleasure twist like wire in his groin. He preferred to top, but there were exceptions. The thought of Kelly's cock in him and Kelly's hands on him wasn't... horrible.

Not tonight, though. This was Clayton's bad idea, and he wanted Kelly under him, tight and begging for more.

"I want to make you come," Clayton said as he padded over the wooden floor. Kelly watched him with pale, unfocused eyes as he ran his thumb along his twitching shaft. "I want my name in your mouth and my cock in your ass when you come. I want you to turn around."

Kelly took a quick, shallow breath and did as he was told. He faced the wall and braced his arms against the back of the sofa. Long muscles clenched from his forearm and up into his shoulders. The taut bands of muscle in his back ran down into the tight, sweat-glazed curve of his ass.

"You should get better jeans," Clayton said as he shed his boxers.

Kelly glanced over his shoulder. "What? Why?"

Clayton shrugged as it dawned on him that he had no reason to give anyone else reason to crawl into Kelly's pants. He'd had to take the ass on faith. They could too.

"Everyone should," he said vaguely.

His cock was slick and slippery with lube and come, and each slow twist of his hand along the length of it sent a jolt of pleasure back to settle in his balls. Clayton bit his lip as he ran his fingers down Kelly's spine to the crack of his ass and then inside it.

It was still a bad idea, the outnumbered but sensible part of him muttered... but not quite loudly enough to interrupt the proceedings. Clayton acknowledged it anyway. It was definitely a bad idea, but he could live with that.

He rubbed his lube-slick fingers around the tight pucker of Kelly's ass in slow, teasing circles.

"What do you want, Kelly?" he asked.

Kelly rocked his hips back against Clayton and then raggedly admitted, "You." He groaned. "I want you inside me. Sometime today."

Clayton snorted and slapped the taut curve of Kelly's ass hard enough to leave a pink, splayed imprint of his hand on the firm flesh. He pushed his fingers inside Kelly at the same time, and the tangle of sensation made Kelly squirm and garble a curse as he stumbled over the words.

Kelly's ass was tight and hot as Clayton worked the lube in deeper. He shifted closer, one knee up on a cushion and one hand on Kelly's shoulder as he spread him wider. Kelly made a choked sound deep in his throat and pushed back into Clayton's hand.

"I meant cock," Kelly muttered as he dropped his head. His arms were braced and tight, all clenched muscle and fingers twisted into the cushions he leaned on.

"You have no patience," Clayton teased. He hooked his finger and grazed the rubbery node of the prostate. The shudder of reaction ran up Kelly's back and escaped him on a strangled mewl. Again, a little harder that time, and again, until Kelly's arms trembled, and his elbows folded under his weight. Clayton used his grip on Kelly's shoulder to hold him up until his arms would do the job again. "See? Good things come to those who wait."

Kelly snorted. "You're a dick."

He didn't add it to his tally, but that made Clayton grin as he slid his fingers free. "I thought you wanted my dick."

Whatever Kelly had been about to say turned into a breathless "sonovabitch" as Clayton pressed the head of his cock between lube-slick cheeks. He felt the ache of pressure throb raw pleasure back to his balls as he pushed, and then the tight grip of Kelly's ass squeezed around his cock.

"I like your ass too," Clayton said roughly. He ran his hand over the curve of it and down to the heavy length of Kelly's thigh. The clenched muscles twitched under his hand. They were so tight they trembled. "Why haven't we done this before?"

Kelly laughed, and Clayton felt it in his cock. It felt even better than he'd imagined.

"Because this is a really bad idea," Kelly said. "And usually we have better sense?"

It was hard to argue with that. "Worry about that tomorrow."

Another laugh, and Kelly's ass clenched around Clayton's cock as though it wanted to wring him out. He set his jaw and held himself very still as he willed himself back under control.

"Sounds more like me than you," Kelly said.

Clayton rocked his hips forward in a short thrust and buried his cock an inch deeper inside Kelly. Under him, Kelly gasped and flexed his fingers against the heavy leather of the cushions.

"Maybe you don't know me as well as you think," Clayton said. "I could have a wild side."

He didn't. It had been pruned off years earlier, along with everything else he inherited from his mother. The roots of her tendency to make bad decisions were obviously still there, but not her commitment to them.

"Gotta admit," Kelly said raggedly, "I kinda figure your wild side involves shallow graves in the desert."

Clayton snorted and rocked his hips again, his cock slick and hard as it slid out and then back into Kelly. Each time he worked himself deeper until his balls were pressed against Kelly's ass and sent a throb back to settle in the hollow of Clayton's hips. He folded his body along Kelly's back, hung one arm loose over his shoulder, and bit a kiss against the sweaty column of his neck.

"Not yet," he said.

He nudged Kelly's head around and kissed him deeply, the plunge of his tongue a slick mirror of the thrust of his cock. The groan dragged up out of Kelly's throat and slid into Clayton's mouth. He pushed into Kelly with long, quick strokes that jarred roughly through both their bodies.

Kelly peeled one hand off the back of the couch and braced his hand against the wall. His body jolted with each rough stroke of Clayton's hips.

It felt like the heat of it was backed up into Clayton's balls—a sweet, slippery pleasure that grew tighter with every thrust.

Clayton reached down to wrap his hand around Kelly's cock. It was heavy and hot against his palm as he jerked it roughly. Kelly whined into Clayton's mouth with raw, satisfying need.

"God, Clayton, please," he begged as he pushed back desperately against Clayton.

The tight ball of pleasure in Clayton's groin popped, and he came hard, his balls wrung out with satisfaction.

He rested against Kelly's back, all that muscle solid under him, and pressed a wet, breathless kiss against his jaw. Then he pulled out, cock still heavy, and pushed Kelly down onto his back. He sprawled out, lewd and loose against the cushions. His cock thrust up from the sparse curls at his groin and curved slightly up toward his stomach.

"Great," Kelly cracked. "I get the wet spot?"

Clayton crawled onto the couch and straddled him. He pushed Kelly's legs apart and ran his hands up his inner thighs to palm the heavy swing of his balls. A quick squeeze left Kelly with no wisecracks as he arched his hips up off the couch.

"You don't have to always run that pretty mouth," Clayton said. He leaned down and wrapped his lips around the head of Kelly's cock. The sharp, musty taste of come bloomed on his tongue as he flicked it over the wet slit. Kelly squirmed under him, so he hooked one arm under Kelly's thigh and around to grip the sharp jut of his hip bone. He slid his head down slowly, his lips and tongue busy against the hard shaft.

Kelly groaned and raked his fingers through Clayton's short-cropped curls. He didn't shove or grab. His hand was just there as though he just wanted to touch. Clayton sucked on his cock and worked his hand back between Kelly's thighs and pushed his finger roughly against the tight thread of his taint.

"Clayton. I'm gonna—" Kelly choked out the warning as his body clenched around his orgasm.

Clayton pushed his tongue flat against the underside of Kelly's penis in a long, rough lick. If he hadn't wanted to taste Kelly, he'd just have used his hands. Another lick, and Kelly tipped over the edge with a strangled noise that could have been Clayton's name again. Come pulsed over Clayton's tongue, thick and salty-sharp with a metallic aftertaste of warm pennies.

He swallowed and lifted his head. Kelly's cock slid out and lay against his thigh. Clayton crawled up Kelly, caught his chin in one hand, and kissed him deeply.

"You have a bed?" he asked. Kelly raised his eyebrows, and Clayton smirked against his lips. "I think I have one more bad idea in me."

OR, AS it turned out, one and a half.

Clayton opened his eyes as an alarm blared out bad morning-DJ patter and stared blankly at the half-painted ceiling for a second. It didn't take long for the pieces to slot back into place.

Fuck, he'd spent the night after all. Clayton closed his eyes again and swore to the black insides of his eyelids. He didn't do that. It was easier to show last night's company the door when it was *your* door and you didn't have to ask where the toilet was or the address to tell the Uber.

"If you're thinking of chewing your arm off," a sleepy voice mumbled next to him, "try not to get blood on the floor. S'a bitch to sand out of the wood."

Clayton glanced over to the other side of the bed where Kelly was sprawled facedown on a pillow. The sheets were tangled under his stomach, and the bar of sunlight from the window picked out the vivid colors that flowed down over his shoulder. Give it a few minutes, and the golden rays would make their way down to frame the tanned, now familiar curve of his ass. A twitch of interest in Clayton's cock reminded him exactly how he ended up there.

The last vestige of last night's self-destructive "fuck it, then" attitude tried to assert itself with the reminder that he didn't *need* to be in the office for another three hours. Clayton squelched it. Last night had been what he needed—to exorcise the ghosts of the past, to finally get Kelly out of his system—but it had also been last night.

"Do I want to ask how you know that?" he asked.

Kelly rolled over and stretched out with a cat's thoroughness on the bed, all loose muscle and curled toes. The jab of hunger in Clayton's gut was heavy and insistent. Apparently his cock hadn't got the memo about them being over Kelly yet. Kelly scrubbed a hand over his face and up into his hair.

"How do you think I was able to afford this place?" he asked with a sly grin.

Clayton paused for a second as he tried to work out if Kelly was telling the truth or not. He decided it didn't matter. It wasn't likely Clayton would ever have any reason to come back to the sunny little house. If he did, he wasn't going to make it upstairs.

Not, the bad-idea vestige muttered the reminder, that it mattered. Downstairs had worked fine last night.

"I do need to go," he said.

Kelly scratched his stomach, yawned, and nodded toward the bathroom door. "You can use the shower first if you want."

It made sense and would save Clayton a sticky drive back to his apartment. But the image that flashed into his head and dried out his mouth was of steam, white tiles, and Kelly shoved wet and willing against them. Clayton definitely never did that. The morning alarm, usually his own but the point stood, was the cutoff point for one-night stands. After that, he moved on to the next day.

"Thanks, but I'll shower at the office," Clayton said with a glance at his watch. "I'll need to get an early start if I'm to fit Nadine's hours into the day. Look—"

Kelly waved him off. "No, don't worry," he said. "I'll get started on chasing up the info you need today, and I'll give my cousin a call. If I tell her what's going on, she'll get the safe house cleaned up and stocked up by tonight."

"Ah, yes. I need the financial information as soon as possible," Clayton said, briefly on the back foot as his brain switched tracks from "awkward conversation" to "work." He scratched his head, the short curls sweaty under his nails, and laid the course of Nadine's case out in his head. "I don't want all James's assets to suddenly up and disappear."

Kelly shrugged. "That part is up to you," he said. "I'll get you the ammo, though."

He rolled over onto his side, braced his weight on his elbow, and grinned down at Clayton.

"I needed last night." He leaned down and kissed Clayton with a quick buss that was considerate of morning breath and the taste of last night still on their tongues. Then he pulled away before Clayton could give in to the urge to kiss him back. He flashed a grin. "I think I got a smile out of you once too."

"You're an idiot," Clayton growled.

That just got him a shrug as Kelly rolled out of the bed and headed for the bathroom. The urge to follow him jabbed at Clayton, tempted and tightened his balls. He ignored it and got out of bed to pad downstairs in search of his clothes.

It turned out they were just where he'd left them—on Kelly's floor. Clayton tugged his trousers on and found his shirt. He frowned at the wrinkles worked into the fabric, but since he wasn't about to ask Kelly to borrow a T-shirt, it would have to do.

He'd just shrugged it on over his shoulders and was halfway through ordering a car when he heard someone put a key in the front door.

"Fuck's sake," he muttered under his breath. The woman on the other end of the line huffed at him. "Not you. Sorry. Ten minutes is perfect. I'll be waiting."

He hung up, but before he could do anything, the door opened and a small, neat woman with a cloud of dark, curly hair and a fussing baby in her arms let herself in. She stopped when she saw him and cocked an eyebrow up from behind her large black glasses.

"Well, hello," she said with a slow, wicked grin. "I'm Aggie. And you're... new, aren't you?"

Clayton cringed. He did *not* need to meet the... babysitter or friend or whoever Aggie was. He gave her a tight smile as he finished buttoning his shirt.

"Very new," she said, still with that grin.

"Kelly will be down in a minute," he said. "If you want to—"

She handed Maxie to him. Clayton scowled down at the armful of baby, who scowled back up at him from under a fluffy crop of downy black hair.

"I'm not—"

"Kelly!" Apparently you didn't get to finish a sentence around Aggie. She leaned around the banister and yelled up the stairs. "Did you forget I was coming over?"

Upstairs the shower cut off, and Clayton heard Kelly groan, "Fuck."

CHAPTER SEVEN

WATER DRIPPED on ugly floor tiles—he meant to get around to changing them once he painted downstairs—as Kelly scrambled out of the shower. He grabbed a towel from a rail and gave himself a quick wipe down as he hopped toward the door.

"'Course not," he lied down to Aggie as he dropped the towel on the bedroom door and hunted around for his jeans. "Just lost track of time."

"You and Mr. New getting acquainted?"

Kelly rolled his eyes. He loved Aggie—she was the only relative he had who busted his balls over his sex life as much as she did his brothers—but she was incorrigible.

"His name's Clayton," he yelled down. His jeans were, of course, downstairs. *Crap.* He grabbed a cleanish pair from the laundry and scrambled into them, and dry denim caught on his damp legs. "Be nice. He's still a flight risk."

"He's holding Maxie. We can get an APB out on him if he runs."

Guilt tried to poke him over the whole "forgot about the baby" thing, but he shoved it back into its box. It wasn't as though Maxie were his son. If anyone should feel guilty, it was Byron, if he ever worked out how.

Kelly finally got his jeans up over his hips. He left them to hang there while he finger-combed his hair back from his face and checked his eyes in the mirror. Old habit, that, but you only ever want to freak out one boyfriend that way—or freak out whatever you called a one-night stand that had been a really fun bad idea. Just this once Kelly figured he could rebound without letting Catholic guilt turn it into a three-year relationship.

Clayton, said the office gossip mill, didn't do commitment. His longest "relationship" had supposedly topped out at a couple of months, which was just what Kelly needed right now. Between Maxie and his mom, he had enough complications in his life without adding Clayton in any long-term, doomed-to-end-badly way.

He loped downstairs into one of Aggie's hugs. It was all unexpected strength—she was a pathologist, and Cole liked to boast that she could deadlift more weight than a firefighter—and the smell of baby powder over pomegranates.

"I like him," she hissed in his ear, not particularly subtly. "He's hot, and he knows how to hold a baby."

Kelly glanced over her curls at Clayton and grinned at the vaguely trapped expression that had settled onto his stern, sharp-boned face. Clayton held Maxie with cool competence in the crook of his arm and looked on the verge of chewing off his own arm to get away. A dull throb of interest caught in Kelly's balls, along with the pleasant ache of last night that still settled in shower-loosened muscles.

Not exactly the time, though.

"He's married," he told Aggie with cheerful mendacity. "Two kids, a mortgage, a time-share in the Caribbean. I'm just his bit on the side."

That little bit of character assassination made Clayton glare at Kelly. Apparently he didn't want to be thought of as either husband material *or* a cheating asshole.

Aggie stepped back and looked thoughtfully at Clayton as she tapped her fingers against her chin.

"So what you're saying is that he owns property," she said.

Kelly shrugged an "I tried" at Clayton from behind her and then took pity on him. His family were hard enough for him to swallow sometimes. It wasn't fair to drop Clayton in with no warning, first thing in the morning.

He took Maxie from Clayton and tucked the baby into the bend of his arm. Maxie sneezed and waved his fists in the air in some sort of ineffable baby protest about his life.

"You should go," he said. "Your wife will wonder where you've gotten to."

Clayton gave him a hard look and then turned to extend a hand to Aggie. She took it with a dimpled smile.

"It was nice to meet you," he said pleasantly. A muscle jumped in his jaw, and he added firmly, "And I'm not married."

Aggie laughed throatily. "Oh don't worry. Nobody takes Kelly seriously. He's the joker of the family. It was lovely to meet you, Clayton." She paused and gave Kelly an arch look. "Maybe I'll see you again at the barbecue next weekend."

"Shhh," Kelly told her. "You'll scare him off."

He left her to snigger to herself while he grabbed Clayton's shoulder and led him to the front door.

"Give me a while to get Maxie sorted," he said as he opened the door to let Clayton out. "Then I'll get to work on pinning Jimmy's finances down. Don't worry about Aggie. She's not going to track you down. She *could*—she has access to CODIS—but she won't."

Clayton stood on the doorstep, lean and awkward in second-day black, and folded his cuffs back along his wiry forearms.

"Is there anything in LA that your family doesn't have their fingers in?" he asked dryly. "Look, Kelly, about last night…."

Kelly grimaced. He really didn't need his sister-in-law to hear him get the "it's not me, it's you" talk on his own front step. There was some dignity he'd like to hang on to. He grabbed Clayton's shirt and tugged him in and down for a quick, rough kiss that scraped stubble and lips.

Temptation tugged at him for a second, but Maxie's squirm of protest interrupted the kiss before Kelly could turn it into more than just a distraction tactic. Kelly casually bounced the baby in the crook of his arm as he leaned back.

"Was fun," he finished for Clayton. He grinned. "I always figured it would be. Good to know I was right."

Clayton licked his lips with a slow swipe of his tongue over his lower lip and glanced quickly over Kelly's shoulder. Whatever Aggie was doing—probably peeping around the door—seemed to convince him that he could let Kelly down gently later on.

Or maybe it was the car that pulled up on the road, double-parked behind the neighbor's rusted-out Chevy, and honked its horn.

"Let me know when you find anything about Nadine's situation," Clayton said briskly. He tilted his head to see into the hall and dipped his chin in a brief, sardonic nod. "Nice to meet you, Aggie."

"You too," she called out, unfazed at being caught peeping. "Remember the barbecue. I'm making a very nice Japanese restaurant deliver sushi."

"Ignore her," Kelly said. "It'll be burned hot dogs and raw ribs. Go while you can."

Clayton's mouth twitched with amusement, but he did as he was told and headed down the path toward the Uber. From behind the wheel, the driver watched with the bland apathy of someone who'd already seen six far more interesting walks of shame that morning.

There was, Kelly mused, probably something he could do about that.

He leaned against the doorframe, bare-chested and barefoot with a baby on his hip, and tried to look sultry.

"Have a good day, baby," he called after Clayton. "Call me. Okay? The kids miss you."

The driver looked a bit more interested. Clayton didn't look back, but he did give Kelly the finger over one shoulder as he stalked over to the car.

Kelly laughed and went back into the house. He closed the door behind him and grinned at Aggie, who frowned at him from the doorway.

"What?"

"He seemed nice. Now you'll never see him again."

"You mean he seemed hot," Kelly countered. "You don't know him. He's not that nice."

His conscience pricked at that a bit. Nice wasn't the first word that Kelly would use about Clayton, probably not even the fifth. It was too… soft a word, and nothing much about Clayton Reynolds seemed soft. Certainly not, Kelly's brain sniggered and nudged at him, last night. But Clayton was a good person, even if it was only for free.

"I mean, it just wasn't a meet-the-parents sort of thing," Kelly said. He looked down at Maxie and offered him a finger to gum. "You get it, Maxie. Sometimes your uncle just needs to have a bit of fun, right?"

Maxie sneezed and looked horrified by himself in answer. That could be agreement in baby, for all Kelly knew.

"You can't fuc… fun away your feelings," Aggie told him, her tongue tangled on the midsentence childproofing as she picked his clothes up off the floor on the way to the kitchen. "I saw the way you looked at him. When you were a little fat kid, you looked at Rice Krispies treats the same way."

Kelly snorted. "You've been married to my brother too long," he said. The fat-kid phase had only been for a couple of years, before he accepted that he wasn't going to burn it off with a growth spurt. "Ever considered divorce? I can recommend a good firm."

The pause from the kitchen was long enough that Kelly wondered if he'd actually offended her. He was just about to apologize when Aggie quietly responded in a calm voice, "Sometimes."

"What the fuck?" Kelly blurted out. He followed her into the kitchen and watched her shove his clothes into the washing machine. It had been hers originally, handed down when he moved in there. He just hadn't gotten around to it yet. "You and Cole are…. Jesus, I don't know. Not happy?"

She snorted and dropped the lid of the machine. "Don't be ridiculous. We've been married twenty years. Of course we're not happy all the time. Nobody is happy for twenty years unless they have a syndrome or good drugs."

"Divorce unhappy, though?"

"No. Not really," Aggie said dismissively. She turned to look at him and rolled her eyes. "Stop that. You look like you just learned Santa's not real. Me and Cole don't always agree. The last few weeks, we've just been… not always agreeing more than usual."

Ah. Kelly shifted the probable source of discontent in his arms.

"I don't mind the kid," he said. "It's not for long."

"Maybe you should mind," Aggie said sharply. "Maybe there's a lot you should have minded. Byron…. Byron could shit in a tin, and your mother would call it pecan pie. Maybe you should all mind that."

The words blurted out of her as though they were scared she'd bite her tongue before they could escape. She looked surprised once they were out, not like she regretted what she'd said, but like she hadn't realized there was that much to say.

"Maybe we should," Kelly said. "What good would it do, though? The shit's still in the pan, and Byron's not-quite-ex still killed herself, and Mom won't cop to any of it. It's easier to just… roll with it."

It wasn't the answer Aggie wanted, but they both knew it wasn't one she could argue with either. Kelly might be the youngest of his mom's kids, but that didn't matter. It was Byron who was the spoiled baby of the family, the last-born planned. Kelly had been the result of a careless anniversary and a dearth of condoms.

"I don't get it," Aggie said bluntly. "Cole won't even talk to me about it. He just says that I don't understand, that you have to make allowances for Byron. Why? Because he's a cop? You're all cops. Because he's undercover? He could quit."

"What's he want?" Kelly asked.

"That's a question. Not an answer."

"Neither was that."

Aggie tilted her head back, her curls loose around her shoulders, and took a slow breath through her nose.

"Sorry," she said. "I didn't mean to bring it up. I thought I had it out of my system."

"What is it?" Kelly pressed. He pulled a chair out from the kitchen table with his foot and sat down. It was stupid. Babies, particularly Maxie, weighed almost nothing, but the sack of sugar heft of them still made your elbows ache after a while. He sat Maxie up on the table, left one hand there to support his head, and pulled a face at him. "If it's Maxie, the kid is fine with me. Anyhow, by the time you arranged cover at the morgue, he'd be crawling."

That made Aggie snort. She scrubbed her hands over her eyes. "By the time I arranged cover, he'd be in preschool. No. Even Byron knows he's on a losing streak there. He wants money."

Maxie frogged his legs and waved his arms in the air. It could mean anything from "Feed me" to "I'm currently pooping." Or maybe the kid just knew the combination of Byron and money was a bad one. They'd *all* learned that young.

"Why?" he asked.

Aggie snorted, crossed her arms, and tucked her fingers in under her elbows. "He knows better than to ask me," she said. "And Cole won't tell me. He wants to sell the house."

Shit.

He waited for a moment, but nothing better came to mind. "Shit."

"Yes," Aggie said. She looked at Maxie with an odd tangle of affection and regret. She pushed herself off the counter and walked over to stroke her finger over the top of Maxie's powder-fluff head. "I love that house. More than your brother."

"You mean Byron?"

There was a pause, and then Aggie twitched a dark eyebrow up, enough to hint at a few lines in the smooth skin. "For now," she said tiredly. "Ask me again if we sell my house."

"Aggie—"

"I'm joking," Aggie said quickly. "You know I love Cole. I put up with your family for him. It's just… it's just all of you. I should go, hon. I'm going to be late."

She kissed Maxie on the head and ruffled Kelly's hair.

"Bring that tall streak of pretty to the barbecue. I'm still a doctor. If anyone gets the vapors, I can cope with it."

Kelly rolled his eyes and shifted Maxie up onto his shoulder. "It would give *Clayton* the vapors. He's not the type."

"Fine, but I'll see you there anyhow," Aggie said. She patted her pockets to check her keys were there as she headed out of the kitchen. "And if Byron bothers to show up, maybe I'll finally get what you all see in him."

Kelly patted Maxie's back and hoped not.

THE SHOE had gone under one of the parked cars. A client's, judging from the classy BMW lines of it. None of the investigators drove anything that eye-catching. It was all tidy, middle-aged Fords and dusty old pickups. In their line of work, you didn't want people to take too much notice of your wheels. Kelly knelt on the tarmac and breathed in the smell of oil and damp as he groped under the chassis for the miniature Nike sneaker.

"I don't even know why you need shoes," he muttered. "You can't even walk, Maxie, never mind dunk."

"White boys don't dunk, Kelly."

Kelly turned his head and frowned at the very fancy, snakeskin stilettos posed by Maxie's baby seat.

"I think that's jump," he said as he sat back.

Larry cocked a hip, crossed her arms, and raised a perfectly plucked eyebrow at him. She was the only woman he knew who could make a wrap dress look sharp enough to take an eye out on.

"You can't do that either," she said. "Since you're on vacation, I assume this is some new and exciting enrichment experience for Max?"

"It's just a favor." Kelly ducked back down to peer under the car. There it was. He stretched his arm in and grabbed the shoe. "I just need to hit the database, make some calls. I'll be out of your hair before lunch."

Larry plucked the shoe out of his hand and bent down to pick up Maxie. She hooked the baby carrier over her elbow as she clicked her way toward the elevator. Maxie, the little traitor, made an excited seagull noise and flapped his hands in her general, brightly colored direction.

"Vacation," she tossed over her shoulder. "A fixed holiday period. A break from study, work, or day-to-day life. Not just starting a bit late."

"A friend just asked me to run a background check for them." Kelly scrambled to his feet, brushed the oily grit off his jeans, and followed her. "Nothing exciting."

Larry glanced over her shoulder. "Same favor as last night? For Reynolds?"

"Sorta."

Her smile was sour with sympathy. "Joe was out there this morning. She said the poor woman looked scared out of her wits. Logged them into her Netflix account for free."

That was Larry for "I won't ride your ass about invoices." Kelly appreciated it. They were technically partners—Kelly and Jessop right on the letterhead—but… well, Kelly was a bit Hardy Boys and Larry was more Forensic Accounting, second edition.

Larry reached the elevator and jabbed the button. She turned around as the doors slid open and handed a reshod Maxie back.

"And the reason they wear tiny shoes, Kelly," she said as she stepped back into the elevator, "is because they're fucking adorable."

"Jesus, Larry," Kelly grumbled as they got into the narrow, black-glass-lined box. "Don't swear in front of him. His first word is gonna be grandma, not 'fuck it.'"

She smirked and adjusted the band of her watch on her wrist as they slid upward.

"You're going to miss him," she said, "once your brother gets his shit together."

Kelly leaned back against the cold wall. He could feel the growl of the motor against his shoulder blades.

"He eats, he poops, and he sleeps," he said. "If I miss him that much, I can just ask one of my brothers to move in for a while."

The thought slid through his head that it would be Cole if his oldest brother didn't sort things out with his wife. It was a weird thought. Cole and Aggie had always seemed as rock solid as Mom and Dad to Kelly.

He missed the first part of what Larry said, but his ears dragged his brain back online for the last half of the sentence.

"…how easy you get used to things, Kelly."

"I could get used to sleeping through the night," Kelly cracked as the door opened.

Their office manager greeted Larry with an armful of files and a frown for Kelly.

"You're supposed to be on vacation," Randall chided. Then he produced a slip of paper from his pocket and handed it over. "Our doctor has already been out to see your client. That's his cell number if you need to get in contact."

"Thanks." Kelly glanced at the number and then tucked it into his pocket. He hitched Maxie's carrier up and held it out toward Randall. "I need to run a couple of searches. I don't suppose you want to—"

Randall shied backward as though Kelly had just tried to hand him a burning sack of dog crap. He wagged a finger at Maxie.

"Not in my job description," he said. "Babies are disgusting. They poop themselves right in front of you."

He snatched the now-signed files from Larry, gave Maxie a look and a shudder, and stalked off back to his office. Kelly shrugged after him and turned to Larry with a hopeful lift of the baby.

"Larry?"

"Tempted," Larry said as she chucked Maxie under his chin. "But if I go home smelling of baby again, the wife will kill me. Anything else, though. Just ask."

She slapped him on the shoulder and strode off toward her office.

"We should have something for parents," he called after her. "Like a baby coat check."

"That's day care," Larry said as she reached her door. "And we have a generous leave policy instead."

She closed the door with a firm click. Kelly looked down at Maxie, who shoved a chubby fist in his mouth and drooled. Kelly sighed.

"Right. Well, I'll do the hard work," Kelly said. "You fetch the coffee." Maxie yawned at him.

"I know, I know." Kelly scratched the back of his neck and headed to his office. "You're a baby. You can't handle hot liquid. Well, you're going to have to start pulling your weight sooner or later, kid."

SOMEONE HAD been using Kelly's desk when he was out. There was an empty coffee cup sitting on the glass surface and granola grit in his keyboard. He'd already shaken it out over the trash can, but he could still feel the stubborn crunch of it every time he hit the Space bar.

"How hard is it not to touch my stuff, Maxie?" he asked as he typed with one hand and jiggled a blue dog with crinkly ears at the baby with the other. "It doesn't seem like it would be hard."

Maxie made a noise that was halfway between a croak and a giggle and bounced in the carrier.

"Was that a laugh?" Kelly asked as he looked away from Jimmy Graham's life story on the computer. He made the blue dog—might be a dragon now that he looked at it—bop around until Maxie creaked out his excited noise again and kicked his feet. It was definitely, Kelly decided, meant to be a laugh. He grinned and bopped Maxie gently on the nose with the dragondog. "Look at you. You happy to be at work, Maxie?"

Okay. Maybe Kelly would miss Maxie once Byron actually decided to deal with his new single fatherdom. For a wiry, monkey-looking infant, Maxie had grown on him.

"Just remember in the future that I'm your favorite uncle," he said as Maxie managed to shove a handful of rustling blue velour ear into his mouth. "Don't listen to what your dad says."

Maxie stared at him with huge blue eyes and gummed contentedly at the noisy ear. Kelly left him to it and went back to strip mining Jimmy's life. The first background check had laid the groundwork, but this was a deep delve.

Or it would be, but Jimmy Graham didn't seem to have anything under the surface. Kelly scratched his jaw and reached for the coffee. The stink of stale cinnamon was all that saved him from a mouth full of someone else's backwash. Kelly grimaced and leaned over to set the cup out of easy reach on the edge of the desk.

There was something off. Kelly sat back in the chair. It creaked as his weight shifted back in it. He had enough here for Clayton to get Jimmy's assets frozen. That was all he'd been asked to do.

He glanced at Maxie, who was still happy as he drooled all over his toy. He tried to imagine Maxie in a barren, sweaty little safe house—scared, worried about his mom, not quite ready to trust anyone. It made Kelly's stomach knot with a musty new fear that didn't care that it wasn't really an issue.

"It can't hurt to turn over a few more rocks," he said as he tweaked Maxie's again-naked toes. "Once I've sent this over to Clayton. Just to see what comes scuttling out. Well, I'll see. You get to stay with Mrs. Ryder and her kitties. No stakeouts till you're older."

CHAPTER EIGHT

YOU COULD shuffle the houses on Nadine's block like checkers and no one would be the wiser. They were nice houses—low and wide with long stretches of window—but they were all the same neat, bluntly geometric houses on the same neat squares of land. Some of them were painted one color, but one of them had replaced the lawn with a rectangle of small white stones and large gray paving slabs. That was just cosmetic. Underneath, the bones were all the same.

It had taken Kelly two days and an hour longer than it should have—a traffic jam on the I-405 caused by, as far as Kelly could tell once he got that far, a Spongebob hairbrush some kid had tossed on the road—before he could get a chance to poke deeper into Jimmy's life. Two days and four stiffly professional emails with Clayton, Kelly's ever helpful brain reminded him.

He ignored it as he walked up to Nadine's house. Someone had filled the garden with roses. Kelly assumed it was Nadine. Jimmy didn't seem the type. They had wilted over the last few days. Their fat pink heads sagged on thorny stems, and the grass was covered with shed petals. The smell of decomposing flowers hung sweet and heavy in the air, like perfume gone sour.

Kelly ignored the No Trespassing sign mounted on the chain-link fence and let himself in. In his street, the curtains would have twitched three houses in either direction. Here there was nothing.

Nadine said that Jimmy would probably be away for work this week, but Kelly knocked on the front door and waited anyhow. There was nothing as embarrassing as being caught. He glanced around at the empty street, tucked his hands in the pockets of his jeans, and walked around the side of the house.

A tantrum had hit the backyard.

A large wooden sheet was hammered over one side of the patio doors, and a kitchen chair lay on the grass. Bits of broken glass lay glitter bright on the lawn. An old swing—older than Harry from the look of it—had been kicked out of its concrete block foundations. It leaned drunkenly against the high back fence. The broken seat dangled sadly from the long chains.

Kelly toed over a large bit of glass and grimaced. It looked like Jimmy had noticed his wife had left him.

He picked his way through the debris to the back door and peered inside. There was a dent in the white wall and an empty bottle of whiskey on the floor that might have caused it. A broken closet door leaned on barely moored hinges.

Something about the scene plucked at the back of Kelly's brain. It wasn't the destruction. It was the way it just petered out. Kelly had turned up at houses to serve soon-to-be exes and found the sort of destruction that only resentment and almost unhinged preservation could commit—everything in the house ripped out and smoldering on the lawn, crap from every dog in the neighborhood smeared on their spouse's clothes. When people lost it, it usually took exhaustion to set in before they found it again.

This was a mess, but it was a halfhearted mess. Either someone had interrupted the spree or Jimmy had just realized it wasn't going to get him anywhere and gave up. When they were kids, Kelly remembered Byron doing that. He'd gone to six therapists to help him deal with his temper, but the only thing that ever really stopped him midrage was the realization that it wasn't going to work this time.

Of course, Jimmy wasn't a spoiled ten-year-old. Kelly took a quick series of pictures of the mess with his phone and headed back out to the street.

No one was in the house on either side. Two doors down, a tall, tired-looking woman in crumpled nurse's scrubs opened the door and squinted through the security-chained gap. She listened patiently until he mentioned Jimmy's name. Then her face closed like a trap.

"I don't know them," she clipped out. "We don't talk. We have no business."

"You didn't see anyone come to the house last night?" Kelly asked. He pulled his phone out of his pocket and flicked it on. The glower of some of Jimmy's known associates was already pulled up to view. "Maybe one of these men?"

The nurse thinned her lips in irritation. Her eyes didn't even flicker down to the phone screen.

"I work. I come home. I sleep." She drew back into her house and added through the nearly closed door, "I mind my own business."

The door clicked shut. It wasn't slammed, but it managed to convey the same finality.

Kelly tried five other houses. Only two doors opened, and neither of the residents had seen anything.

"I just rent," a sleepy-eyed blond man—pretty enough to make Kelly have to kick his brain back on track—shrugged helplessly. "I don't want to get involved."

The last door was the most promising. The middle-aged woman who answered the door, her hair up in a towel and the smell of bleach on her cuffs, snorted.

"Oh, I've seen plenty," she said irritably. "That good-for-nothing—"

Her husband interrupted her before she could finish. "Let it go," he told her, and then he scowled at Kelly. "No offense, but you ain't going to be here tomorrow. He is."

The door slammed shut.

Kelly puffed his cheeks out on a dispirited sigh and stepped down off the porch. He turned and scanned the area. Two little girls at the end of the street worked earnestly to cover the whole of their drive in muddy pastel chalk. An old woman in a bright Hawaiian shirt and shorts limped out of one of the houses, down to the street, and sat down carefully on the bench to wait for the bus. Her hair was tarmac black. It was worth a shot.

Kelly jogged across the road. The old lady saw him and shook her head.

"Boy, what good is it for me to see something?" she asked once he was close enough. "That man is bad news."

"How do you know who I'm asking about?"

She snorted and set her Disney bag in her lap. Tanned, liver-spotted skin tightened over her knuckles as she gripped the handles. "You want to ask about Petrosyan, then?" she mocked him. "For leaving his garbage cans at curb all week? Or is the Harpers, on account of their daughter having an odd head?"

"Fair enough."

Kelly sat down on the bench and stretched his legs out. The plastic was hot through his T-shirt.

"Kelly," he introduced himself. "I'm a PI. I'm representing Jimmy Graham's wife."

"Margaret Sirkasian. And she finally came to her senses and left him, then?" the woman asked. Her voice tried for tart, but she couldn't fight the underscore of relief. "About time. I told her." She pursed her lips together in annoyance.

"You told her...?" Kelly prompted.

Margaret gave him a dry look and then sighed. "I told her that men make their sons in their image," she said. "My husband was a shit. My sons are shits. Good boys—as their mother, I have to say that—but cheats and liars. Harry deserved better than to grow up like his dad."

"You and Nadine are friends?"

"Were friends," Margaret corrected him. She fished a roll of candy out of her bag, popped one, and offered the tube to Kelly. It wasn't entirely clear what they were—the half name left on the side was in a foreign language—but he took it anyhow. Maybe it was mint. "*He* didn't like that. Couldn't stop me. I'm not scared of some low-level errand boy for the local crooks. Too damn old."

Kelly rolled the candy over his tongue—he didn't know what it was, but it tasted like roses—and nodded.

"So he made Nadine?"

Margaret crunched her sweet. "I would happily blame that man for a lot—noisiness, creepy friends, intimidating people—but he didn't need to make her do anything. What I said, she didn't want to hear, so I wasn't good company. No one wants to be friends with an old woman who isn't good company."

"I think now she'd admit you were right." Kelly tucked the candy in the side of his mouth. He got his phone out again and flipped the pictures up onto the screen. "Did you ever see any of these men around?"

Margaret was the first one who actually looked at the men's faces.

"I know him." She tapped the phone with her finger. "He dated my niece for a while. Cried when she left him and sent chocolates every day. I don't know if he wanted her back or just to make her fat. Kris... something. Moushian? The others I might have seen around, but *he* has a lot of friends for a shit."

"What about a couple of nights ago?" Kelly asked. "Did you see anyone come to the house? Go inside?"

"None of them," she said.

"Who?"

She sucked her sweet at him and raised perfectly plucked storm-gray eyebrows.

"It was something to do with Jimmy," he said. "But they scared Nadine."

Margaret closed her eyes and grimaced. "Men like that don't scare women," she said. "Is she all right?"

"She's… safe now."

Margaret took his phone and tapped carefully at the screen with her forefinger. "I don't know their names, the men who came here," she said. "This is who Jimmy worked with, though—Gregor. He was always around here, always trying to play the big man. I called the police on him once for pestering a girl, and he threatened me to keep my mouth shut. Showed me his hammer."

The contempt was ripe in her voice. She shook her head and tapped the screen again.

"I don't know why he bothered. Police never did anything about that man or his friends. No one ever does."

She gave Kelly his phone back. The name and address were typed out in lowercase letters.

"Thank you," he said. "I'll tell Nadine. I think she'd be glad to know you still wanted to help her."

Maybe if Marie had known how many of her old friends—lost over the years to Byron's wandering dick and inability to share attention—had come to cry at her funeral, she'd have called them after the divorce. She might have ended up in rehab instead of a coffin.

Margaret snorted and handed him a tissue. "Just spit it out if you don't like it," she told him. Then she levered herself up off the bench with a glare for him when he tried to offer his arm. She nodded as the bus stopped, a blur of red down the street. "My bus."

The bus pulled up and sank down, the hiss of its suspension almost a sigh, and she climbed on. She paused after she paid the fare and looked around.

"Tell Nadine she made the right choice," she said. "For Harry. And I'm not one to hold grudges."

The door's closed, and the bus pulled away as she stumbled to a seat.

Kelly checked his phone. It said "Frank's Body-Sheep," but she'd taken more time to spell out the name. Gregor Kevoian.

He googled the address on the way to his pickup.

KEVOIAN DIDN'T look like he'd fit under a car. He was a big man with a bigger gut that sagged down over the waistband of his jeans. No chin, though. He scratched the patchy black stubble on his jaw and glared at Kelly down the lumpy beak of his nose.

"I don't know what the fuck Jimmy is doing these days," he growled as he stuck a cigarette in his mouth and flicked the flint on the lighter. The unlit end bobbed as he talked, never quite in the guttering flame. "You want him, find a friend of his."

Kelly lifted his hand to block the sun. Behind Kevoian he could see a handful of cars up on blocks to be worked on, from a gently aged purple Toyota to a glossy black shark of a Firebird. None of the mechanics were at work, though. They stood in oil-stained overalls and muttered to each other as they watched their boss.

Kevoian's name might not be over the door, but he was definitely the boss.

"I heard you were his friend," Kelly said, at his most affable. He held up crossed fingers. "You and him were like this. That's you on top."

That was worthy of a snort. Kevoian finally got his cigarette lit. He drew on it deeply, and the threads of tobacco sparked. Then he plucked it from between his lips as he exhaled, pinched the cigarette between thumb and forefinger, and tucked it into the callused cup of his palm. Smoke eddied up through his fingers.

"Then you're lying about knowing Jimmy," he said. "Because he ain't got no friends."

"Colleagues, then?" Kelly said.

Kevoian narrowed his eyes, and Kelly turned his hands palm out in a shorthand for harmless. "I'm not a cop," he said.

"Reporter?"

"Private investigator. I work for his wife."

Kevoian laughed and took another puff on his cigarette. He squinted through the smoke. "Silly cow finally found out he's catting around on her?" he asked. "About time. I thought she was blind as well as stupid."

Kelly didn't correct him. For some reason, you mentioned domestic violence, and people clammed up as they muttered "don't know what goes on behind closed doors." A whiff of scandalous sex, though, and they'd be at the door to peep through the keyhole.

"I heard Jimmy worked for you." Kelly exaggerated what he'd been told to fluff Kevoian's feathers. It worked. "I'm just... running down some of his revenue streams. The more legitimate ones."

"Not a cop?" Kevoian checked.

"Too short," Kelly shrugged with a grin.

Kevoian laughed and looked over his shoulder into the garage. He jerked his thumb at Kelly. "Get a load of this. He wanted to be a cop but couldn't see over the counter."

The other mechanics sniggered on cue, and Kevoian turned back to Kelly. He thumbed his nose and sniffed.

"Me and Jimmy," Kevoian said, "we had a parting of the ways. He thought he was some hotshot, that he was too good for my... how'd you put it?"

"Revenue streams?"

Kevoian pointed a blunt, nail-bitten finger at Kelly's nose. "That's it," he said. "Revenue streams. He's got some new colleagues these days, but don't get his wife's hopes up."

"Oh?"

"From what I hear, all of Jimmy's revenue streams are about to dry right up," Kevoian said. "In a permanent sort of way. It looks like he didn't learn his lesson from double-crossing me, and his new friends? They ain't as understanding as I am."

Kelly's job was a lot like a conversation with his mom. People talked themselves into confidences, a bit of flattery went a long way to grease the wheels, and once it was done, it was done. It felt like Kevoian had dried up, but Kelly gave him a prod just in case.

"Still my job to make a list," he said. "These new partners of his, do they have names?"

Kevoian smirked, his teeth yellow behind his lips, and flicked the cigarette on the ground to grind it to shreds under a steel-capped toe.

"Let me think. It was.... Fuck Off," he said, "and Shortass."

Clever.

Kelly shrugged and stepped back. He pulled a pair of sunglasses from his pocket and slid them on to cut the glare.

"Thanks for your help," he said. "I'm sure Nadine will appreciate it."

Kevoian snorted and spat a wet glob onto the ground in front of Kelly's boots. Then he turned his back and stalked into the garage. The other mechanics shrugged, looked disappointed it hadn't escalated to a fight, and wandered off.

Well, that was less useful than Kelly had hoped, but more than he'd expected. He tugged his phone out of his pocket and pulled up his texts as he walked away. Cole had worked Glendale for a few years. He'd know who Kelly should chase up for information on tensions between the local gangs.

The answer that popped back almost immediately was "Why?"

Kelly rolled his eyes. He started to reply but put it on hold as he reached his pickup. A bright white citation was snapped under his windshield wiper.

"Shit."

That was just what he needed. Kelly leaned over, yanked it off the window, and tossed it onto the passenger seat as he climbed up into the oven-hot cab. He was just about to start the engine when the sharp rap of knuckles on glass interrupted him.

A lean, dark man in a baseball cap gave him a blandly handsome smile through the window and rotated his finger in a "roll it down" gesture. It didn't seem like a good idea, but when Kelly glanced out the front window, another man—sunbaked blond with the same bland look—stood in front of the pickup. His grin had something of a shark around the corners—all white teeth and no humor at all.

"Yeah, well, I was always too pretty for my own good," Kelly muttered as he took his glasses off.

He dropped his phone and kicked it under the seat. Before he could do anything else, the driver's-side window exploded. Nuggets of hot glass hit Kelly in the arm and on the side of his face. Chunks of it caught in the neck of his shirt. He swore and twisted around to see tall, dark, and blandsome use a hammer to wrench what was left of the window out of the frame. Then the man reached in and popped the door open.

"You know, the door wasn't locked," Kelly cracked. Tension always made him stupid. "That's going to have to go on my insurance."

Blandsome didn't find him funny. He grabbed the collar of Kelly's shirt and dragged him out of the cab.

"You've been asking too many questions," Blandsome said as he smacked Kelly against the hood of the pickup. "We think you need to learn to mind your own business."

"This is literally my business," Kelly said. He mock-patted his hips. "I've even got a business card here somewhere."

Blandsome sneered as he glanced over at Beefcake One. "He thinks he's a comedian. Maybe we should—"

Kelly shoved his hand between Blandsome's legs, grabbed, and twisted as hard as he could. The noise that came out of Blandy sounded like the air escaping a balloon, and the color washed out of his face. Before he could recover, Kelly headbutted him in the face.

He didn't get the satisfying gristle-pop noise of a dislocated nose, but Blandsome still grunted and staggered backward with blood drooling from split lips.

"Stupid fucker," Beefcake One said mildly. "You should have just taken the beating."

He lunged at Kelly, who dodged out of the way. Beefcake hit the side of the car with a heavy thud, muscle against alloy, and bounced off. Kelly threw a nice punch—clean from the shoulder, knuckles right on target—that Cole would have been proud of. It caught Beefcake in the jaw, hard enough to rattle, and Kelly slammed a second, short and nasty, punch into his gut.

That one he thought hurt his knuckles more than Beefcake's gut. Beefcake grunted, shook it off, and rammed Kelly. The heavy width of his shoulder hit Kelly in the stomach and drove him off balance. Kelly grunted and hammered his elbow down between Beefcake's shoulder blades. It hurt him enough that Kelly managed to twist free of him.

Blandsome spat blood on the pavement and pulled a baton out of his jacket. He extended it with a flick of his wrist, and Kelly backpedaled with his hands held up to ward Blandy off.

"C'mon, now," he said. "No need to—"

He'd forgotten about Beefcake Two. The punch came from nowhere on the left and caught him on the cheekbone. He felt a nasty snap-pop and a chill draft behind his eye. *Fuck.* His ears rang with a sharp, off-tune note, and he couldn't quite keep his legs under him.

His knees hit the pavement with a crack and a dull pop of pain that quickly faded. Kelly braced his hand on the ground and tried to push himself back up. Blandsome stamped a booted foot on his fingers and ground down.

Kelly swore and bit down on the inside of his cheek.

"You don't belong down here," Blandsome said. "We know you. We know your vehicle. Remember that."

The club cracked down across Kelly's thigh. Then one of the beefcakes kicked him in the stomach. Kelly grunted out a pained breath and threw himself into Blandsome's legs. The impact was enough to knock Blandsome back a step, and his foot lifted off Kelly's fingers. It didn't do any good. The next kick landed in Kelly's ribs with a hollow thud of impact and knocked him down.

Kelly sucked in a painful breath and curled in on himself as kicks and punches rained down on him. Beefcake One was right. It was three on one. He should have just let them deliver the beating. It would have been over quicker. Now he just had to wait it out.

CHAPTER NINE

"AFTER CONSIDERATION my client is unwilling to surrender his interest in the talent agency," John Barton said. There was a hint of weariness in his voice, as though he were as tired of his client as everyone else was. "His contribution to business might not have been easily measured, but his support for his wife was invaluable."

In the seat next to Clayton, Charity Tate snorted. It was an excellent snort, full of contempt and from somewhere just below her sinuses. Before she could say anything, Clayton raised a finger. She snorted again but sat back in the chair.

"Fine," Clayton said.

"What?" both soon-to-be-ex spouses blurted out.

Charity added, "The hell it is" for emphasis.

"Since we can't come to a settlement," Clayton continued calmly, "the judge can decide. I can also convince my client to repursue her strong claim on Mr. Tate's—" He fanned out the paperwork and ran his eye down the list of property. "—beach house and vineyard."

Anger flushed Declan Tate's skin ruddily over his cheekbones, a deep, livid color like someone had slapped him from the inside.

"That bitch doesn't even like wine," he spat.

"So you say," Clayton pointed out. "Yet every single merlot produced there is named after my client, and I have witness testimony that she spent considerably more billable hours at the vineyard than you ever did."

"Because she was fucking the manager." Declan spat the word out between tight, white lips.

"A liaison she regrets." Clayton ignored the mutter of "do not" from Charity. "And that she only entered into due to the alienation of affection caused by her husband's long absences and his affair with her niece. I think blood relative trumps employee there."

The color in Declan's face managed to darken further. It didn't look healthy. The almost congested red was stark against the pallor of his temples and jaw. He was a wealthy man, a generous man where charity galas and glitter-spangled, celebrity fundraisers were concerned, but the divorce had brought out the worst in him. The way that not getting his own way brought out the worst in a toddler.

"You think you can fucking blackmail me," he spat across the table. "That goddamn bitch has always planned to take me for everything I've got."

Clayton nudged his knee against Charity's under the table, but she held her tongue. She always did behave better once she'd gotten a rise out of her ex. She just smirked at him with a smug pleat of matte-red lips and leaned in to whisper something in Clayton's ear.

"If you lose me the agency, I'll marry you," she murmured. Her breath was sticky hot against his neck. "Then fuck your life up too."

She squeezed his arm and sat back, still smiling. Across the table Declan clenched his fists and then snarled and lunged up out of his chair. It fell over backward, and he stepped over the legs on his way out of the room. John looked relieved that the chair was the only thing on the ground.

"I will talk to my client," he said as he gathered up the papers and dumped them in his briefcase. Before he closed the lid, he hesitated. "Clayton. My client is very… determined that he's been wronged in this. He wants recompense."

The polished latches clicked under his thumbs, and John nodded quickly and chased after his client.

"He wants recompense," Charity parroted, a mockery of John's careful Nevada accent. She slouched down in her chair, all long, onetime-starlet body and red suit that matched her lips. "He has feelings. Oh, poor baby."

Clayton filed his own paperwork into heavy, firm-branded folders. "He was implying that your husband could do something stupid," he said.

"I have excellent security," Charity said. "And my new boyfriend is a fight choreographer. So…."

"Just be careful."

She tapped a nail on the desk and sniffed. Then the vim visibly drained from her, and she sighed. "You know he's wrong."

Clayton nodded as he stood up. "I think it's an equitable enough settlement," he said. "Like I said, I could have gotten you more."

"The winery is a black hole for money," Charity told him dismissively. "The wine tastes like vinegar, and the manager is keeping his whole extended Italian family afloat with jobs. I don't want it. And I wasn't always in this for what I could get. I did… really… care about Declan. He just… he cared about the person he wanted me to be."

Clayton looked down at her in surprise. In his experience Charity wasn't a reflective woman. Of course, the first time he met her, she'd driven straight to the office after finding her husband in bed with her twenty-year-old niece. So she'd started out angry.

"You think I'm lying, don't you?" Charity asked him.

"No," Clayton said. He offered her a hand up from the seat and then went around the table to right Declan's chair. "In my experience most people go into marriage with the best of intentions. It's just that once it breaks down, they forget that sometimes."

Charity nodded and unhooked her sparkly clutch bag from the back of the chair. "I guess," she said. "I mean, don't get me wrong, Clayton. I want to hurt him. If I could claim custody of his penis, I would have it mounted over the toilet. It wasn't always like that, though. You think he'll back off my agency?"

"He thinks you want the winery," Clayton said, one hand in the small of Charity's back as he showed her to the door. "Between that and the threat of losing control to a judge, he'll settle."

Clayton left her at the elevator and headed back to his office. His brain purged the particulars of the Tate case as he weighed the rest of what he had to do that day. He flicked chasing up Nadine's restraining order to the top of the list since it wouldn't take a lot of his time. After that he needed to reject the changes to the prenuptial agreement that Harris's fiancée had instructed her lawyer to make. Hardly unreasonable, since he doubted Harris's lawyer would want to argue the legal case for contractually obligated reciprocal oral sex.

Today Heather had gone for a slicked-down page-boy wig and Rat Pack suit. She popped up from behind her desk as she saw Clayton approach.

"Clayton—" she blurted out.

"Could you chase up the court clerk to see if the judge has granted the temporary restraining order for Nadine?" Clayton asked. "And when the hearing will be for the permanent one? If there are any problems, kick up a fuss. I don't understand how our original DV-100 got misrouted to the wrong judge. That doesn't happen."

"I will," Heather said. "Clayton—"

"I'll also need someone to serve the order to her husband," he said as he pushed the door to his office open. "Apparently Kelly was going to track him down today, so hopefully he can do that. On the Neilson case, my client wants to appeal the custody order, so could you pull the original paperwork—"

The words caught in Clayton's throat as he caught sight of Kelly perched on the edge of the couch at the side of the office. He expected the clutch of awkwardness—it had been a long time since he'd gone to bed with someone who might expect more—but not the cold drench of sick anger that hit as he saw the bloodstains dried into Kelly's T-shirt and jeans. Bruises dappled Kelly's arms in dull, ready-to-bloom pale blues, and he was hunched over with a tissue wadded against his nose.

So he wouldn't bleed on the couch. The floor would still get you a slap around the back of the head, Clayton recalled from his childhood, but if you got it on the furniture, you were in for another beating. Which was counterproductive, really.

"WHAT THE fuck happened to you?" Clayton rasped out. It sounded like the anger was aimed at Kelly, but he couldn't pin it down to shut it up.

"He won't *say*," Heather blurted from behind Clayton. "He just limped out of the elevator and said he'd wait for you. Look at his poor face."

Kelly lifted his head and grimaced around the tissue.

"You make it sound like I lost a nose," he muttered, his voice thick.

Clayton stalked over and caught Kelly's chin so he could tilt his head back enough to get a good look. His nose was still there, but the rest of his face showed wear. There was a livid, road-rash scrape on one cheek, a lump on his jaw, and a black eye patch crooked over one eye. Clayton had seen worse. It still shouldn't have been on the face he remembered under his fingers, its only scar an old and faded one in his eyebrow.

"Ow," Kelly muttered.

"What happened to your eye?" Clayton demanded.

"Popped out."

"Oh my God," Heather squawked. She clapped her hands over her mouth and squeezed the words out through her fingers. "Should I call 9-1-1? I should call 9-1-1."

"Very funny," Clayton said. "Did it fall in the bog with Liam's family?"

He reached for the patch, and Kelly caught his hand. "Yeah, don't. It's not pretty. I mean it's not gross, but—"

"Seriously, your eye fell out?" Heather said as she fidgeted in the background. "I should call someone."

"No," Kelly said.

"Yes," Clayton corrected. "You look like hell."

"What do I do?" Heather dithered.

Kelly lifted his chin out of Clayton's grip and leaned back. He gingerly peeled the tissue away from his nose and then balled it up when blood didn't spurt again. "Seriously," he said. "I'm fine. Could you just get me some wet wipes or something?"

After a moment, Clayton nodded at Heather. She looked relieved to have something to do and skittered out again. He sat down next to Kelly and worked his fingers through the scruff of his sable-dark hair— no sticky patches, no tender lumps of bone.

"They didn't want to kill me," Kelly said.

"So you're just being an idiot, then?"

Kelly cracked a grin and then winced as he poked at his nose.

"Did you know the LAPD don't have a height requirement?" he asked.

Clayton paused for a second and then reluctantly freed his hand.

"I did not know that." He got up off the couch and walked over to the cabinet where he kept the "well, shit" whiskey. It wasn't good whiskey. It wasn't even okay. But every new dad he'd ever had drank it, and the sour burn of it fit a bad mood. "You've always said that's why you aren't a cop."

"I lied. The LAPD don't care if you're a shortass," he said. "They do expect new recruits to have all their parts, and I was short one eye."

Clayton poured a glass and brought it over. "Drink that."

Kelly sniffed it first and blinked at the acid sting of it. He braced himself and took a swig. It made him wince.

"How did it happen?" Clayton asked. The question sounded more suspicious than sympathetic, as though he wanted to check the story for inconsistencies.

"I was a kid. It was traumatic. I don't really remember," Kelly said. Something about the way he said it sounded off to Clayton—not a lie, necessarily, but something he'd said so often it had lost any connection to the actual event. "To be honest I don't think about it most of the time."

"Until someone punches you in the face?"

Kelly shrugged his acknowledgment of that.

"Yeah. They knocked the fake eye right out of my head." Kelly held the whiskey out and tilted it in invitation. Amber liquid sloshed up the sides of the glass. Clayton took it and drained what was left in the tumbler. It still tasted like drain cleaner smelled, but the raw punch of it helped him focus past the anger and mild confusion.

"Nadine's husband did this?"

"Not exactly." Kelly rubbed at the edge of his eye patch as though it itched. "This was courtesy of what I think were some undercover cops."

Clayton licked harsh liquor from his lips. "They were police? You're sure?"

"You know what undercover means, right? They didn't show their badges," Kelly said. He leaned back and wrapped an arm protectively over his ribs. "I grew up around cops, though. One of my brothers is undercover. They moved like cops. Tall, dark, and blandsome used his nightstick like a cop."

"Blandsome?"

"It was a beating, not a hookup. We didn't really get around to introductions."

Clayton's mouth twitched. He had a feeling his definition of hookup and Kelly's were a bit different. There had been a few where he really hadn't seen their faces. There was just hot-breathed agreement and hands in a dimly lit club. Meanwhile, he'd hardly ever been beaten up by someone whose birthday he didn't know.

That was just one reason he wasn't what a ridiculous romantic like Kelly needed.

"So what does that mean?" Clayton thought about another glass of whiskey but decided against it. One was a bracer. Two was just day drinking. He set the tumbler down on the edge of his desk. "They're investigating Jimmy too? They don't want you to scare him off. He wouldn't be the first man to deal with a divorce by not leaving a forwarding address. That's why I'm pushing to get his finances frozen."

Kelly looked dubious. "Maybe."

"But?"

"More likely it's an ongoing investigation, *and* he's an informant," Kelly said. "I'd talked to a few people. He wasn't popular with his neighbors. The cops were called a couple of times, but nothing was done. No record of it on the search I did on the address."

Clayton frowned. "It's not proof," he said.

"I know," Kelly said. "Something is going on, though."

He snapped the elastic band of his eye patch to make his point. Clayton couldn't argue with that, and some form of interference would explain the unprecedented misplaced DV-100.

"I'll talk to Baker," he said. "He used to work for the DA's office. He's still got friends there. If there's something going on, they'll at least have seen the ripples."

Kelly nodded. "I'll—"

"Nothing," Clayton said firmly. He ignored Kelly's attempt to protest and talked over him. "I asked you to do a favor, run a few searches on a two-bit abuser. This has clearly gone beyond that. Stay out of this, Kelly."

It was good advice, but Kelly just snorted rudely at it. "Bite me," he said as he pushed himself up off the couch. "I'm not doing it for you. I like the kid, I feel bad for Nadine, and I'm going to help them."

Clayton brushed his thumb over the scrape on Kelly's cheekbone. "I don't need this on my conscience, Kelly," he said. "I don't need you."

Hurt flickered over Kelly's face—the sort of emotion that anyone other than heart-on-his-sleeve Kelly would have hidden—and then was gone. Kelly shrugged.

"They do."

The door popped open, and Heather scurried in with a pile of paper towels and a first-aid kit clutched under her chin.

"I found these in the… umm…. Sorry."

Clayton resisted the urge to snatch his hand back. He wasn't doing anything intimate, just showing basic concern for an injury. He calmly stepped back and smoothed his shirt down over his stomach in an absent, habitual gesture. The crisp cotton under his fingers was a reminder of who he was now, and who he had been, as well.

"Get yourself cleaned up and go home, Kelly," he said flatly. "If I need anything else, I'll call Larry."

Clayton ignored Heather's half-voiced protest and stalked out of his office. Anger was hot and ragged in his gut, and it grated against itself as he walked. Kelly was a good person. He fell in love and planned holidays to Bali. He took in a baby to give his brother a break.

Now some assholes had decided to hurt him in order to do an abusive husband a solid.

It was the sort of thing Clayton had left home to get away from.

BAKER SAT back in his ergonomic leather chair and pushed his thin wire-framed glasses up onto his forehead. He folded his hands across his stomach and tapped his thumbs together.

"The Graham case?" he said as he rocked his weight back. "Now, I could pretend to be confused, like it's slipped my mind, and force you to actually lay it out for me. Hopefully, in the process, you'd realize how unreasonable you are. Or I could just point out that I thought we'd agreed that the firm wasn't wasting any hours on that. Decisions, decisions."

Clayton folded his long body down into one of the chairs on his side of the desk. Unlike Baker's custom-fit, lumbar-support-enabled piece of hi-tech seat technology, they were all metal tubes and crisscrossed knots of leather.

An uncomfortable client, Baker liked to say, paid attention. Luckily Clayton was used to them.

"We can just assume you did both," he said. "Then I could explain why I'm putting my neck on the line here."

"Well, I had assumed that was something to do with the bloody Kelly boy in your office." He smirked at Clayton's surprised look and pretended to buff his nails against the lapel of his jacket. "I have eyes everywhere, Clayton."

"Heather told you?"

"Heather told me. So—" Baker checked his watch. "You have ten minutes to convince me I shouldn't give you a lecture and stick you with our most miserable clients. From now."

He pointed a silver pen at Clayton in the Go signal and waited.

"I think we have a problem with the LAPD."

There was a pause, and the flicker of interest in Baker's deep sea-blue eyes. He'd taken the hook. From all muttered accounts—and even Clayton wasn't in on the full story—Baker's exit from the DA's office had been acrimonious.

"Okay. Bait taken," Baker said. He also hadn't quit as a DA because he wasn't sharp enough. "Twenty minutes. Go on."

Clayton outlined what had happened, from the delay at the courthouse to Kelly's professionally delivered beating. The anger leaked back into his voice as though it had waited for the chance. Judging by his pursed lips and the ticktock sway of the pen, Baker noticed it too.

It wasn't a case that Clayton would have wanted to take to court, just supposition and coincidence. There was something, but he didn't know if it would be enough to convince Baker.

"Basically Kelly thinks they were cops. If he's right, we have a problem," he wrapped up.

"Not to be a downer, but if he's wrong, you still have a problem," Baker said. "How's Kelly?"

"Still an idiot," Clayton said. His conscience gave him a kick, and he grimaced. "That's not fair. He's not an idiot, just... Kelly. Which is like an idiot, just on purpose."

Baker chuckled and shook his head. "You know, one day you're going to have to admit you're a little bit in love with him."

For a second, Clayton entertained the wild speculation that Baker's "eyes everywhere" extended to Kelly's living room. They didn't, of course.

"Don't tell me that you've fallen off the Romantics Anonymous bandwagon," Clayton sighed.

Baker snorted and stood up. He unhooked his tailored jacket from the hanger behind his desk and shrugged it on. "Romance is when you think the object of your affections is better than they are. Love is when you can't convince yourself they're an idiot, no matter how hard you try."

"I don't love Kelly."

"Of course not," Baker mocked lightly. "You don't believe in love."

"I'm a divorce lawyer," Clayton said. The words had sounded light when he framed them in his head. By the time they got to his tongue, there was a bitter tang to them. "I believe in prenups."

Baker paused as he fastened the buttons on his jacket. "Love can last, Clayton. My parents were madly in love for fifty years," he said. "From the moment they met."

"You hated your parents."

"Well, they were homophobic assholes," Baker said. "But just because they hated me didn't mean they didn't love each other."

Clayton rolled his eyes. "An improving story," he said impatiently. Then he tried to drag the conversation back on topic. "What do you think

I should do about this case? I've been threatened before, but that's usually direct. No one has ever sent the heavies in after our investigators before."

"They were also racist," Baker said. At Clayton's confused look he shrugged. "My parents. I don't like to leave it out. Right now, do your job and concentrate on your caseload."

"I can't ignore—"

Baker talked over him. "I'll make some calls," he said. "See what I can find out about this Jimmy Graham. There are still a few debts I can call in. Leave it with me."

"Thank you," Clayton said as he stood up. "Now I owe you one. Like you said, this isn't the firm's case."

"I was a very good DA," Baker said. He looked unusually serious, almost grim. "I left because I couldn't be a good DA anymore for... various reasons. So I expect the people who stayed to do their jobs and protect people to not sell an abused woman and her child out for the sake of dubious information from a dubious source. If you're right about this, it's our case. If the other partners object, I'll deal with them."

For years Clayton hadn't really been able to imagine the flamboyant, dryly amused Baker in a criminal court. Now he could.

"I'm going to talk to Nadine this evening," Clayton said. He made a mental note to relieve Heather of that job. She'd already gone above and beyond, but he wasn't going to put her in danger. "If you have any questions...."

Baker looked thoughtful as he adjusted his cuffs and checked his reflection in the mirror. A tug at his collar settled it to his satisfaction. "Actually I'd rather speak to her myself," he said. "I know what to ask. Later. Some favors are better called in in person."

After Baker left, Clayton glanced at himself in the mirror. His suit was just as—almost as—expensive as Baker's, but instead of bright colors and patterned linings he'd gone for charcoal gray and a black shirt.

That was the thing, though. It wasn't that he didn't believe in love, he just didn't believe that it lasted.

After all, he went to its funeral every time he went to court.

CHAPTER TEN

ONE OF the few things Clayton missed about his home was the dark. In Utah, night fell like a stage backdrop to the desert. In LA, it never really got dark. The lights just got brighter. It did get late, not too late to hit a club, to find a pretty ass in black leather, but definitely too late to weave through the ribbons of traffic on the highway and definitely too late to growl a bike down the neat little street to Kelly's ridiculous yellow house.

But here he was anyhow.

In his head, a figment of Baker smirked and raised his eyebrows in a knowing expression. Clayton snorted as he pulled in and knocked the kickstand down with his heel. Baker didn't know as much as he thought he did, and Clayton didn't have anything to admit, to himself or anyone else. He'd just spent too many nights as a kid worried that the purple knot on his mom's temple would kill her, or the bottle she'd taken to his latest dad would turn her into a murderer. Old habits wouldn't let him rest until he made sure that Kelly hadn't passed out and choked on his own tongue.

Clayton pulled his helmet off and hung it off the handlebar of the bike. He scrubbed his hand through his sweat-matted hair and frowned at the familiar, dusty-windowed pickup parked up on the curb. If Kelly had gone back and driven his truck home, Clayton was going to use that as evidence that he was an idiot and not just a romantic.

He climbed off the bike and headed up to the front door. It stood ajar, and the sound of raised voices and a baby's distressed wail filtered out into the warm night air. Clayton stiffened as the hackles on the back of his neck rose. Maybe it wasn't Kelly who drove his pickup back home. Any ID in it, and the men who'd ground Kelly's face into the pavement earlier could have found their way here. If Kelly was right about the police being involved, they wouldn't even need the ID.

It meant there wouldn't be any point in a 9-1-1 call either.

Clayton grimaced, pushed the door open, and cautiously stepped into the hall. The three men in the main room turned to stare at him.

"Who the fuck are you?" the taller, blonder version of Kelly demanded harshly.

"What are you doing here?" the oldest of the three said as he put his hand on blond Kelly's shoulder. He didn't look much like Kelly, but he looked a lot like the blond.

"He's actually welcome," Kelly said sardonically from behind them. He still had the eye patch on, and it lent an oddly rakish touch. "Unlike you two."

Brothers. Of course. Kelly had his own family—a big, tight-knit, Irish family. He didn't need Clayton to make sure he was okay. That was one responsibility Clayton could hand off without a qualm.

"You asked us over," the blond pointed out to Kelly.

The older man stepped forward and held his hand out. He looked more like Kelly when he smiled, but it didn't quite reach his eyes under ginger brows.

"You must be Clayton," he said as Clayton took his hand. "I'm Cole. That's Wilde."

A backward tilt of his head indicated the other brother. Wilde chuckled and turned to look at Kelly. "So this is him?" he said. "Thanksgiving Clayton?"

"Shut up," Kelly muttered. Color spread across his cheekbones.

Wilde laughed, and Cole ignored him as he narrowed his eyes at Clayton.

"You met my wife the other day. Agatha."

"I did."

The grip on Clayton's hand tightened. "And doing a favor for you is the reason my brother got beaten up."

"Yes."

The blond laughed again. "C'mon, Cole, be fair. He's gotten worse from us. Remember when Byron pushed him off the roof to see if he could fly? We thought he'd killed him."

Cole grimaced. "Shut up, Wilde. What if they punched him on the other side of the face? He could have lost his eye."

"Again," Wilde cracked. He jabbed his elbow into Kelly's side. "One is a misfortune, two looks like carelessness, eh?"

He laughed at his own joke. Both Cole and Kelly rolled their eyes. In the background Maxie, on his back in a padded playpen, hiccuped and wailed some more.

It felt like family, at least the ones Clayton had experienced, where he was the outsider who gave in-jokes their point.

"I didn't mean to interrupt," he said coolly as he took his hand back. "I just wanted to make sure he didn't need anything."

Cole stared at him. "That's what family is for."

"Well, I wanted some dick," Kelly drawled. "People frown on family who provide that."

Clayton nearly laughed. A flush hit Cole's face and was easily visible through his pale skin. "Do you have to talk like that in front of the baby?" he asked. "You want Mom to be waiting for *Nana*, and Maxie's first word is *dick*?"

"We'll just tell her he meant his dad," Kelly said flatly.

There was a pause. That was family too—the fault lines that took a lifetime to navigate. Wilde broke the tension with a laugh and slung his arm around Kelly's neck.

"Or you could just be grateful that it distracted her from lecturing you on why you have to wear your special glasses."

"We're keeping Clayton," Cole said shortly.

"I'm keeping Clayton," Kelly corrected. He shrugged Wilde off and gave him a shove toward the door. "You're going home. Worry about your own love lives."

Wilde snorted. "My wife is still in Idaho. Apparently we're all toxic, and she's got to stay on a commune to detox. Like *her* family's a prize." He paused on the way past Clayton and tilted his head to the side. "I mean, obviously, you get there's six of us, and we're cops, and we can make your life awkward if anything else happens to our baby brother? We got that across with the 'tude? Because I can puff my chest out and make some empty threats if you need a bit more."

"Enough, Wilde!" Cole bit out.

Wilde winked at Clayton and left. He tossed a "Nice to meet you anyhow, after everything the kids had to say about you," over his shoulder on his way out, and Cole scowled after him.

"He might think everything is funny," he said to Kelly. "I don't. You're supposed to be taking care of Max. You said you could do it. You told us we could depend on you. I told Dad that you could do it, that we could trust you to step up and help Byron. If you can't, if you'd rather screw around and get into fights, maybe... maybe Max should be with me and Aggie. I think Byron would be happier with that."

He left.

Clayton wished he could as well. The day had been bad enough without being conscripted into someone else's drama. He didn't do scenes. He didn't do families. Casual hookups and one-night stands kept his life simple. That was how he liked it.

"Sorry," Kelly said. He rubbed his hand over his face and dragged a smile up out of somewhere. "This is why I can't date casually. You're one unannounced drop-in away from meeting my parents, and once that happens, we have to go steady. It's the law."

He crouched down to fuss over Maxie and deposit a much-loved, spit-wet dragon into the baby's sticky embrace. It was enough distraction to stop Maxie's wails, but he kept up staccato, hiccuped sobs of irritation.

"I thought your problem was that you believed in love at first sight," Clayton said.

"That doesn't help," Kelly admitted with a rasp of laughter. He sat down on the ground and leaned back against the couch. The cut on his face had scabbed with a bruise smeared blue and tender around the edges, and his nose was tender-looking around the bridge. "Did Baker find anything out?"

Clayton wanted to tell him. Maybe that was why he was there instead of reading case files at home or picking up a one-night stand at Revolver—so he could talk about Nadine's odd pride in her abusive husband's criminal ideals and how Baker had picked her story to bits so elegantly that she hadn't even realized he'd done it.

It would be a bad idea, and he only allowed himself one of those.

"You should listen to your brothers," he said. "I told you this afternoon that you have enough on your plate. If the police are involved in this somehow, your family won't exactly appreciate you going against the grain."

"If the LAPD wanted me to keep their dirty secrets, they should have let me sign up," Kelly said. "And I've got six brothers. I can fall out with two of them for a while."

"Three," Clayton pointed out. "It sounds like Maxie's dad isn't going to be happy either."

Kelly smiled, but it didn't have the usual joy. "Oh, trust me, that I can live with."

The bitter edge to his voice wasn't something that Clayton associated with Kelly, but that was what family did. It brought out the worst in people sooner or later.

"You had anything to eat?" Clayton asked.

The abrupt shift in topic made Kelly blink, and that old bitter resentment was replaced by confusion. "No, not yet. Why?"

It wasn't a date. Clayton pulled up the Grubhub app on his phone and scrolled through the nearby restaurants for something that looked good. It was just food. That didn't have to mean anything.

BEER AND pizza, eaten on the floor. Last time Clayton had eaten like that he was a student with a box of cold slices from his part-time job and no money for heat. The pizza was better now, and LA came with its thermostat stuck on high.

"…Nadine denies everything, in good faith, I think," Clayton said. "But once Baker started to question her, he picked up on a pattern of behavior he thinks suggests something."

Kelly folded his pizza in half and took a bite. He wiped cheese-greasy lips on the back of his hand.

"Police harassment, but no charges," he said once he swallowed. "Traffic tickets go away. Domestic calls never stick."

"Only thing that doesn't fit is that his parole got revoked a few months ago," Clayton said. "He had to serve out five weeks. Maybe a judge didn't get the hands-off memo."

Kelly shrugged and tossed a burned rind of pizza crust into the grease-stained box on the coffee table. The eye patch made his face look leaner—almost stern—until he flashed one of those stupidly happy smiles of his. Clayton didn't object to the new angles.

"Byron—he's the one who's undercover—used to have to serve out his sentence whenever he needed a breather or to recalibrate to the real world," Kelly said. "Hell, around the same time that Jimmy was shipped off to jail, Byron's cover had to go to traffic court in West Virginia so Byron could bury his wife. The judge on Jimmy's case might have been told to deny him bail because the cops wanted to stick him a jail cell with someone to get them talking or put pressure on Jimmy if he'd been balking at doing dirty work for them."

Clayton found it hard to imagine one of the Kelly brothers as an undercover cop. The three he'd met seemed like the sort of men who lost frequently, and with good grace, at poker. Whether it was dislike or sympathy, their feelings were as easy to read as a page in a court filing. He couldn't imagine any of them on the tightrope of lie and truth that an undercover cop had to walk.

Maybe that was why none of Byron's brothers seemed that sure they trusted him.

"What I don't get is why they care whether or not Nadine leaves him," Clayton said as he dragged his imagination away from the potential black-sheep Kelly brother. He picked a slice of mushroom off the box and popped it in his mouth. "Her only criminal involvement is through her husband. Her father was a construction worker—he's dead—and her mother works in a factory. It shouldn't have any impact on the police investigation if she leaves Jimmy."

"If he's a long-term informant," Kelly said with a rueful expression, "it might just be a favor to Jimmy, something to keep him happy. Like you said, Nadine's got no connections. There's no benefit to Jimmy's handlers if she owes them a favor."

That left a bad taste in Clayton's mouth. It tasted sour enough that he was done with his pizza. He flicked the box shut on the remaining slices of kale and mushroom and tried to wash the taste away with a mouthful of beer and a change of subject.

"Are all your brothers named after poets?" he asked. "Byron. Wilde. Cole… ridge?"

Kelly looked at him and eventually said, "I'm not telling you my name." He got to his feet. "You don't need to know my name. No one does. Want another beer?"

Clayton considered the bottle he had drank. Another would give him an excuse to stay, plausible deniability if he broke his "only one bad idea a year" rule.

"No," he said. "Thanks."

Kelly shrugged and took the empty pizza box with him into the kitchen. Metal rattled, plastic rustled, and the fridge lit up as Kelly opened it.

Up on the shelf, the baby monitor blinked placidly. Maxie had been quiet since Kelly took him upstairs. The pizza-delivery girl, all freckles and funky moped helmet, had said "aw" as she watched through the door. Clayton hadn't corrected her. On the other side of the monitor, the framed picture of Kelly's Irish ex grinned sunnily at the camera.

He looked like he was in love, but where was he now?

"Not here," Clayton muttered to himself. He stood up and walked over to lean against the kitchen door. On the way past, he put Liam's picture facedown on the shelf. The kitchen was a mess—not dirty, but half-finished. A polished silver fridge stood alone against the wall, and the skeletons of unfinished cupboards leaned against the back wall under the long grubby window. The floor was freshly surfaced with sea-blue tiles, and the smell of fresh cement still lingered in the room. Kelly popped the cap off the soda he'd grabbed instead of a beer as Clayton tried again. "Wordsworth?"

"I wish," Kelly muttered, low enough that Clayton probably wasn't meant to hear. "And nope."

"It's the Romantics, though," Clayton said. "They were a limited run. I'll work it out eventually."

Kelly turned and gave him a wry look over the bottle as he took a swig. "You're assuming that I'll tell you if you're right."

"Fair's fair."

"I don't tell anyone my name."

"So Liam didn't know?" Clayton asked as he walked over the sea-blue tiles. One had cracked already and been sealed back down with sticky tape in a haphazard fix that would probably be there for a while. "He lived with you and never saw your name on anything?"

There was a raw edge to the question that Clayton didn't like, a scrape of jealousy or possessiveness. He wasn't sure which, and he didn't have the right to either.

"He met my mom," Kelly said. "Unfortunately, she hadn't forgotten my name yet. My birthday sometimes, but not the name."

Clayton took the soda from him and balanced it on top of the bare-bones framework of the counter-to-be.

"I'm not suddenly going to become a good fit," he said as he hooked his fingers in the waistband of Kelly's jeans. If Baker really did have eyes everywhere, he'd think the abrupt shift in topic was bizarre. But the two of them knew what Clayton meant. "It'll be fun—a lot of fun—and then it'll end. I want you, but I'm not your next Prince Charming."

He tugged Kelly forward and bent down to kiss him, roughly and quickly and deeply. Kelly's mouth tasted of sugar and salt, soda and pizza. It felt intimate in how commonplace it was. Unpracticed, like it was a real thing. Clayton curled his hand around the nape of Kelly's neck and tucked his thumb under the sharp hinge of Kelly's jaw. He could feel the eager beat of Kelly's pulse through stubbled skin and felt the hot tide of lust under his own.

It took a minute, but Kelly leaned back. He licked Clayton's spit off his lips and shook his head.

"I didn't ask you to be," he said.

The pang of hurt caught Clayton by surprise. It was the right answer, but that wasn't the point. Just because you knew you couldn't be someone's future didn't mean you wanted them to agree with you, particularly when it came from a man who fell in love at the drop of a hat.

To cover the moment of hypocritical injury, Clayton pushed his hand back into Kelly's short, wavy hair and dragged him back into the kiss. "Good," he muttered around Kelly's tongue. "Blake?"

The snort of laughter tangled between their mouths in a trickle of sound and the curve of Kelly's smile mapped out against Clayton's lips. Kelly stripped his jacket off on the way out of the kitchen and folded it almost neatly over the back of the chair on the way past.

"I'm not telling you," Kelly said between kisses as he tugged at Clayton's tie. "But you think I'd kick up this much fuss over Blake?"

Clayton murmured his acknowledgment of that point against Kelly's lips. He didn't know why Kelly's name mattered to him. If he really wanted to find out, he could ask Baker or check out his PI license with the state. Hell, he could just wait and check Kelly's driver's license when he was asleep.

But he wanted Kelly to tell him—a lawyer's habit, Clayton supposed. He ignored the Baker-like snort that *hmphed* in the back chambers of his brain. It wasn't going to tell him anything he wanted to listen to, and Kelly's eager mouth and wandering hands were much more fun to focus on.

They navigated their way to the stairs.

BRUISES DAPPLED Kelly's body like shadows against his skin as he stripped out of his clothes. Clayton stood behind him and explored the tender edges of the injuries with his fingertips as he mentally cataloged them. The narrow, stark lines of the sap were mostly on his arms and across his back. The edges had only started to blur as the bruise spread outward, while the boot-shaped splotches of black and blue stained his thighs and forearms.

"Next time," he murmured as he leaned down to kiss Kelly's bruised shoulder, "try to avoid some of the punches."

Kelly snorted and snapped his fingers. "Dammit, I knew there was something I forgot."

Clayton found an unbruised span of shoulder and bit it, just hard enough to make Kelly shudder. He slid his hands down over Kelly's stomach, across hard muscle and a sparse scruff of dark hair, to the eager curve of his cock.

"At least this still works," Clayton mocked as he wrapped his fingers around the shaft and felt it twitch. Under his trousers Clayton felt his own cock thicken in response. His balls were tight and heavy as they pulled up toward his groin. "You're lucky."

Kelly leaned back against Clayton's chest, relaxed as a cat. He reached behind him and cupped his hand around Clayton's neck and laced his fingers through the short-cropped curls.

"I know how to get beat up," Kelly protested lazily. He kissed Clayton's throat wetly, all tongue and the promise of teeth. "You think the short one-eyed kid with the cop dad didn't get picked on?"

Clayton dragged his hand back along Kelly's cock in a lazy caress that bunched the sheath of skin under his fingers and made Kelly's hips jerk. A strangled "son-of-a-bitch" grated between Kelly's teeth as his fingers dug into Clayton's neck. His breath was ragged as Clayton stroked his cock again.

"I would have made you cry," Clayton admitted wryly.

He didn't add that he would have done it because he was jealous, that he'd have wanted Kelly's big, affectionate, stupidly named family—a mom who cared enough to theme her brood, not just name them after the guy she was going after for child support. And when he hit puberty, he would have wanted Kelly, with his sunny grin and earnest, easy good looks.

The first time he saw Kelly, he wanted him. There was no reason to think it would have been different if he'd seen him earlier.

Kelly snorted out a laugh and turned around. He pulled Clayton down and kissed him and then murmured against damp lips, "You know, you're supposed to say you'd have stood up for me."

The fabric of the eye patch rubbed against Clayton's cheek. It was an odd smudge of black in the corner of his vision, and it didn't *bother* him, but he couldn't shake the idea that it was a costume.

"If I wanted to stand up for the downtrodden," Clayton said as Kelly nudged him backward toward the bed, "I wouldn't specialize in high-asset divorce settlements."

The mattress was soft, and the sheets were crisp and white. Clayton sat down and caught Kelly's lean hips in his hands. He tugged him in closer, pressed a wet, leisurely kiss against bruise-flowered ribs, and felt the heat of blood against his lips. He slid his hands down to Kelly's thighs and across the long tight bands of muscle.

"Says the man who offered to pay my hourly rate out of his own pocket on a pro bono case," Kelly said as he pushed Clayton back down onto the bed. "You talk a good game, Clayton, but we all know you're a good guy."

"That was not idealism," Clayton said. "That's a sop to my conscience so I can spend the rest of my time making an hourly rate that would make you cry."

"Liar."

There was absolutely no basis for the certainty in Kelly's voice. He didn't know Clayton—not really. Clayton could have said something sharp and sarcastic enough to cut through even Kelly's bulletproof confidence. But before he could string the words together, Kelly slid down onto his knees and wrapped his mouth around Clayton's cock.

That—soft lips and wet heat around the hard length of him—scattered Clayton's self-destructive impulse. He propped himself on one elbow and watched as Kelly slicked his cock with spit and tongue as he gripped the base of the shaft.

Pleasure cramped in Clayton's thighs and stomach. It was hot and heavy, like an overworked muscle. The sight of his cock, wet and shining as it slid between Kelly's lips, was hot even without the ball-clenching sensation of a tongue flicking across the crown of his cock or the thumb pushed up against his taint.

The throb of hunger between his legs curled Clayton's toes against the wooden floor and twitched back to his ass. He bit the inside of his cheek and reached down to lace his fingers through Kelly's hair. It stuck up between his knuckles in unruly tufts and tangles as Kelly let Clayton's cock slide out of his mouth and licked his way back down the length of it. He stroked his hands along Clayton's thighs, his thumbs rough as they traced up to the thin creases of skin at his groin, and mouthed wet, eager kisses against his balls.

"Fuck," Clayton groaned and pulled Kelly's head back from his cock. The whine of protest from Kelly, his full lips flushed and sticky with precome, made his balls twist again, and he had to chew his cheek until he tasted blood to hang on to control. "Not yet."

Kelly crawled up onto the bed and sprawled on top of Clayton, all heavy muscle and bone. His thick insistent cock nudged against Clayton's thigh as he bruised kisses across Clayton's shoulders. Clayton kicked his trousers off—the stray thought that Heather was going to kill him if she had to make any more runs to the dry cleaners slid through his head—and caressed the sweat-damp slope of Kelly's shoulders.

"I don't want to fuck," Kelly said.

"Could have fooled me," Clayton said. He bit back a groan as Kelly reached down between their bodies and grabbed his cock for a squeeze. "Got the wrong end of the stick entirely."

"You know what I mean," Kelly said. "I have a bruised ass, and besides, it feels weird with Maxie just down the hall."

Clayton cupped the ass in question and rolled over onto his side. He kissed Kelly and tasted himself. "You worried he'll hear?"

A wry smile tugged the corners of Kelly's mouth out of the kiss. Clayton chased them as though he could catch it with his lips.

"More worried that I'll have to look a cop in the eye and tell them a coyote got my baby," Kelly said. He rubbed his thumb along the underside of Clayton's cock, and a sliver of hot sensation dragged under the skin. "Well, Byron's baby. That'll just make it worse."

Clayton tightened his grip on the ripe curve of ass and slid his thigh between Kelly's legs until it pressed against his balls. A low, strangled sound escaped Kelly, and he thrust his hips forward, his cock hard and hot as it ground against Clayton's stomach.

"But this is okay?" he asked.

"Didn't say it made sense," Kelly said raggedly. "But yeah. This is fine."

Clayton laughed against his throat, ignored his grumble, and dragged him closer. The sheets tangled under them and caught under their hips as they moved against each other. Sweat tasted salty against Clayton's lips as he smeared hungry kisses over Kelly's mouth, jaw, and shoulders, and their cocks bumped and slid past each other with each thrust. Under him, Kelly moaned and clutched at his hips and the backs of his thighs with eager hands.

The tease of grazed contact, satin hard cocks, and the rough brush of body hair caught in Clayton's balls and pulled. He needed more.

He pinned Kelly down on his back against the now-crumpled sheets. Somehow the eye patch made Kelly's face look softer, dazed and distracted with the pleasure that flushed pink across his cheekbones and parted his damp, kiss-swollen lips. Clayton wrapped his hands around Kelly's wrists and pressed them down into the mattress. He rolled his hips against Kelly's in slow, hard thrusts that pressed their cocks against each other hard enough that the throb of it almost hurt.

Kelly arched his hips up into each thrust. His body was tense and tight under Clayton's, the muscles clenched under pale Irish freckled skin. He gasped Clayton's name as he came. The come spilled slick and wet across his stomach and smeared over Clayton's cock with each thrust.

Clayton lowered himself onto his elbows, mindful of the patchwork of purple and blue over Kelly's ribs, and kissed him deeply. He could still taste himself—cock and the thin musk of precome—on Kelly's tongue as he came roughly on his stomach.

"Fuck," Kelly groaned.

Clayton grinned and dragged a kiss along Kelly's rough stubbled jaw as he rolled off him. His hand trailed through the sticky mess on Kelly's stomach. "Bit late to change your mind."

"Funny." Kelly stretched and winced as the bruises caught under his skin. He folded his arm behind his head, under the pillow, and closed his eyes. His eye, Clayton supposed. "You're still a liar."

Maybe he was, Clayton supposed as he ran his hand down Kelly's heavy thigh. His cock was limp and sated, but it twitched as Clayton's fingers passed it. As much as he didn't want to be a little bit in love with Kelly, lust didn't make you want to taste someone's smile.

Probably not what Kelly meant, though.

"You're a good guy," Kelly said. He blindly reached out, tucked his hand under Clayton's head, and tangled his fingers through Clayton's short, sweaty hair. "And I like when I make you smile."

Just a little bit in love.

CHAPTER ELEVEN

THERE WAS nothing like baby sick on your shoulder to remind you that you weren't really a sex god. Kelly rolled the dice on a repeat performance and shifted Maxie to his other shoulder. He grabbed a wipe from the box and reached back to clean the hot barf off before it dripped down into his boxers.

"Okay, we've discussed this before," he said as he tossed the wipe into the bin. "This is your last chance. If you need to be sick, you put up your hand and ask me to take you to the toilet. Deal?"

Maxie frog kicked his legs and burped.

"My client will consider the offer and get back to you," Clayton said from behind Kelly with lazy amusement in his voice. It sent a trickle of awareness down Kelly's back, from the nape of his neck to his tailbone. "In the meantime he'd like to ask for a raise in his diaper allowance. The quality is not what he's used to."

Kelly snorted. "Don't give him ideas," he said. "Mom already bought Egyptian cotton towels to clean him with."

He leaned over to carefully put Maxie back in his crib. He was more confident than he'd been when his mom first handed him the gremlin-looking Maxie, but he couldn't quite shake the fear that one day he'd just let the baby slip out of his hands and fall on his head.

"He's obviously well-cared-for," Clayton said. "Your brother is lucky to have family who can help out. What your other brother, Cole, said yesterday… if I've caused any problems, I'm sorry."

Kelly snorted. "Byron's one good point is that he doesn't care who I sleep with," he said. "Cole was just…. He's the eldest. He thinks it's his job to manage us all, make sure we don't do anything to upset Mom and Dad. The fact that we're all grown now seems to have escaped him."

The question hung in the air, just begging to be asked. They studiously ignored it. That was what Kelly liked about lawyers—they knew when not to ask questions. Like "Did you do it?" or "Are you going to lie on the stand?" and "Does who you sleep with upset your mom and dad?"

Kelly wound the mobile back up and turned it on. It started to twist, and the primary-colored plastic cartoon animals bobbed on the end of their strings to the tune of "Hush, Little Baby." In the crib, Max watched it with wide, curious eyes and flapped his arms and legs about as though it were a Jazzercise class.

The thing was supposed to help him sleep, but Kelly wasn't sure it did.

He left Maxie to it and turned around. The sight of Clayton propped elegantly against the doorframe flash-dried his mouth. Last time, he hadn't had a chance to appreciate Clayton's morning-after presence. It had been sex, sleep, and then awkwardness.

Now he had the opportunity to really appreciate the sharp, handsome face and the long, lean body, still smudged and marked from Kelly's mouth, hands, and cock. Not that Kelly didn't appreciate the suits. He'd spent a *lot* of time appreciating the suits, the way all that expensive tailoring made Clayton… sharp enough to cut yourself on. But a half-naked, fresh-from-his-bed Clayton was something new to appreciate. He looked just as dangerous, somehow, but there was a warmth you didn't always see through the obscenely expensive suits.

Maybe that was just the hair, irrepressibly bouncy once the product had sweated out of it.

"Hey," Kelly managed once he realized he was staring. "Surprised you're still here. After last time, I thought you'd have snuck out before anyone came to visit."

Clayton looked amused. "Maybe that's where I was going."

"Yeah? Well, in that case, you forgot your pants," Kelly said. He nudged Clayton out of the room and closed the door behind him. "You probably do need to go soon, though. I can make you coffee?"

"Huh," Clayton said.

"What?"

"So *this* is what it's like on this side of the bum's rush."

Heat flushed Kelly's face. He scratched his head and snorted out an uncomfortable laugh. "Sorry. I didn't mean to…. I'm just not used to casual. Usually by now I'd have gotten you a toothbrush and a key. I might have overcompensated."

Clayton tucked a knuckle under Kelly's chin and tipped his head back. The kiss was soft and close-lipped, but Kelly still felt the tingle of it all the way down into his cock.

"I'm not going to climb out the window if you ask me to stay for breakfast."

Kelly hooked his fingers over Clayton's hipbones. "How about if I ask you to come back to bed?"

That didn't need an answer.

Back in the bedroom, Clayton sat down on the bed and pulled Kelly into his lap. He ran his hands down over the tight curve of Kelly's ass to grip the back of his thighs.

"So this." He leaned in and pressed his lips to the spray of bright ink marked over Kelly's collarbone. It had taken two sessions to finish the parrot and color it in, and the collarbone and the point of his shoulder had hurt the most. "Anything to do with the eye?"

Kelly had almost forgotten. He reached up and scratched at the edge of the eye patch where the glue had irritated his skin.

"Yeah, I used to be really into pirates," he admitted.

"I've seen that stack of DVDs downstairs," Clayton informed him as he bit sharp kisses along Kelly's collarbone. It reminded Kelly briefly of a slowed-down version of that old ink-gun pain, only wrapped in honey. "You're still into pirates."

He twisted his fingers in Clayton's curls and leaned his head back. He could feel the interested nudge of Clayton's cock against his ass, and maybe the bruises weren't that bad.

"I used to be more into them," he corrected. "Not exactly a whole lot of one-eyed role models for a kid, you know, so my dad worked with what he had. Pirates. The cops of the sea. Only had one eye, but it never slowed them down."

Clayton gave a low, rough laugh that Kelly felt vibrate through the hinge of his jaw. "Did he regret that once you got the tattoo?"

"That's probably the least of his regrets about me," Kelly said. The guilt pinched almost immediately, because that was ungrateful. His dad wasn't always great, but there were worse parents in the world. "Besides, he's got a pint of Guinness tattooed on his thigh, so he can't really talk."

"I haven't met your dad, but I'm going to go ahead and not imagine that," Clayton said.

"Good call."

A phone rang—two phones, one a beat behind the other. The clash of ringtones rattled through the house and set off a cat-wail of indignation from Maxie.

"Fuck."

Kelly rolled off Clayton's lap and reached for the dresser where he usually left his phone. Empty. He turned to scan the room.

"Downstairs," Clayton said as he grabbed his trousers and shook the phone out of his pocket. He unlocked it with a swipe of his thumb. "Daniel?"

Baker. That wasn't good. If your boss called you at three in the morning, it was never good. Kelly grabbed a pair of sweats from the back of a chair and loped downstairs. It smelled like old pizza and beer. Kelly skidded on the wooden floor in his bare feet, caught himself against the couch, and spied the glow of his phone under the table.

He grabbed it and checked the display on its way up to his ear. Larry. When your partner called you at three in the morning, it wasn't good either.

"What?" he said.

In the background he could hear an alarm blaring officiously and a dog barking furiously. "We have a problem," Larry said.

Someone knocked the door with the hard, determined rap of someone who expected you to get up out of bed to answer them.

"Hold on," Kelly said to Larry.

"It's the safe house," she said. Whoever was outside hammered the door again.

"Fuck." Kelly scrambled gracelessly into his sweats on the way to the door. The elastic waistband caught under his cock and then bounced over it. "Is anyone hurt?"

There was a grim pause. "Not yet."

"Wait. Let me get rid of whoever this is," he said. "A minute?"

She sighed but didn't argue. Kelly pinned the phone under his chin and yanked the door just before whoever it was could hit it again.

"What?" he snapped. The young red-haired cop on his doorstep looked familiar, but he blanked on the name. One of his mom's matchmaking projects. Cathleen? Cara? Something with a *C*. "Sorry. I didn't mean to…."

She lifted a hand to wave that away. "Your brother's been hurt." She sounded anxious. "He's in the hospital. Your dad asked me to come get you."

Fear hit Kelly in the gut, almost like a punch. He should have known. There'd been two calls like this when he was a kid. Dad had been shot and three years later Dad had been caught in a fire—same knock on the door, same wet, sympathetic eyes on the cop outside.

"Who?" he asked.

She pulled a sympathetic face at him. "Byron. He was, ah… it was a hit and run. We were…. He called me to ask for help with something. The case he was working on had gotten complicated. He thought someone might have made him. We were going to meet, but before we could, the car hit him. I saw it happen. They took him to Cedars-Sinai."

Claire. That was her name. She rubbed her hands nervously on her thighs, and Kelly wondered how much blood had been on them earlier.

In his ear, Larry snapped his name. "I need you to come and deal with this."

Claire pointed to the car. "I'll drive you to the hospital."

"Give me a minute, Larry," he said.

"I just gave you one," she snapped. "Look, I didn't mind you using the safe house, but this is your case, not the company's. I can't—and don't want to—deal with this tonight."

"I know. I just… shut up for a minute." He hung up on her. Later on he'd pay for that, but he couldn't deal with so many voices in his ear. "Was he badly hurt?"

There was a pinched bracket on either side of Claire's mouth. "He was unconscious. There was blood. I… should have checked, but it… it wasn't like in training."

Kelly rubbed both hands briskly over his face as though he could scrape away the cobwebs in his brain. As she glanced at his bruised chest, her surprise and suspicion reminded Kelly that he had an excuse to take his time.

"I need to go get dressed," he said. The hiccupy fury of Maxie's wail from the second floor reminded him that wasn't all. "Get Maxie sorted. I'll meet you at the car."

He closed the door in her face—which wasn't going to help the suspicion—and headed back up the stairs. His phone rang as he reached the landing. It had probably taken Larry that long to find out where she threw it.

"Sorry," he led with. "Something happened with—"

Clayton stepped out of the bedroom, his shirt open at the collar and sleeves rolled back as though he'd been at work late and not just fucked. He plucked the phone out of Kelly's hand.

"Larry, Clayton Reynolds," he said. "Daniel called me. Kelly has a family emergency. One of his brothers has been rushed to the hospital and…. Yes. I will. I appreciate that."

He hung up and handed the phone back.

"Go to the hospital," he said. "It's your family."

"What about Nadine?" Kelly asked. "If her husband or his 'friends' found where she was…."

Clayton sighed and rubbed his hand through his hair. Still a tangled mess of short cherub curls, it was the only thing that resisted being cool and collected.

"If they did, she probably told them where she was," he said. "Baker said that there was no sign of forced entry. She left Harry there, told him that she had to go and see someone. Harry set the alarm off by accident."

Kelly frowned and ducked past Clayton. He grabbed an old T-shirt from the dresser and dragged it on. "I can't see her going back to Jimmy," he said. "She made up her mind."

"And I hope she hasn't changed it," Clayton said. "But it's not always that easy. He's had a long time to learn how to manipulate her. She hasn't had long where she felt in charge of her own life. I'll call you when I know more."

"You could just call anyway," Kelly said. "If you wanted."

Clayton flashed one of those rare smiles and leaned in to skim a kiss across Kelly's mouth. He casually, intimately brushed his hand down Kelly's arm. "I'll remember that."

He left, but the warmth of his hand lingered, and the room still smelled like him.

Kelly rubbed his arm. It was weird to feel like you missed someone who'd only—right at that moment—left. He and Clayton hadn't even been—something more than nothing but less than something—for long enough to justify missing him at all.

"Don't make yourself into a liar," Kelly told himself. "No fairy tales here."

It took him a couple of minutes to find his spare eye. At some point he'd decided the safe place to put it was under the cap from an old eyewash. He gave it a dust and popped it into place and gritted his teeth against the ache of his bruises. It would have been easier not to bother with the eye, but there was a chance his mom would miss the bruises. The patch was a bit more in your face.

He grabbed his sneakers, pulled them on, and scrambled down the stairs. He was at the door when his brain registered that Maxie was still crying.

Shit. He'd forgotten.

Kelly went back up the stairs two at a time despite the ache of bruised muscles. As Kelly bent over the cot, Maxie stared at him as though he realized he'd nearly been abandoned.

"Sorry. We're going to go and see your dad," Kelly said as he lifted Max up. "That'll be new, won't it?" Maxie sneezed a bubble in answer, which Kelly supposed he could take either way.

Downstairs the door creaked open, and he heard Claire take an uncertain step into the house. "Mr. Kelly?" she said. Her voice had the brittle edge of trauma. "I really want to get back to the hospital. Are you...."

Kelly wiped Maxie's nose on a bib and tucked him into the crook of his arm. "Coming."

But not in the way he'd planned.

IT WOULDN'T be fair to say that Kathleen enjoyed crises, but she was good at them. Maybe it was just practice. As a new-minted mother when Cole and Worth were young, she might have gagged at open wounds and panicked over broken bones. But by the time Kelly came along, she'd slapped a dressing on what was left of his eye and drove him to hospital because it would take too long for the ambulance to get there.

A simple car accident wasn't enough to rattle a woman with that sort of pedigree.

When Claire and Kelly found her, she was red-eyed but composed. She'd abandoned the waiting room in the ER for a seat in the cafeteria, and a cup of nursed coffee was going cold at her elbow as she ran her family's life through her phone.

"...tell him to drive safely," she said as they reached her. A strained smile acknowledged their arrival without interrupting the call, and she nodded to the chair opposite. "Last thing we need is someone else in the ER. Okay. I love him too and you too."

She hung up and set the phone down.

"Dad?" Kelly asked.

Kathleen wrapped both hands around the plastic cup and nodded. She had her pajama top on over her jeans—cartoon kittens caught midpounce on robin's-egg blue satin. Her face was bare and shiny, the wrinkles at the corners of her eyes and around her mouth harsher than Kelly remembered them.

"Jim was at a training seminar in San Diego. Thank God, I talked Worth into going down with him." She fretfully checked the top button of her pajama top and first undid and then redid it. "Thank God I made Worth go down with him. He thought I was being paranoid, told me he was fine, but he's not up to the drive, not after a shock like this. Claire. Thank you so much for coming."

That was what she said. Kelly mutely translated it to what actually happened. Out from under Kathleen's healthy regime for the day, Jim had gotten legless in a bar—there was always one—with other old cops.

Kathleen held her hand out and clutched Claire's bony, freckled fingers tightly as she murmured how it would be fine, that Byron had a strong will and so many people cared about him. It was almost a prayer—two gingery women standing in front of a shadowy, plate glass window.

Kelly let them get on with it. It was the lie that bothered him. Maybe that was unfair, but his dad was a drunk, the life and soul of the party, until he'd got to America and people tutted "alcoholic." He never beat anyone or broke anything. The worst he'd ever done was try to book them all on a flight back home after a particularly bad year. The only one he hurt was himself.

So why lie about it to two people who probably knew better?

"What about Wilde?" he asked. "Cole?"

Kathleen shook her head. "They have to work. I told them to come in the morning. They can sit with Byron while I go home to change," she said. Her eyes fell to Maxie, his blanket hung half to the ground as he unraveled it one overheated squawk at a time, and her mouth trembled.

"There's my boy." She held her arms out. "Give him here. He wants his granny, doesn't he?"

"He's tired," Kelly said as he transferred Maxie. It was the truth, but it felt like an excuse, a reason for Maxie to sniff and whinge as his grandmother cuddled him and tucked his blanket in.

"Look at this? What has your uncle done to you, sweetheart?" Kathleen tutted as she swaddled Maxie up again and twisted the blanket and folded it around him like a straitjacket. He was tucked in so tightly that Kelly wasn't sure if it was internal pressure or frustration that turned his face bright red and made him wail. "That's better."

"He really hates that," Kelly said.

Instead of listening Kathleen gave the end of the blanket a tuck to tighten it further. She half turned to Claire and shook her head in mock dismay.

"He's a good boy. He tries," she said. "But he's not…. Well, Kelly's never been interested in getting married and having a family. He prefers the bachelor life, don't you, dear?"

Kathleen sat down and nursed the furious Maxie with a fingertip instead of a pacifier. Behind her back Claire grimaced awkward sympathy at Kelly, her pretty face surprisingly elastic and mobile.

"This is how he lost his mom," Kathleen said as she slowly rocked Maxie in her arms. She patted his bottom in a slow, almost hypnotic rhythm. "I drove up and sat with him while we waited for news. Do you think he remembers? So much tragedy for such a little person."

Claire frowned, ginger eyebrows twitched together. "I thought…. Byron said he was there. That he sat with Maxie while his wife died."

"Oh, he was there too," Kathleen said. "That was later, though. At first it was just me and Maxie. Just like today."

She took a shaky breath, and a tear fell on Maxie's blanket.

"I'm so sorry," Claire said as she hugged Kathleen's shoulders sympathetically. "I didn't mean to remind you of…. It'll be okay."

It was habit to let Kathleen have her rose-tinted version of history, to reframe Wilde's drug problem as him being a layabout when he was a teen, that Byron was hyperactive, that they'd moved because of Dad's job… that Kelly was just a committed bachelor, not that he dated bachelors.

Her memory wasn't just a cockeyed optimist's take on events, though. It was an outright lie. Kelly remembered the calls from Mom to him and Cole and to Dad as she harried them to get Byron to the hospital. Every call had expressed relief that they'd fixed the last insurmountable obstacle that stopped Byron getting into a car to see his wife die and frustration that they hadn't fixed the next one.

Not once had she listened to "He just doesn't want to go."

Kelly bit the inside of his cheek in frustration. His teeth caught on the raw graze from earlier, and he tasted copper and salt.

"I'll go check in with the doctors," he said as he swallowed the blood. "See what's going on or if they've got any updates on how Byron's doing."

Kathleen pressed her lips together, took a shaky breath, and nodded. "Thank you," she said. "They, umm... they said he was still unconscious and they wouldn't know more until he wakes up. And he will. He's got his boy here. He'll wake up for him."

She looked down at Maxie while Claire awkwardly patted her shoulder and asked about tea. Kelly left them to it as he dumped Maxie's bag of stuff on a chair and headed out to look for information. He ruefully rubbed his thumb over the edge of his bruised eye as he nudged the door open with his shoulder.

Kathleen probably wouldn't even have noticed if he left the eye patch on.

CHAPTER TWELVE

IT WASN'T often that Byron came out worse in anything. A fight with a car was apparently the exception that proved the rule. He lay on the bleached-white hospital sheets, bruises stippled from his jaw up to his temple and his leg slung up in the air and held together with a cage of pins and struts.

His toes were swollen and purple where they stuck out of the dressing. It reminded Kelly of a corpse he'd found once—a missing person turned suicide who got dressed to go to the beach and hanged themselves in a derelict store instead. It took them four days to track down the hole in the bucket where all the family money had dripped out, and the woman's feet had been that color when they finally got there.

Despite all his issues with Byron, Kelly felt a jolt of relief that his brother was still breathing. At the end of the day, he was family, and blood was thicker than water.

The doctor in charge of the ward was a middle-aged woman with tired eyes and shoes that squeaked as she walked around the bed.

"Your brother was in and out of consciousness when he came in, and he does have a hairline fracture of his skull," she said briskly. It wasn't that there was no sympathy in her voice, but it had to wait its turn. "That can cause a traumatic brain injury, but at the moment, we're hopeful that there's been no bleeding in the brain. He was in surgery…"

She paused as she bent over to check the IV plugged into Byron's arm and the stand he was hooked to. Then she picked up the thread of her sentence as though she'd never dropped it.

"…due to complications from his broken ankle. There was significant internal bleeding, and it was necessary to operate immediately to ameliorate the pressure. It went well, and, for now, there's no reason to be pessimistic about his outcome. Detective Kelly is doing well, Detective Kelly." She delivered the last line with sharp irony.

"Sorry," Kelly said. "Only one in the family who isn't."

The doctor raised a perfectly arched eyebrow and tapped a tooth-dented pen against the soft crescent of bruised skin under her eye.

"That's a prosthetic?"

Kelly rubbed his eye again. He didn't remember binocular vision—he imagined it was like being a chameleon—and it didn't bother him that one was glass. But experience had taught him that most people found the naked socket weird, and the ones that found it hot weren't for him. Yet it still felt strange when someone pointed out that he only had one. It was like being naked, only not in a good way.

"Yeah," he said.

The doctor squinted at him and nodded her approval. "It's nice work. Your ophthalmologist did a good job."

"Thanks."

"Your brother is doing well. He's young, he's strong, and he's got excellent doctors," the doctor said. She pushed the pen behind her ear and checked her pockets for a mint. The red-striped sweet crinkled as she unwrapped it. "For now, there's no reason to expect the worst. Stay with him. I'll send a nurse to let your mother know he's doing better."

She popped the candy into her mouth, patted his arm, and walked away as she crunched. Left alone with his brother, Kelly took a deep breath and let it out. The taste of it lingered on his tongue—bleach, antiseptic, and pain.

There wasn't a lot Kelly remembered about what happened after he lost his eye—mostly stories from the rest of the family, repeated until it was *like* a memory—but he remembered that antiseptic and blood tang on the air and Byron's voice in his ear to keep him company in the dark.

Now it was Byron in the dark, and Kelly the one by his bedside.

"Mom's downstairs," he said aloud. "She'll be here in a minute."

Behind bruised lids he saw Byron's eyes flicker as though he'd heard him. Kelly dragged his hand down over his mouth. The stubble was rough against his fingers. He wished he'd told the doctor not to worry, that he'd go and get Kathleen. If it was Cole, he could have held his hand and talked about the beer they'd get once he woke up.

It wasn't that easy with Byron. Nothing ever was.

The minutes ticked by, and the silence settled on Kelly's shoulders like a weight. Somehow it felt more oppressive than if Byron had been awake. He'd just started to think that he should go and find his mom when Byron coughed and licked his lips.

"Wha' the fuck?" he mumbled as he opened his eyes.

He tried to lift his arm and flinched at the rattle of the IV. Kelly reached out and pressed his hand on Byron's shoulder. The skin under his hand somehow managed to be hot and chilled at the same time… clammy.

"You're in the hospital," Kelly said. "It's okay."

Byron blinked and registered the pain somewhere down under the drugs they'd hit him with. He twisted his mouth awkwardly. "No."

"Just relax," Kelly told him as he got up. "I'll get someone."

THEY LOOKED like a nice little family unit once the doctors were done. The slim red-haired girlfriend on one side of the bed, the doting mother on the other, and the injured hero in the middle with his baby cradled lovingly in the crook of his arm. The only thing out of place was the extraneous uncle in the doorway.

Maxie made a fretful sound and squirmed. He kicked his legs and covered his eyes with his hands, palms out and fingers starfished. In about five minutes, he'd start to wail, inconsolable at being a baby. Habit made Kelly push himself off the wall, but before he could say anything, Kathleen plucked Maxie up off the rough blankets.

"One silver lining is that you'll have time to bond with Maxie now," Kathleen said as she cradled the baby against her shoulder. "You can stay with me and Dad. We'll sort out Wilde's old room over the garage until you're back on your feet. Your dad's right. It's not fair to expect Kelly to take on a baby. He's got his own life."

The flash of resentment caught Kelly by surprise. It stuck in his throat like a ball of nettles despite the fact that this—other than Byron's sliced-open leg—had always been the plan.

"I don't mind," he said.

"A boy should be with his father," Kathleen said firmly. "I remember when you two were little, always getting into fights so Jim would pay attention to you. You'd have thought they hated each other, Claire. All so their dad would come and break it up."

"Always saw right through me, Mom," Byron drawled. He shifted cautiously in the bed and turned a grayer shade of pale as his foot shifted in the sling. "Speaking of Dad, where is he?"

"He won't be long. They were on their way." Kathleen gave Maxie back to Byron, who grimaced as he looked down at the baby. She pulled her bag onto her lap to hunt through it, through receipts, a roll of coins, a crumpled handful of cardboard loyalty cards, and finally her phone. She tilted it toward the lamp on the bedside table to see the screen. "Oh. Worth wants one of us to meet him in the north tower to tell him where we are. He and your dad are driving around now."

It was a good excuse. "I'll go," Kelly said. Claire protested halfheartedly from her perch by Byron. She wasn't family. Kelly should stay with his brother. He waved his phone at her. "I should check some stuff with work anyhow, and they don't want you to use your phone in here."

He stepped into the hall. Behind him Kathleen tutted over the fussy Maxie, and then she noted to the room at large, "See, he can't get a moment to himself. It's not like the other boys. When you run your own business, you can't just put in for time off and forget about it. They've run him ragged the last few weeks."

That was Kathleen for you. She was only ever nice about her boys to other people. Kelly stalked away down the hall, away from his brother's bedside and the ugly knot of feelings he had no right to have.

A woman with a crying little boy in tow and a confused toddler on her hip came out of one of the rooms. She wiped her face on her sleeve and gave the boy's arm a tug as they headed down the hall. Devastation was no barrier to a child's bladder.

Kelly felt a pang of… guilt… that his brother was going to be okay while someone this woman loved obviously wasn't going to be. It was stupid. Maybe it seemed like Byron sucked other people's luck out of them, but he didn't really.

Not from a hospital bed anyway.

The toddler started to cry hiccuped sobs of confused misery as they reached the elevators and stopped. His mother made a feeble attempt to comfort the child and then gave up. She just tilted her head back and watched the elevator count down the floors while the child wailed.

Kelly took the stairs. It had been too rough a day to close himself in a tight metal box with strangers and their hospital-sour grief.

His phone buzzed in his hip pocket as he reached the parking lot. Kelly pulled it out to see, half expecting his dad's number.

It was Clayton. The sight of his name made Kelly feel better than it should have, even though the call was probably just work related. It frustrated him. Even if Clayton hadn't made it clear that he just wanted something casual, Kelly didn't need a new boyfriend. There was work, there was Maxie, and love should be *easy*. He already knew nothing about Clayton would be easy.

Besides, it was work, nothing personal.

Nadine texted me. She said she's changed her mind about the divorce. Didn't ask about Harry.

That made no sense. Kelly texted back quickly.

Think she's safe?

No answer. Kelly stared at the unresponsive screen as he wondered what to do, torn between reluctance to let Clayton down and loyalty to his family. That it was even a question made him feel worse, but…. Dad and Worth would be there soon, so Kelly wasn't needed. The bitter thought occurred to him that he never really had been. He'd only been the delivery method for Maxie.

It wouldn't usually bother him. Kathleen loved all her boys, but right then, he was tired and sore and not in the mood to kick his self-pity into gear. He was halfway through an offer to head over to help Clayton when he heard his name clipped out sharply.

"Captain, we don't know what happened," a man's voice said, distorted as it echoed off the bare concrete of the parking lot. "We haven't had a chance to talk to Detective Kelly yet."

Despite the distortion, the voice plucked at Kelly's memory. It sounded familiar somehow. He took the last few steps carefully and nudged the heavy stairwell door open with his foot. The first thing he saw through the crack was the blandly handsome profile of the man who'd given him a very professional beating the day before.

"Look, I agree with you on the basics. The Glendale situation is unstable," Blandsome said. "However, we can turn this accident to our benefit. Blame it on Kevoian, get him out of the equation, and there's no one else but Jimmy to fill the gap. They'll have to use him."

Adrenaline itched under Kelly's skin and tried to twitch his muscles, but fight-or-flight wouldn't be particularly helpful right then. He absently pressed his thumb into the edges of his black eye, and the dull pressure was a throb in the empty socket. Fight hadn't exactly worked out that well for him before either. He glanced at the man with Blandsome. He had short gray hair and a darkly tanned face. He wasn't one of the Beefcake brothers. Doubt pinched for a second—maybe he was wrong, the man's defining feature was how bland he was—but then he glanced down. Those were the same boots, the worn-to-creases jump boots with a T-shaped notch in the toe that had given him a kicking earlier.

Shit.

It made no sense that they were there… unless Byron's accident hadn't been an accident. If whoever Jimmy's new partners were assumed that the Kelly who'd asked questions about them was a cop. Kelly grimaced around the sour-lemon tang of guilt. He'd never live that down.

Except he wouldn't need to, would he? The pieces were all there— the undercover protection detail, the lonely wife, the sudden absence three months ago—and despite Kelly's best efforts, they started to fall into place.

There was a third man with them, but he was behind the white pillar. All Kelly could see was a black-clad shoulder and a bristle of a beard.

"I know how many years you've put into Jimmy," the man said. His voice was low, a rasp of controlled irritation, and the hair on the back of Kelly's neck itched with recognition. "I don't want to burn that identity any more than you do, but at the same time, I won't put one of my officers at risk. Even if I agreed, how you going to explain that Jimmy suddenly has a cast?"

Blandsome glanced at Salty, who shrugged and answered for him. "People have accidents," he said. "We just say he did."

The third man snorted and stepped out from behind the pillar. Kelly already knew who it was. Like Mom had said, how many times had he been lectured in that low, irritated voice over his grades or fighting.

Jim Kelly, his white hair shorn short and his beard grown out since Kelly had last seen him, stalked over to the elevator and jabbed his finger against the call button.

"I don't like this, Lepson," he said flatly. "You're pushing this cover to the edge."

Blandsome shrugged. "That's not really your call, is it, sir?"

Jim grunted. "You wouldn't be here, Lepson, if I couldn't pull the rug out from under you. If this accident wasn't an accident, then your team has fucked up and put one of your undercover cops at risk."

"He signed up for it," Salty pointed out.

Kelly tasted bile in the back of his throat, a hot wash of angry acid. He forced it back down and closed the door carefully. One thing being

Byron's brother had taught him was to always think before you jumped in—not that he could see any way this wasn't what it looked like.

He sat down on the hard edge of a concrete step and looked at his phone. The half-written message to Clayton hung in the minimized window. He took a deep breath, deleted it, and started again.

She's not with Jimmy, he typed instead.

Because Jimmy was upstairs on starched white sheets as he waited for his dad to tell him if his cover was blown or not.

Son of a bitch.

CHAPTER THIRTEEN

THE COFFEE stall outside the courthouse sold Advil. They were overpriced and came in single-serve packets. Clayton didn't care. Lack of sleep and the offensive brightness of the morning had combined to drill a spike of pain from the crown of his head down to his spine. He swiped his card.

"...it's going to be another hot day in old LA," the radio balanced on top of the cooler warned chirpily. "Temperatures are predicted to hit one hundred degrees this afternoon, increasing the risk of...."

The vendor flicked the radio off and *tch*ed his tongue. "Some idiot will start a fire," he told Clayton as he passed him the Advil, or maybe it was to the woman who'd just stepped up to grab her coffee. "Some idiot always starts a fire."

She grunted sourly and grabbed her cardboard cup. "Some idiot should be made to pay for the damage."

"Some idiot does," the vendor snorted as he jabbed his thumb at his chest. "Me."

Clayton ripped the pack open with his teeth and dry swallowed the pills instead of opening the bottle of water he'd bought. He could feel the tension in his jaw as he swallowed. The dull ache of clenched muscle and ground teeth amplified his headache.

The pills wouldn't get rid of this sort of headache. It would hang around until it burst like an abscess and left him blind with pain for an hour. Until then, though, he had to function, and the Advil dulled enough of the ache to let him do that.

He headed into the courthouse. Briefcase, phone, and wallet went through the X-ray without incident, and then the security guard beckoned Clayton forward.

The metal detector went off as it picked up the pins that held Clayton's left forearm together. It always did, just like he always got pulled aside for a brisk pat-down by security guards who already knew him and his forearm.

It usually didn't bother him. It was a minute out of his day and one he could effectively bill. But he had to bite his tongue on a sarcastic comment as the jug-eared guard with crescent-shaped sweat stains dark under his arms as they dried in the air-conditioned chill, slid the wand up the inside of Clayton's leg.

How many minutes had he wasted on this over the years, he wondered bleakly. If he totted them all up, how many billable hours could he invoice his mother's… third, fourth? The one with the rusted-out Camaro and the creepy eyes?

Too many.

He'd hoped he could save Harry from doing the same math, because eventually Jimmy would get tired of terrorizing his wife and turn to his son. In Clayton's experience abusive assholes could always find a new low to sink to.

The wand beeped as it ran over his forearm, and the guard gave him an apologetic shrug and sent Clayton on his way.

On the other side of the security checkpoint, Baker waited for him on one of the benches. His arm was slung along the back as he watched people go by. A few of the defendants who saw him looked nervous. Some of the lawyers too, for that matter.

"I shouldn't have taken this case," Clayton said without preamble as he joined him. "It's too close to home."

Baker moved his arm and sat up. "Aren't they all?" He shrugged when Clayton gave him a sharp look. "Background checks are standard, and you bounced around a lot of homes."

"Houses," Clayton corrected him. It took more than a roof and a Wi-Fi password to make a home. He waited for the old wash of shame at the fact that someone knew about his life, knew his mom had fucked her life up. It didn't hit. Maybe the headache hadn't left any room for it, or he'd finally knocked that chip off his shoulder.

"Besides," Baker added, "unless you're a rich old woman, if you dedicate all your do-good impulses to one cause? There's something personal there."

The back of Clayton's throat still tasted of powder and chemicals. He finally twisted the cap off his water and took a swig. The label said the additives were cranberries and green tea, but it just tasted flat and vaguely green.

"I didn't do much good this time," he said.

Baker slapped his shoulder. "Harry isn't back with his father yet," he said. Although an emergency placement with Maureen and her dogs would only hold for so long, and if Nadine didn't come back, that only left Jimmy or foster care. "Nadine can still change her mind."

It wasn't fair to be angry at Nadine.

Clayton knew the statistics and the talking points. He'd heard— he'd *said*—the sound bites about how many times a battered spouse tried to leave before it took. He even knew how true they were. Yet, when he walked into that empty house last night, the sound of a children's movie on at past three and a stool dragged over to the kitchen counter where Harry had tried to heat up something to eat, he felt the slow pressure of anger start to build.

Like he'd told Baker, it was too close to home. He could still remember how cold and strange it was to be alone in your house overnight—or longer. His mom had spent two weeks in Vegas once— and the responsibility of it being a secret to keep from your neighbors and the school.

So he was angry. That was his problem, though. Nadine was still, until he confirmed her text, a client.

"I hope she does," Clayton said. "If she does, what did you find out about Jimmy Graham?"

Baker frowned. "Cobwebs," he said. "Old dead flies. No spider yet. I talked to Judge Ebel, and she confirmed—off the record—that she'd been... requested... to delay any movement on your petition for a restraining order. It's in your office now, by the way."

"Thanks."

Baker shrugged that off. "I checked around, and there are a couple of cases in Glendale that got, ah, short-sheeted, so to speak. Plea bargained out, dismissed on grounds that any lawyer would only introduce as a Hail Mary pass. Just generally a lot of bad luck making anything stick right now."

"So Kelly was right. He's an informant?"

"I would be very surprised if he weren't," Baker said. He adjusted his tie fussily as he looked around to make sure no one was close enough to hear him. "I checked with an... associate who's spending time in the Los Angeles County prison. He used to have some influence, and, based partially on what he didn't say, there's been enough mutterings about how lucky Jimmy is to earn him the moniker Greasy Graham. Nothing that would stick enough to get him a shiv in the shower, though."

If you'd asked Clayton a month ago, he'd have put money on never hearing Baker say the word *shiv* without him putting air quotes around it. His matter-of-fact pronunciation was only made more surreal by the smile and nod he offered some acquaintance on the way by.

"Not ideal," he understated. "It's possible I could still use it as leverage, though. Might tighten Jimmy's means, but being outed as an informant would tighten a noose around his neck."

Baker winced. "That's… risky," he said. "If they call your bluff…."

"They'll find out it's not a bluff," Clayton said calmly. "I'm not an ADA, Daniel. My first responsibility is to my client, not the man who manipulated her or the police department that had my"—the words caught in his throat for a second as he experienced the fleeting urge to call Kelly something else. He squashed it and finished the sentence—"investigator beaten up."

Baker still didn't look happy. To be fair, it was bad business to end up on the wrong end of the LAPD. It would give the other partners grounds to curtail some of the more extravagant concessions they had made to recruit Baker to the firm, not to mention the punitive traffic tickets and possible criminal charges that would result if Clayton weren't careful.

"I know how much I owe you, Daniel," he said. "I'm not going to drop you in it with this. If it comes down to me using this information, I'll take full responsibility."

Baker snorted.

"You're my employee and my friend," he said as he clapped a hand on Clayton's shoulder. "You owe me billable hours and no scandals for the first, and nothing for the second. Unless you want to tell me what you were doing at Kelly's house in the small hours of the morning?"

It had been a long time since Clayton was innocent enough to blush. The last time, he thought, was during his first visit to The Zone when he moved to LA. But it certainly felt like he had blushed hot stripes across his nose and cheekbones. He glared at Baker.

"He might have had a concussion," he said self-righteously.

Baker snorted out a laugh that started in his nose and turned into a belly laugh that crinkled the corners of his eyes. He flapped his hand apologetically at Clayton, who rolled his eyes and checked his phone.

He had fifteen minutes until court and two messages that must have arrived when his phone was in the security tray.

"Fine," he said. "I might have something of a crush on our neighborhood pirate. Happy?"

Baker wiped his thumbs under his eyes. "Are you?"

It was the sort of question that Clayton was never sure how to answer. He was good at his job, and he had everything he wanted when he left Utah—a place to live that he didn't have to share, enough money in the bank to feel secure, and he wasn't dependent on anyone's goodwill.

Happy enough for him. For most people, though, happy meant a warm house and a warmer lover—someone who made them smile, who they made smile.

It was eating pizza on the floor while he watched Kelly's mouth curve into that wide, thoughtlessly warm smile and missing what he'd just said because his brain was elsewhere. It was half lust and half a slow, bittersweet warmth—because it wouldn't last.

But in that moment when Clayton had almost forgotten that it would never work, it had felt like happiness.

He tapped the first message firmly with his thumb. "The sex is good," he said blithely. Because that was the first rule you learned in a house like the one Clayton grew up in—never admit that you care about anything, and people wouldn't know it would hurt to lose it.

Baker snorted and rolled his eyes at him.

The text was from Nadine. It stuttered down the screen in strings of consonants, unbroken by full steps. A frown creased Clayton's eyebrows as he pieced together familiar abbreviations and what looked like off-the-cuff shorthand.

"Something wrong?" Baker asked.

"Nadine," Clayton said slowly. He scanned the message again to make sure he hadn't missed anything. "She just repeats that she's back with her husband. It was a mistake to try to divorce him, and that she wants me to stop work on it."

"Not odd for some parents. We've all had clients who fought the bit out over a three-year-old Lexus before they even mentioned custody."

"No. She loves her son," Clayton said. "It wasn't Jimmy hurting her that made her leave, it was that Harry saw it."

Baker leaned back and crossed his legs. He absently tapped the case of his Kindle against his forearm.

"Maybe she thinks he's better off without her?" he said.

"Or she's under duress," Clayton said. "She was already afraid of Jimmy, but maybe he's decided she wasn't afraid enough."

"Or he just has her phone," Baker said. "It's a text message. She might have typed it out on her end, but there's no fingerprint on ours. It's also not a formal termination of your services."

Clayton shot an irritated glance at Baker. "I'm aware of that."

A registered letter would serve as formal termination. Clayton requested an in-person meeting instead. At least he'd be able to see that Nadine was all right and hopefully judge if she was under duress or not.

He hit Send and swiped through to Kelly's message. The blunt statement on the screen made him frown.

"Kelly says she's not with Jimmy," he said.

"How does he know?"

"No idea." Clayton stared at the message and then glanced at the time. "I need to get to court. Daniel, I know I've maxed out my favors, but could you get Larry to see if she can find any trace of Nadine? Credit card? Phone? Basic movements?"

Baker unfolded himself from the bench, tucked his Kindle into his jacket, and slid one button in.

"That's five minutes out of my day. I can do it on the way to doggie day care. Well, I can tell Heather to do it for you. Still not a problem." He slapped his hand on Clayton's shoulder. "You know, you don't have to be single to be a successful divorce lawyer."

The phone went back in Clayton's pocket, and he gave Baker a wry smile. "Yet somehow we all are," he said. "Most people, even people like Nadine and Jimmy, get married with the expectation of forever. You and me, we know ten years is unfeasible. Today's client didn't even make a full month." He shrugged and turned to go.

"I'm not saying you're wrong. God knows, I've never made it work, although that could be my terrible taste," Baker said. "But, ah, I wasn't the one who brought up marriage."

No, he hadn't. Clayton grimaced to himself. That was why he didn't get involved with people like Kelly—they were contagious. Two nights in Kelly's bed, and suddenly the idea of dates and... more... didn't seem so far-fetched.

But it still was.

"Just call Heather," Clayton said over his shoulder. "And don't give up the day job. You're a better lawyer than you are an advice columnist."

The last thing he heard from Baker was a chuckle.

ALL IT took to turn a quickie divorce ugly was one drunken confession the night before—in this case, an admission that Clayton's client had hooked up with her wife's bridesmaid during their wedding in Vegas. Now the bridesmaid had a clean conscience, Clayton's client had a black eye, and Clayton had a suit full of bleach. Mostly bleach.

He parroted Baker's advice to himself as he stalked into his office with a grunt for Heather on his way past. *It could have been worse. Nobody cried and nobody died.*

Clayton peeled off his tie. It had started the day a muted gasoline blue. Now it was blanched gray and yellow white. He stuffed it into the pocket of his suit and shrugged the jacket off, cautious of any still-wet drips. He folded it inside out and laid it over a chair.

The jacket had absorbed most of the mess, but his trousers were smeared with it too. Long stripes and splatters faded down to a muddy gray, and some of it had soaked through his shirt. It had dried on the drive back and glued the fabric to his stomach. Clayton grimaced as he fastidiously peeled it off.

"I'm sorry," Heather blurted outside suddenly. "You can't go in there just yet. Just a minute."

"That's okay. I can wait," Kelly said. There was an uncharacteristic thread of tension in his voice. "Just let him know I'm—"

"It's fine," Clayton interrupted, his voice raised to carry. "Let him in, Heather."

His stomach itched where the—he thought it was egg—and bleach had dried on his shin. He rubbed at the irritated patches of red as he turned to the door.

Kelly ducked through and paused as he caught sight of a half-naked Clayton. He cocked his head to the side and bit his lower lip as he gave Clayton a quick once-over. An appreciative smile lit up his face, but it faded quickly back to a serious expression.

It looked odd on Kelly's face—as though it had a weight to it.

"What happened to you?" Kelly asked.

"A twenty-two-year-old who didn't sober up in time to realize this was a bad idea to do in court," he said. "Hazard of the job, although usually it's paint."

Kelly rubbed his thumb along his cheekbone. Blood had settled under his eye, and the bruise was a mottled blue and green that spread up onto his eyelid. "Want to swap for the hazards of my job?"

"Your face will heal," Clayton said. He tossed the shirt over the chair with his jacket. "My suit is never going to be the same. Close the door?"

Kelly nudged it shut until it clicked and then leaned back against it. He shoved his hands into his pockets—at some point he'd gone home and changed into black jeans and a faded-to-gray band shirt—and watched Clayton strip out of his trousers. His eyes tracked a hot path down Clayton's body from his shoulders to his fitted black boxer briefs.

Eye, Clayton supposed, although it was hard to remember. His spare suit was already hung on the filing cabinet, fresh from the dry cleaners. Heather had even left him a fresh, crisply starched shirt. It was pale pink—not his shade—but she said if she had to buy them, she got to pick the color. He really needed to up her Christmas bonus this year.

"What did you mean earlier," he asked as he unfolded the shirt. The tension visibly settled back onto Kelly's shoulders. "You texted that Nadine wasn't with Jimmy? I agree that things are off, but what makes you think he's not involved?"

Kelly started to say something, stopped, and then bit his lower lip. The sudden tactile memory of exactly what Kelly's lip felt like between Clayton's teeth—the taste and plush curve of it—made Clayton's mouth go dry. He cleared his throat, pulled his attention out of his pants, and waited for an answer.

"I should have waited," Kelly said finally, "until I'd talked to Harry, until I made sure that...."

"Made sure of what?"

Kelly grimaced and rubbed at his bruised eye. He pressed the heel of his hand down against the bony orbit hard enough that it had to hurt.

"I... it sounds crazy."

Clayton pulled up his trousers and left the unfastened waistband slung low over his bony hips. Then he crossed the room to pull Kelly's hand away from his face. He gave in to the impulse to lean down and kiss him while he was there.

The curve of Kelly's mouth felt exactly like he remembered it. After a moment's surprise, Kelly relaxed into it. His muscles loosened, and he twisted his hand to lace his fingers through Clayton's.

"What was that for?" he asked. A smile still shadowed his mouth when Clayton finally leaned back.

"So far today I've lost a client I really believed was going to divorce her abusive husband and had rotten eggs and bleach thrown on me," Clayton said. "I wanted something to go my way."

"Kissing me?" Kelly asked skeptically.

It wasn't the whole truth. Clayton knew his own track record and Kelly's. Sooner or later Clayton would kick the legs out from under... this, because he might as well get it over with. It would fall apart anyhow—that was the only useful thing his mother had taught him apart from how to make a grilled cheese sandwich—but at least if Clayton killed it himself, it wouldn't hurt as much. And Kelly would find someone else, someone who wanted to be his Prince Charming. He wouldn't not look back. "If we had time," he said as he slid one hand over Kelly's hip to cup his ass, "it wouldn't be just a kiss."

Kelly snorted out a laugh and then grimaced as whatever was on his mind caught up with him again. He braced his hand on Clayton's shoulder and pushed him back a step.

"You might change your mind about that," he said. At Clayton's inquisitive look, Kelly apologetically shrugged one broad shoulder. "I don't think I'm about to make your day any easier."

He looked like he meant it, but kissing Kelly had never made Clayton's life easier. It was just worth the trouble. But it did feel odd have this conversation in his stocking feet.

"Okay." Clayton pointed to a chair. "Sit down and let me finish getting dressed. Then you can tell me what you found out this morning."

Kelly slumped in the chair and stretched his legs out in front of him. He stared at the scuffed toes of his boots as Clayton zipped his pants over the ache in his balls and pulled his shoes back on. Clayton slid his arms into the sleeves of a fresh jacket. It felt like armor—a layer of lawyer between him and the world. Usually he appreciated that. The close stitches and tailored fit were a reminder to everyone, Clayton included, that he was what he'd made himself, not what his childhood had tried to make him.

For the first time it felt like a mask.

So what, he thought sharply as he looped a fresh tie around his collar. It was a mask he needed. Or did he really want Kelly—perfect, happy Kelly with his sunny, lucky life—to know that his mom was in jail, he had a half brother in juvie, and his dad was still a no-show?

Kelly had signed up to fuck a lawyer in control of his life, who knew exactly what he wanted and for how long, not some damaged sad sack who desperately wanted to pretend, just for a while, that this relationship wouldn't crash and burn.

Clayton tightened the knot precisely between his collarbones and slid behind his desk. He rested his elbows on the blotter and laced his fingers together.

"If Nadine isn't with Jimmy, where is she?"

"I don't know," Kelly said. He didn't look up as he spoke. His attention was on his bruised knuckles instead of Clayton. "I just know where Jimmy is—probably—and she's not there."

"And? Where's Jimmy."

Kelly shook his head. "If I'm wrong…."

"Are you?"

Finally Kelly looked up from his hands. "No," he said slowly. There was a touch of real, unexpected bitterness in his voice as he added, "But that's never mattered before."

Clayton clenched his teeth on his frustration. The hairs on the back of his neck were on end with a mixture of worry for Kelly, who seemed more affected by whatever this was than he had been by the beating the other day, and a sharp prick of concern for Nadine that was growing by the minute.

"Just tell me," he said. "Where's Jimmy?"

"The hospital," Kelly answered. He rubbed at his eye again. "That's not it, though. The problem is *who* Jimmy is."

"An informant," Clayton said. "We know. I talked to Baker about it, and apparently his sources pretty much confirmed it."

Kelly huffed out a humorless chuckle. "Yeah," he said. "They were wrong. Jimmy Graham isn't a police informant. He's my brother. He *is* the police. And right now he's with my mom. No sign of Nadine."

A dozen different questions occurred to Clayton, each eager to jostle to the front of the crowd on his tongue. *What the hell? Which brother? Why are you only telling me this now?*

"Then who is Nadine with?" made it over his tongue first, as he stood up from behind the desk. "And why is she lying to me about it?"

The only answer Kelly had for him was a shrug.

CHAPTER FOURTEEN

HEATHER TUCKED the phone against her shoulder to muffle the handset as Clayton stalked out of his office. She'd gone au natural today, with a peach fuzz of curls freshly cropped close to her scalp and a simple shirt-and-pants outfit that looked more like a costume than anything else she wore.

There was concern in her voice as she said, "Mr. Baker isn't in the office," she said. "He's in court until this afternoon. I've left a message for him to call you as soon as he can."

"Keep trying," Clayton told her. "If you get through to him before he calls me, fill him in. I have nothing scheduled for this afternoon, so send my files to my apartment. I'll work on them tonight."

Heather nodded her firm agreement and then widened her eyes at him. "It's like something out of one of Grandmom's shows," she whispered. Then she lifted the phone back to her ear. "Yes. Sorry. Could you...."

Clayton left her to wrangle Baker's service and headed for the elevator. He knew that Kelly was behind him, but he wasn't quite ready to talk to him yet. His temper was knotted in his chest like a ball of hot wire, and barbs caught in his ribs every time he took a breath. He didn't trust his temper or cope with it well, and angry as he was at Kelly, he didn't want to say something cruel—or worse, do something cruel.

Kelly held his peace until they reached the elevator. "You need to talk to Harry first," he said. "Make sure I'm right."

"Do you think he hid her under the bed?" Clayton could taste his bad mood in the back of his throat as he snapped. He jabbed his thumb impatiently against the muted-gold call button and tried to choke it down. "I appreciate your loyalty to your brother—"

The words caught in the rough edges of his temper, and he couldn't spit them out. He didn't, and he didn't understand it either. It felt like betrayal. Maybe he didn't have the right to feel that way—he'd made it clear he didn't want any promises—but Nadine and Harry deserved better. They trusted Kelly.

"Nadine's my client," he said. "My duty is to her, not to LAPD. Her safety isn't going to be the collateral damage in protecting your brother's cover. She deserves better than—"

"I didn't—"

The elevator doors opened. An intern and one of the litigation lawyers—Janet, Clayton thought—stepped apart, blushed, and nodded their way awkwardly through the stiff silence. The elevator stank of cheap cologne, burnt coffee, and bad behavior as Clayton got on and hit the ground-floor button.

Kelly blocked the door with his foot before it could close.

"I didn't know," he said.

"He was your brother," Clayton said scathingly. "You expect me to believe you didn't recognize him? That he didn't—at least—touch base with you once he knew I was Nadine's lawyer?"

The doors bumped against Kelly's foot for a second time, and he cursed under his breath and finally stepped through them. Free of interference, the doors bumped shut and the elevator purred its way down. Kelly pushed his hand through his hair, and the tug of his fingers left it stuck up in all directions.

"I sent you all the info I pulled up in my background search," he said. "There were no pictures of him. What descriptions we had could have been for any midthirties asshole. Sure, I knew Byron worked undercover, but not that he had a whole other fucking family."

The angry crack in his voice sounded real, but the actual words didn't. Over the door the floors counted down one at a time.

"I've met your family," Clayton said. "The close-knit Kelly boys, your sister-in-law, and then there's the mom who texts you every hour. None of them knew about your brother's secret life? Really?"

Kelly started to answer, then visibly swallowed the words and tried again.

"I don't know," he said. "My dad knew some. My brother Cole might have. He's the one that Byron usually goes to help clean up the pieces."

"Could Cole be the one with Nadine?"

"What? No!" Kelly shook his head. "It's not like that. Cole's a good guy, a good cop. He wouldn't break the law. He wouldn't hurt anyone. It's just money usually, or sorting stuff out so nothing has to be made official. Just so my mom doesn't find out."

"I bet your mom would be thrilled to find out she had a daughter-in-law that used to work in Hooters," Clayton said. "A grandson she'd never met, who was afraid of his dad. Would Cole want to keep that from her?"

Kelly couldn't bring himself to answer that question. His silence was answer enough. It lasted until the elevator reached the lobby.

"You think there's a chance you could be mistaken?" Clayton asked before the doors opened.

"I think Byron's a very good liar," Kelly said. "If you don't have every box ticked, he'll wriggle out of it somehow. He always does."

"Fine."

HARRY SAT on a mismatched chair in the shelter's kitchen. An untouched chicken sandwich sat on the glass table in front of him, its cheap white bread curled at the corners. Clayton sat next to him and tried to ignore the presence of Kelly behind him in the doorway. They hadn't talked on the way over. Well, Kelly had tried, but Clayton had shut him down.

He was still angry. He still didn't trust himself with it.

"I don't wanna go back to my dad," Harry said. His hands were curled into white-knuckled fists under the table, pressed down hard against his knees. "He's mean all the time, not just when he's drunk or had to work late. All the time. It's best when he's away. Mom's happy then. She doesn't even miss him. I don't know why she'd go back."

Harry slapped the plate off the table and onto the floor in a jerky spasm of anger. The plastic plate bounced, and the sandwich came apart. One of Maureen's little dogs—a wonk-eyed Maltese with an overbite—pounced on cleanup duty. Harry hunched in on himself as though he expected to be yelled at.

"When does he go away?" Clayton asked instead.

Harry sniffed and wiped his sleeve over his face. "All the time. Mom says it's for work. She says he has to work hard for us, and I shouldn't complain just 'cause he can't come to my games and stuff. And I don't care, 'cause I don't even want him there. I just want Mom."

His face crumpled for a second, and he looked miserable and snotty. He was just a little boy, and he was tired and scared. Not crying was hard.

"She'll come back," Clayton told him.

"But she'll be in trouble," Harry said. "For leaving me. Litty's mom left her alone, and… and Litty had to go away and live with her grandma."

"Grandmas aren't so bad," Kelly said. He shifted awkwardly in the doorway as he put his hands in his pockets. He guiltily slid his eyes away from Clayton's glare. "Sometimes they're good people."

"I don't know her. She doesn't even live here," Harry said with all the contempt a small child could muster. "I want to stay with *Mom*."

The tears got away from him in an ugly rush. He folded his arms on the table and buried his head in them, and his shoulders trembled, and the back of his neck turned red as he sobbed.

Clayton reached over and put his hand on Harry's shoulder. He could feel all the bones and misery.

"Your mom isn't going to get into trouble," he said. "I promise. This wasn't her fault."

Clayton was fairly sure that was true. Unless Nadine had done something particularly heinous over the last twenty-four hours, it would be more trouble than it was worth for the LAPD to expose itself in order to pursue a case against her.

That didn't comfort Harry much. He just cringed away from Clayton and hiccuped out sobs as he dragged his T-shirt up to wipe his face. The little Maltese dog abandoned the crust of bread it was chewing and padded over to snuffle at Harry instead.

Harry reached down and patted it with rough affection that flattened its topknot. His fingernails were bitten down to the quick.

"Harry, we still want to help your mom," Clayton said. He waved Kelly over, and Kelly abandoned his post by the door and awkwardly slid into a chair on the other side of the table. "But we need you to look at something for us. Do you recognize any of these men?"

Kelly put his phone on the table and slid it over in front of Harry, who rubbed his face on his T-shirt again, sniffed, and looked at the picture. He squinted and fumbled at the screen with snot-sticky fingers to enlarge the image.

"That's my dad." He poked his finger firmly against the phone. "I don't know the others."

Clayton glanced at the phone. Most of the men he didn't know either, but there was silver-ginger Cole at the back with a dry smile, and the blonder Wilde was wedged in next to the man whose face Harry had picked out with a sticky fingerprint.

He looked like Kelly. He had the same open, roughly handsome face, the same pale eyes, and the same wide guileless smile. But Byron's smile didn't reach his eyes the way Kelly's did, even though Kelly only had the one.

The thought made Clayton glance over the table. The light from the window caught the bruises on Kelly's face and picked out the ones half-hidden under the stubble on his jaw. Last night Clayton had followed the path of the beating with his mouth, from shoulders to thighs.

Kelly hadn't known.

That should have cooled Clayton's temper, but he could still feel its sour tang in his stomach. He shoved it aside for later.

"What about the men who came to your house?" Kelly asked as he pulled his phone back. "Do you remember anything about them?"

Harry puckered his lips together as though he'd just tasted a lemon. He shook his head and hunched his shoulders in as he shoved his hands between his knees.

"You didn't see them?"

"Uh-uh," Harry mumbled through still-pinched lips. He shook his head in a quick, twitchy denial and kicked his feet against the legs of the chair.

Clayton debated whether it would help to push Harry. He was obviously lying, and he was obviously unhappy about it. In an adult, that would make it easy to break their story. Children were more difficult. They didn't see right and wrong in the same way.

"You know, sometimes moms get things wrong," Kelly said. "They might ask you to do something, but it's not the right thing to do. When I was little, I got hurt pretty badly."

Harry squinted at him. "Did you break your leg?"

"Something like that," Kelly said with a quick grin. "My mom knew what happened, but she told me that it would cause too much trouble if I told everyone about it. She told me I didn't remember what happened, and that's what I had to tell everyone."

Harry squirmed in the chair. "My mom says I should always listen to her."

"Most of the time," Clayton said. "But right now she isn't here. We want to help. Did you see anything the night the men came to your house? The night that your mom got hurt?"

For a moment Clayton thought it had worked. Harry glanced up, eyes wet and haunted, and opened his mouth to say something. Then he closed it again and shook his head with a tight, desperate energy. He stared down at the table.

"I didn't see," he repeated in a small, breathless voice. He glanced up through tear-spiked lashes. "Just what Mom said."

Clayton bit back frustration. He wanted to smack his hand down on the table, to make the glass rattle and everyone jump. It was effective. He remembered that from when he was a kid, the way his skin cringed across his shoulders as whatever man was there—the debt collector, his mom's latest boyfriend, his grandfather before cancer won the fight with the mean old bastard—filled the sweaty, trailer kitchen with the smell of anger and the sound of flesh on Formica.

Just like him, Harry would know to heed that sound. It was like a snake's rattle, that sound. The next thing they hit was always you.

Clayton swallowed the hot, angry words in his throat. This was why he didn't like to get angry. It... bled... all over everything.

"Just think about it," Kelly said easily. He braced his elbows on the table and shrugged loosely. "It's never too late to tell us something, Harry."

"I didn't lie," Harry muttered quickly.

"Maybe you just remembered something," Clayton said stiffly, careful to keep his voice neutral. "Sometimes people don't remember things directly after something happens. It takes time for the memory to come back. Nobody would be upset that you hadn't remembered before."

Harry squirmed in his seat and then blurted out, "I have to go pee." He waited, knuckles white where he gripped the edge of his seat, until Clayton nodded. Then he scrambled down and dashed out of the kitchen. The little dog followed him, and its excited yap was audible even after the thud of Harry's sneakers had faded.

"If Nadine wanted him to lie about what he saw, then he must have known them," Kelly said after a second. "Jimmy—Byron—did a lot of business at the house. His associates were always over there. Maybe Harry recognized them from that?"

Clayton rubbed his fingertips over the hinge of his jaw. It was clenched so tightly he could feel the knot of muscle under his skin.

"Or she lied to us," Clayton said. He lifted one shoulder in a shrug. "And in my experience, when a battered spouse lies to me, it's usually to cover for their partner. It wasn't their husband, the door did it."

Dead anger tasted like cold tea in the back of Clayton's throat. It wasn't fair, but for most people, blood was thicker than water.

That was going to put him and Kelly on opposite sides, and it hurt more than he'd ever admit to Baker.

"You think Byron did—" Kelly shook his head. "No. He wouldn't do that. Besides, she was already leaving him. There was no reason for her to cover for him anymore."

Clayton shrugged. "She felt responsible, she felt guilty, she still loved him. It's hard to leave an abuser physically, but it's harder to leave them behind emotionally."

Doubt flickered over Kelly's face. It was more than Clayton had expected, but it wasn't enough.

"I don't…. No," Kelly said. "Byron's a lot of things, but he doesn't lose his temper like that."

"I hear that nearly as often as I do the door excuse," Clayton said.

"If he did it, and I'm sure he didn't," Kelly said, "then where's Nadine?"

Clayton got up from the table. He didn't think there was any point in waiting for Harry. Pressure would only make it easier for the boy to stay mute. Let him think about it for a while. Maybe he'd remember something useful he could tell them.

"I don't know," Clayton said as he headed for the door. "Where are the guys that beat you up?"

The silence behind him managed to be deafening.

"Go home," Baker had said when he finally got in touch. "Don't let them know we're onto them. Let me handle it."

Clayton weighed his frustration at being called off as though he were Baker's dachshund against the promise of banked anger in his mentor's voice. It turned out he trusted Baker. He wasn't sure when that happened or if he liked it, but he did.

So he left Kelly to keep an eye on his brother and went back to the office. At that point there hadn't seemed much point in going back to his apartment. In the echoing silence of the nearly empty office building—twice a cleaner had rolled a cart to his door, nodded a surprised acknowledgment, and left again—Clayton worked out his frustration through hard work and professionally approved cruelty.

He finished eviscerating a settlement offer from an opposing attorney, drew up a list of special interrogatories for discovery on his "should have been divorced this morning" case, and sent a blunt threat to Declan Tate's attorney to either finalize the divorce settlement or get ready to go to court. Some people looked at pictures of kittens or meditated. He took apart marriages for stress relief. It worked, but he supposed it didn't make him a very nice man.

The closest he'd come was the few days when he entertained the notion that he could *have* a nice man.

Clayton snorted at himself and dropped the paperwork to arrange a witness summons into Heather's email. Unless he resorted to busywork, his desk was cleared until tomorrow.

That just left him with his thoughts, and he wasn't particularly interested in them. He stood up and stretched. There was a kink in the middle of his spine that refused to loosen, a dull knuckle of pain just under his shoulder blade.

Clayton twisted his arm around and tried to locate the knot with his fingertips. The long hours bent over the computer had been a mistake, but what the hell. It could accompany all the other mistakes he'd made lately.

He left the office—the cleaner would be relieved he could do his job next time he rolled past—and walked down to the floor's narrow kitchen. It was packed up for the night. The yogurt bar was dry and the day-old pastries cleared up, but the fridge was still packed with rolls and the pods of coffee were always available.

Clayton had only come for coffee, but his stomach rumbled a reminder that all he'd eaten that day was pain pills and a stale cookie at Maureen's. He grabbed a bagel and some salad and ate it as he waited for his espresso to perk.

"That's not very environmentally friendly," Baker noted from behind him.

The unexpected interruption nearly made Clayton choke on a mouthful of uninspiring greenery. He coughed his airway clear and turned to give Baker an annoyed look.

"Five years on, and that's still not funny," he said.

Baker looked tired. His tie was tugged loose from his wilted shirt collar, and he'd rolled his sleeves back. He made a point to fold them to show off the fancy print on the underside of his cuffs, but he still looked tired, and he summoned up a dry little smirk.

"You can't begrudge me my one small pleasure," Baker said. "You kids down here always forget that I'm the partner with a work ethic. Are you going to drink that?"

Clayton plucked the cup out of the machine and handed it over. He fed another pod in and hit the button to reset it.

"Thanks." Baker used his foot to drag a stool out from under one of the high tables. He propped his hips on it and took an appreciative sip of the coffee. "I needed that. I'd forgotten how... unforgiving... criminal law could be."

The bagel sat heavily in Clayton's stomach. He balled up the quarter that was left and tossed it into the bin.

"Where do we stand?" he asked. "With Nadine? The police? Make that everyone."

Baker took another drink of coffee and rubbed his index finger against the line creased between his eyebrows.

"Well, in retrospect, probably shouldn't have called the DA a dried-out sack of cat turds when I quit before he could fire me. Insult to injury, literally. To be fair, though, once I'd danced a bit for him, he heard me out. The case got rolled over to Internal Affairs, who were not happy to find out one of their undercover cops was a wife-beating bigamist." A sardonic grimace curved Baker's mouth down, and he tossed back the rest of the espresso. "I suppose it's cynical to assume their dismay has less to do with the bigamy and beatings and more to do with the fact that the wife has a very good lawyer?"

The second cup of coffee was finally ready. Clayton plucked it out of the machine, ignored Baker's hopeful look, and found a spoon to stir in a dose of sugar.

"It's cynical. Doesn't mean it's wrong."

"They don't want to let Detective Kelly—any of them—know that he's under investigation, so for the moment, it's just a missing person case," Baker said. "Eventually, though, Detective Kelly will be in a lot of trouble, Clayton."

"Good."

Baker raised his eyebrows. "Is that going to cause trouble for you?" he asked. "With your Kelly."

"He's not my Kelly." Clayton took a drink of coffee and tasted the graininess of not-quite-dissolved sugar on his tongue. "It's his family, Baker. When push comes to shove, he's going to back up his brother to keep the peace."

"Maybe you've misjudged him."

Clayton paused, coffee cup halfway to his lips, and gave Baker a challenging look. "When was the last time you misjudged someone?" he asked. "Because it's been a while for me. Kelly can't even pick a color for his living room without his family's involvement. He's not going to go against them on his brother's reputation. And for what? A woman he doesn't know and a man he's fucked occasionally?"

The logic was unassailable. Even Baker seemed to admit that as he sighed and levered his long body back upright off the stool. He rinsed the cup in the sink, shook the water off, and left it upside down on the drainer.

"I don't usually interfere in people's lives," Baker said. He acknowledged Clayton's snort with a shrug. "Mocking isn't interfering. Just… give him the chance to disappoint you. Even if he does, you won't be the one who burned the bridge."

"That's not the advice you'd give a client."

"Maybe I should." Baker dried his hands and rolled his sleeves down. "Maybe I will. Right now I'm going to go home and see if my boyfriend has written me off or not. You should get some sleep. Nadine's case is in the right hands, and tomorrow you need to finalize the prenup and the Tate divorce."

He clapped Clayton on the shoulder and left. Clayton took a swig of too-sweet coffee and supposed he might as well follow suit.

The cleaner had been and gone while Clayton drank his coffee, and he left a tidy office and the scent of orange oil in his wake. Clayton grabbed his jacket, left his briefcase, and flicked the lights off on his way out.

It was quiet as he left the building—quiet for LA anyway. The sound of traffic and people had dropped to a low murmur and the occasional burst of laughter in the background. Clayton paused to shrug his jacket on.

It was late but not too late to find someone to burn his bridges with. St. Felix wasn't exactly a pickup joint, but that didn't mean you couldn't find company if you wanted it. He wouldn't look out of place in his suit either.

A one-night stand with no complications, no ridiculously warm laugh, no parrot tattoo, and no crooked brother, would put his relationship with Kelly where he should have left it—six feet under.

It was that or go back to his apartment and think about how he'd rather be in Kelly's bed, in Kelly's warm, half-finished house with the baby monitors and the wall Clayton could talk him into painting red.

Playing house. Like he'd ever fit in that sort of life.

The bitter thought made up Clayton's mind for him. He tugged his tie loose with one hand as he stalked toward his bike. His attention was focused on the night ahead, so he barely noticed the shadowy figure who lurked at the corner—not until they moved toward him.

Crap. Well, it wouldn't be the first time he was mugged. He had already reached for his wallet—all he held was a couple of bills for tips and a credit card he could cancel in five minutes—when the figure stepped into the light and he recognized her.

"Nadine?" He jogged over to her and caught her by the shoulders. "Where have you been? Are you all right?"

She didn't look it, but then she hadn't before. He hadn't counted her bruises, but her cuts were still stitched, and the cast on her arm was intact, if grubby. Her unplastered fingers dug into his wrist as she grabbed him. Her knuckles were bruised and skinned. At the safe house she hadn't quite been ready to take the gaudy wedding set off. Someone had taken that out of her hands.

"I... I... that doesn't matter," she stammered out. "I don't want a divorce. You have... you have to cancel it all. Okay? Just make it not happen. Please."

"Why?" Clayton asked. "Who's making you do this? Why do they care?"

She hiccuped a breathless laugh as she looked around. "Doesn't matter. Nobody." It wasn't just a lie, it was an afterthought. "I just don't want to get divorced. He's a good man, really, just under a lot of stress. I don't want to make it any worse, and we need... we need money."

Her eyes were wet with tears as they darted nervously toward the road again. A big blue SUV was parked at the curb. Clayton hadn't paid it any attention earlier.

"Okay," Clayton said slowly. He freed his wrist from her fingers and turned her toward the building. "I just need you to sign some papers. Then you can do whatever you want."

Nadine resisted the pressure of his hand. "I can't," she whispered. A tear escaped, and she angrily swiped it away with her fingertips. "They hurt Jimmy. If they don't get their money, they'll hurt me. Or Harry."

The mention of his name made her face crumple for a second, and she looked just as achingly vulnerable as her son.

"Harry's safe. You don't have to worry."

Nadine's sniffed and shook her head. "They know where he is," she said. "They took pictures of him. Of my *son*."

She wrenched her arm free of his grip and backed away.

"Look. Just come with me. You'll be safe," Clayton tried to reassure her. It was his turn to glance at the car as the door opened and expelled a lean, wiry man in a faded gray sweatshirt with sweat stains at his collar and under his arms. He looked like a rat, but a tough one. "The police know what's going on. They'll protect you. They'll make sure nothing happens to Harry."

She folded her bare, bruised mouth in a humorless pleat of a smile.

"You already promised me that once," she said. There was no real venom in her voice, but the accusation still caught Clayton somewhere raw. "I shouldn't have listened. They just want money, and I'll give it to them. I don't care what happens to Jimmy now. To hell with him... and you. I just have to take care of my son."

She turned and walked briskly back toward the car. *Shit.* Clayton pulled his phone out of his pocket and dialed 9-1-1 as he went after her.

"You don't know what's happened," he said as he caught up with her. He grabbed her elbow and pulled her back a step. At the car, the tough rat glanced back inside at someone for instructions. "Jimmy can't hurt you anymore. Neither will they."

She swallowed hard. "I can't risk it," she said. "This is all my fault anyhow. Better me than Harry."

The rat pushed himself off the car and swaggered across the sidewalk. He held one hand behind his back, and the muscle in his arm flexed as he gripped something.

"She's coming with me."

The phone connected, and the tinny voice of the operator asked what his emergency was. Clayton ignored it as he tightened his grip on Nadine's elbow.

"If we go inside, there's a security system… guards," he said. "They won't be able to touch you. I can get Harry here too. We can protect you. If you leave with them, we can't."

She looked down at her arm and then up at him. "Are you going to make me stay?" she asked. "Going to drag me in there against my will?"

He hesitated but finally made himself let go of her. Even if he were willing to manhandle her, the men in the car would catch them before they got far. Clayton shifted his attention to Rat Boy.

"You have no idea what you're getting into," he said. "Let her go. Do what you like to Jimmy. That's no skin off my nose. He's the one you have a problem with. Obviously."

Rat snorted. "Not for long," he said. "And shut up. Get in the car, woman."

Nadine took a step, hesitated, and looked back at Clayton. "I don't need to be rescued," she said. "I'm sorry I got into this. I'm sorry, but just do as I ask."

"I told you to get in the car," Rat snarled. He grabbed her shoulder and swung around to march her to it.

It wasn't a gun shoved into the back of his jeans. Just a hammer.

Clayton cursed briskly and lifted his phone to his ear. "Hello?" he said to the worried-sounding operator. "There's a woman being kidnapped outside the Symons Building. It's a blue Nissan…"

He backed up to see the tags on the SUV. "Rogue. License is—"

"Fucker," Rat muttered and shoved Nadine roughly toward the car. He yanked the hammer out of his waistband and loped toward Clayton. "You should have kept your nose out of this, asshole."

Probably.

Rat swung the hammer in a low, nasty arc. It wasn't aimed at Clayton's head. It was meant to make him scramble away. Back off.

"SWR," Clayton told the operator. "The rest is obscured."

This time the hammer was aimed at his face. Clayton jerked his head back, the prickle of old habits chill on the back of his neck, and the blunt end of it caught his hand. He felt the crunch of something under the skin. It didn't hurt—not yet—but he could feel the tight heat where it would, and he heard the crack as the phone hit the ground.

Rat grinned nastily, and Clayton punched him in the mouth. The crack of bony knuckles against teeth was the last thing Rat expected. Most people would have been cowed by the violence, by the shock of assault. But Clayton had been punched before. Even as an adult, a surprising number of people thought it was okay to punch their ex's lawyer.

Surprise flared in Rat's eyes, and he staggered back. He spat blood onto the pavement, wiped his mouth on his arm, and glared at Clayton.

"When I'm done w' you," he slurred through split lips. "Expensive suits ain't even gonna make you pretty."

He worked his fingers around the rubber handle of the hammer and took a step forward. Despite the rough words, he looked nervous, as though he hadn't expected it to escalate. He flinched in surprise when the lights suddenly came on, and he lifted one hand to shade his eyes.

"Hey! You! Get the hell out of here." It was the first time Clayton had heard the security guard say anything other than "Have a good night." The stocky man had finally noticed the fight and come outside. He ran across the plaza with his gun gripped in one sweaty hand.

It was a Taser. Clayton knew that, but it looked real enough in the moment.

Nadine was already in the car. Whoever the driver was yelled flatly, "Get in the goddamn car. Leave it."

Rat turned and ran. He threw himself into the back of the SUV as it pulled away.

That's when Clayton's hand decided to hurt.

CHAPTER FIFTEEN

"BEER?" JIM asked suspiciously as Kelly handed him the cold glass.

"Ginger," Kelly told his dad. "Mom said the doctor—"

Jim interrupted with a disgusted noise.

"No booze. No smoking. No fried foods," Jim grumbled as he ducked his head back under the hood of his hobby car, an old Willy's Jeepster in vintage denim blue and halfway to drivable. Sweat beaded on the sun-scorched back of his neck. "Don't know if they're making me live longer, or just making it *feel* like longer. It's going to be a bloody awful barbecue."

Despite his grumbling, he sucked down half the jug of chilled ginger beer, wiped his mouth, and burped discreetly. He set the glass on the edge of the engine and shoved his hands into the half-built guts. The car wasn't going to be on the road anytime soon. Kelly had spent hours on it with his dad when he was a kid, just the two of him usually. It was the sort of thing Byron always got bored with quickly.

While Kathleen prepped ribs and barbecue sauce, Jim had fixed the suspension and shown Kelly how to sandpaper down and fill the holes drilled in the bumper. At least until his buddies rolled up with chilled six-packs and gossip from the precinct. Then he'd tossed Kelly a twenty to polish the leather until it was like butter and clear up the drive.

It was only years later that Kelly realized those were bullet holes in the metal. Like so much in his family, the ugly truth went unsaid.

"So, I heard that, ahh, your friend went back to Ireland," Jim said from under the hood. It was the first time they'd talked in weeks. Neither of them had mentioned that. Probably wouldn't either. "For the best really, with you taking Byron's lad in like that."

Kelly sat down on the low wall that separated the drive from what his mom insisted would be her perfect lawn one day, when she had time. He took a drink of his beer—actual beer, no ginger involved—and wiped sweat off his forehead onto his arm. The forecast kept promising the heat would break, but every day the sun defied it. From inside the house, Maxie's persistent, miserable wail registered his opinion of the heat. The steady monotonous note of it caught under Kelly's skin, but if he went into the house, Kathleen would chase him back out again.

"You have to let him cry it out," she tutted last time. "Byron isn't going to spoil him like you did. He needs to get used to that."

It didn't seem like something someone should have to get used to, never mind a baby who couldn't even sit up yet. But Kelly didn't get a say in that. Maxie was Byron's son, and he got to decide—even if that had already screwed up one kid.

"Liam was here on a student visa," Kelly said as he tried to ignore Maxie's piercing, fire-siren frustration. "He was always going to go home one day. We both knew that."

He had. Just like he'd known that Joey planned on a military career before he came out of the closet, that Harve was really obsessed with his ex and that was never going away, and that every other guy he'd ever fallen in love with came with a preestablished expiration date. It was easy to fall in love with them, because it was never going to really matter. He'd never have to choose between them and his family, never have to face what it meant when Kathleen asked him to be "discreet" in front of Jim's friends.

"Thing is, Dad, I've met someone else," he said. His throat was dry, and somewhere he imagined Clayton felt a chill run down his back. "He's… I really like him."

That got him a grunt from under the hood and a brisk request for a different wrench. Kelly picked it up and didn't hand it over. The end of it was scraped and dented from a long-ago impact with a garage wall.

"I thought I might bring him over sometime," he said. Or he *had* thought that—daydreamed that—before he realized what Byron had done. There'd be someone though, one day, even if he couldn't muster much enthusiasm for it right now. "Maybe for dinner."

"Your mom runnin' a café now?"

"She's hosting a barbecue for half your precinct tomorrow," Kelly pointed out in exasperation. "Like she does once a month. Chili's goes through less ribs."

Jim snorted. "That's different. And your brothers, Father Peters, my old partner and his wife? They aren't strangers. They're family."

"Maybe I could bring him next time."

"Well, I don't know if that's such a good idea," Jim said. He stuck his hand out and wriggled his fingers until Kelly handed over the damaged wrench. "What if someone says something?"

"Like what?"

Jim shrugged. "You know what the boys can be like. Some of them ain't... politically correct."

For a while the only sound was the rattle of wrench on metal and the occasional grunted curse from under the hood. Kelly scratched the scabs on his knuckles and tried to remember how to be an adult. It was harder than it should have been while he sat on his dad's drive with the sun hot on the cropped nape of his neck.

"Dad, why didn't you want me to take care of Maxie?" he asked. It was a question he was pretty sure he knew the answer to, but he'd never wanted to face it before.

"He your kid?" Jim asked. "You go against the grain and fuck your sister-in-law?"

It wasn't funny. There was nothing funny about any of it. Even Byron, laid up with his ankle in plaster. It might be deserved, but it wasn't funny. Kelly still nearly choked on his startled snigger.

That was Dad, crude wit and a sly wink as he passed them five bucks and told them not to tell Mom.

This whole situation—from the shame of what Byron had done to the guilt of not telling that Clayton was onto him—would have been easier if Kelly hadn't loved them, or at least been so used to them that it was the same thing.

"Jesus, Dad," he said. "No, I didn't. She hated me."

"Yeah, well." Jim finally came out from under the car. He pulled an oily cloth out of his pocket and wiped his hands. Then he stole Kelly's beer and gestured with the half-empty bottle. "You clean up your own mess, you shoulder your own responsibilities. God didn't put anyone on this earth to pick up after you. That wee fella is Byron's son, and Kathleen shouldn't have gone to you lot to cover for him. Told her that."

He punctuated the statement with a deep draught of forbidden beer and glanced guiltily toward the house as he swallowed.

It sounded good. Kelly wanted to believe it.

"I thought it might be because I was gay," he said quietly. "Maybe you thought someone would say something."

Jim scratched his jaw. His fingers left oily smudges in the gray scruff he'd cultivate until Monday morning. It was hard sometimes to remember that it had been twenty years since he'd shown Kelly how to change the oil in the car or throw his first punch. Back then—when everyone assumed Kelly just didn't want to kiss girls because of cooties—he thought Jim knew everything. The Word of God that Father Peter preached on Sundays had nothing on the Word of Jim, as far as Kelly was concerned.

"Okay, yeah. That crossed my mind," he said. "You know what it's like. People think things, don't they? Come up with things. You hear it all in my line of work. We get calls all the time from people who've seen a man outside a school or heard a toddler throw a tantrum when a man picked them up. Most of the time, it's their dad or uncle, but we still have to go ask questions. All it takes is one of your ma's church friends to say it's odd that you don't mind changing Maxie's diapers, and then, well, people always like to think the worst."

"Yeah," Kelly said resignedly. "I guess they do."

He left the beer with Jim and headed inside. Maybe he had to come to terms with adults being fallible. Maxie could wait a few years before he had to realize that.

WHEN THEY were kids, Byron caught chicken pox from a kid at school. Actually Kelly caught it first, but no one mentioned that in retellings, and even he tended to forget that detail. Kathleen had given Byron a bell to ring if he needed anything.

Every ten minutes he rang that bell. In the end Cole took it from him and buried it in the back garden somewhere. Actually it might still be there. No one had found it again.

For years that insistent tinkle-tinkle had held pride of place in Kelly's brain for the most annoying sound ever. Apparently now there was an app for that, with a variety of different bells.

The gong was the one that set Kelly's teeth on edge.

Everyone looked up as the bong echoed down the hall at maximum volume.

"Aggie," Kathleen asked as she grabbed a packet of ham out of the fridge. "Go see if he needs anything, dear?"

The muscles in Aggie's jaw clenched. She stuck her hands in the soapy water in the sink and then shook them off.

"I'm a pathologist, Kathleen," she said. "Unless he's going to die, I'm not much use to him."

Kathleen *tch*ed at her. "He's sick, dear. Be nice."

Aggie's lip curled her opinion, but she dried her hands on a tea towel and stalked off.

"You could just ignore him," Kelly said as he held Maxie on his knee with one hand cupped behind his head and mock bounced him. "He'll get used to it."

Jim probably wouldn't have noticed it, but Kathleen caught the echo of her own words. She threw a handful of pickles onto the sandwich and slapped the top slice of bread on top.

"He has a broken leg," she said. "What's he going to do, hop down to dinner? I'm just glad he feels like he could keep something down today."

Kelly rolled his eyes and turned his attention back to Maxie. Taking off his socks and his weird little baby jeans had stopped the tears, but Maxie's cheeks were still raw and pink from frustration. Kelly used the hem of his T-shirt to wipe them and pulled a face for him.

It was apparently the funniest thing that Maxie had ever seen, and he gurgled out a delighted baby crow and waved his arms and legs about in uncoordinated glee. Kelly had to laugh along as he caught one of Maxie's hands and kissed it.

It was sticky but the tickle of it made Maxie laugh again.

"He likes you," Kathleen said. She ruffled Kelly's hair with an affectionate hand. "You're going to be his favorite uncle one day."

Kelly lifted Maxie up so he mock stood on Kelly's denim-clad knees. "Hear that?" he said as Maxie kicked him. "I'm the best uncle, even if you don't know it yet."

Maxie burped a skeptical spit bubble and stretched up onto his tiptoes. At some point over the last few days, he'd done some weird baby thing and looked more like a baby than a grumpy alien infant. He was still skinny, and still had a dubious air for the whole life thing, but he seemed sturdier.

"This is why I wanted a big family," Kathleen said wistfully as she turned back to make the coffee. "So you'd have this—family to step in and help out when needed. When I had you boys—my family all the way back in Donegal and your dad's in Derry—it was lonely. I'm so proud my boys are all still close, that you can all come together and support each other."

Guilt pinched Kelly hard somewhere soft and vulnerable. He didn't appreciate it. It wasn't as though he owed Byron anything, and he hadn't for a long time. Even if he did—even if it had been Cole or Wilde—what had been done to Nadine and Harry was still beyond the pale.

He knew that, but it was just hard to believe it. Or maybe he knew that, once it all came out, his mom wouldn't believe it.

"Mom, maybe I should take Maxie again tonight," he said.

She tutted at him. "Sweetheart, I know you're lonely since Liam left, but Maxie isn't a dog. He should be with his dad."

"Yeah, it's just with Byron being hurt," Kelly said. He stood up and carried Maxie over to the cot Mom had moved out of the spare room— now Byron's again—and into the kitchen. It had bolsters tied all around the side, fat and white and not at all approved by the baby sites that Kelly had read. He ignored the urge to argue and laid Maxie down on top of the blanket, where he squirmed and gurgled to himself. "He needs his sleep, and Maxie doesn't sleep through the night. I suppose you and Dad could get up for him…."

Kathleen snorted. She claimed she could count on one hand the number of times Jim got up to feed any of the boys at night. For a man who'd spring awake at the sound of a teenage boy's foot midsneak on the stairs, he could sleep through a baby's wails like he'd taken a pill.

"I don't know," she hedged. "Cole told me that you had a friend over. Now, I've nothing against you getting back out there. I want you to find a nice boy, someone to settle down with for a while. It's just, well, you can't 'hook up' with strangers when you've a baby in the house. Who knows what they might do?"

"I work with Clayton. I've known him for a while," Kelly said. He swallowed the bitter taste in his throat. "Besides, I don't think he's going to be back."

Kathleen pursed her lips. "Well, then he's a fool," she said. "Any man would be lucky to have you, sweetheart. You've a good job, a good heart, and look at that face. You and Byron are both the picture of your dad as a young man, and he could have been in the movies, you know."

Yes, Kelly had heard both versions of that story. The one Kathleen had polished up for the boys and the other police wives, and the one Jim told if you got enough whiskeys in him at the bar. In Kathleen's version she never mentioned the director was drunk and just wearing chaps when he made the offer.

It still supported the idea that his dad was handsome, Kelly supposed.

"It just didn't work out," Kelly said. "He's not really interested in anything long-term, and neither am I right now. I've got other things to deal with."

It was the truth. It really was. Somehow it just felt like a lie.

Kathleen sighed. "Well, you'll find someone else," she reassured him. "You're still young, and it's not like you have to worry about a biological clock."

From the back of the house, Aggie yelled, "Go to hell, Byron!" and then slammed the bathroom door.

Kathleen pretended not to hear and finished putting Byron's lunch together. "Get the door for me, would you?"

Kelly went over to push it open, his body a long stretch against the wall. "Okay," he said. "What do you think, though? Probably best if Aggie or I mind Maxie tonight?"

Kathleen shrugged an "I suppose" his way as she went out past him. "Just make sure you bring him back in the morning. I want him to get to know Byron better."

She went down the hall to the guest bedroom, and Kelly headed to the downstairs bathroom. It was a good bet. He rapped on the door once—just in case Aggie was actually using it for the intended purpose—and nudged it open.

Aggie stood on the toilet seat, elbows on the window sill, and blew smoke out the cracked window toward the garden next door. She glanced around at Kelly with an expression that managed to be both guilty and defiant at the same time.

"Don't tell Cole," she said.

"It's bad for you."

She snorted and took a drag. "I'm a doctor. I know it's bad for me. Going to jail would be bad for me too. So I had to make a risk assessment." Smoke escaped her mouth as she talked, and she batted it around with her hand. "I'm going to tell you something, and this one you can tell Cole—I hate your brother."

Kelly sat down on the edge of the bath, and his phone dug uncomfortably into his hip.

"Cole or Byron?"

She flicked ash into the cup of her hand. "Both."

"What did Byron do?"

She hung the hand with a cigarette out the window. It wasn't just anger in the set of her mouth and around her jaw. It was something a lot like pain.

"He offered to sell us Maxie," she said.

For a long, disconcerting moment, Kelly felt nothing much—not even the anger and frustration he'd kept tamped down in his gut since the day before. It was just the sort of statement that didn't make *sense* outside of the context of a TV screen and a rugged, trustworthy detective. Normal people with jobs, who ate pickle-and-ham sandwiches their mom made, didn't try to sell a child to other perfectly normal people.

Except apparently Byron did.

"Fuck," he managed at last.

"Yeah," Aggie said. "That's what I said. I don't know. Maybe he didn't mean it and he just wanted to press my buttons. Who'd even say that, though, about their own child?"

The anger leaked back in. Kelly could feel the scorch of it as he breathed, like the burn from bad whiskey. It wasn't useful—a hard lesson from his childhood was that once Byron got you mad, he'd make you look like the bad guy—but he couldn't get on top of it.

"On the bright side, at least it was you," he said. "If he was up and about, Maxie might just have been gone by morning."

Aggie shot him an angry look. "It's not funny."

"I'm not joking."

A tinge of gray washed over Aggie's face. Her fingers trembled as she pulled her hand back in through the window to draw on the cigarette.

"He would—"

"Is this still about the money he wanted from Cole?" he interrupted tightly.

Aggie pressed the heel of her hand against the bony arch of her brow, and the smoke was lost in her dark curls as she mentally shifted tracks.

"Yeah," she said. "I told Cole that if he wanted to sell the house, I'd divorce him, and we could divvy it up fifty-fifty. Up to him. He's pissed off at me—slept in his office for the last three nights—but it seems like he wants to stay married. Enough to tell Byron no anyhow. So instead of a loan, he offered a sale instead."

"What does he need it for?" Kelly asked.

Aggie shrugged as she pinched the cigarette out between thumb and forefinger. "Being an asshole isn't cheap?"

Kelly roughly scrubbed his hands over his face. Most of the time his brain adapted to the missing eye. It filled in details and smudged the edges around the missing slice. His hand right in front of his face stumped it, though, and he was abruptly *aware* of the blind spot and the cool weight of his glass eye.

It made his eye socket itch for some reason. It was a pinprick of misfired nerves, right at the back of the eye. He stood up abruptly.

"What are you going to do?" Aggie asked. She shoved the butt into her pocket and jumped down off the toilet to grab his sleeve. "Don't do anything stupid."

"You don't even…. You don't know the half of it, of what he's done," Kelly snapped. His voice echoed off the tiles, and habit and a desire not to upset his mom made him drop it back down. Not that he was sure she deserved that. "I'm going to kill him."

Aggie winced and tightened her grip. Her nails dug into his bicep. "Don't be stupid. That won't help anyone."

That was always the problem, wasn't it? By the time you caught up with whatever damage Byron had done, it seemed like the least destructive course to just tidy up and move on—every time. Eventually you had to admit there was always going to be a next time.

"I have to do something," he blurted out as he pulled his arm away from Aggie.

The sharp notes of "Mack the Knife" from his pocket interrupted him. He probably wouldn't have killed Byron, though. Kelly hoped not, for his own sake. He wasn't sure Father Peters was up to forgiving fratricide.

"Take the call," Aggie told him. She shoved him down the hall. "Go outside and talk to whoever that is. Do that. We can work out what to do about your brother later."

CHAPTER SIXTEEN

KELLY DIDN'T take the call. Not right then anyway. He let it ring to silence and walked down the street, far enough away from the house that it felt like he'd left. Then he finally called Clayton back. He hadn't outwalked the anger, but he'd gotten too far away to do anything about it.

"I can't do this," he blurted out. It wasn't what he planned to lead with. He thought he'd start with *hello* and segue from there. But the minute the line connected, all the other words sank away and he was left with those four to lead with. "Everyone feels bad for him, and I just want to kill him. My mom made him a sandwich, and I hope he chokes on it. The stupid selfish asshole."

There was a pause on the other end of the line, and then a short, harsh laugh.

"And I expected your qualms to be around testifying against him," Clayton said.

His voice was cool and precise, the lawyer voice. A couple of times, when he was at the court, Kelly had watched Clayton as he politely cut some guy's mistress's story into confetti. It was weirdly hot, all detachment and sharp edges, and it provided an unexpected comfort.

Coolness and detachment were two things that Kelly felt he needed right then, even if he did have to siphon them from someone else's voice on a phone call.

"No," he said. Then honestly squeezed the rest of the words out of him. "Not yet anyhow. I mean, I'm not going to back out or anything. It's not going to be easy, though."

He stopped as he reached the end of the street. If he turned left, he could walk to the café where his dad used to stop on his way home because a burger and coffee on his breath was an easier fight than smoke and booze. If he turned right, there was a park where he used to hang out to watch people with their dogs. He'd always wanted a dog, but they couldn't have one because of Byron's allergies.

Instead of going to either, he sat down on the curb. It was quiet. No one was around. And if someone thought he was a drunk, then it would serve his family right.

"You might not have to," Clayton said. "I need to talk to Byron. The hospital said he'd discharged himself."

"Yeah," Kelly said. "Well, people kept telling him what to do, and he hates that. Mom's got the guest room set up for him until he can fend for himself again. Why do you want to talk to him now? I thought Baker said—"

"What's the address?" It was less hot when that detached, dismissive voice took a layer off your skin. He hesitated.

"Kelly."

"Hey, if you meet my parents, we're going steady. I already warned you about that." Kelly tossed the joke in to buy himself a minute to think. He supposed it wasn't a very good joke. It felt a bit sad. And this wasn't going to be the start of anything, just the end—not that Clayton had ever wanted more, but who wanted even a casual relationship with someone whose family was as screwed up as his. He licked his lips and frowned down at the concrete scoop of the gutter between his feet. Ants crawled around his boots. "Look, I appreciate wanting to punch Byron, but my dad does have a gun. If you're looking for a fight—"

"Not today." He could hear the thin, tightly amused smile in Clayton's voice, almost feel it against his skin. "I just need to talk to him. It's important."

Kelly rubbed his hand over the back of his neck. His skin was hot under his fingers.

"All right," he said finally. It wasn't much of a concession. Clayton could find the address if he tried. He wouldn't even have to try that hard. "Just. My family doesn't know anything about this yet. They still think he's… a good cop hit by a car."

"Close enough," Clayton said. "He's a bad cop hit by a car. Where is he?"

Kelly rhymed off the address. It was the first address he'd ever known, the one he learned to tell the teacher at school and the taxi driver when Mom or one of his brothers couldn't get there. In an emergency it was probably still the address he'd have given as he was wheeled into the hospital.

Expiration-date lovers meant you didn't get to depend on them in a crisis.

All of a sudden, it didn't feel like home anymore.

Clayton repeated the address to someone and then hung up.

"You okay, hon?" a woman asked as she stopped, her sandaled feet a safe distance from him. "Are you sick?"

Kelly pushed himself to his feet. "Sorry. I'm fine," he said. "Just got a call and...."

The woman winced and tapped her cheekbone with a touch of empathy as she saw his face. "Oh, your poor face."

He grinned wryly and rubbed his thumb over his eyebrow. "Rough week."

"Hope it gets better."

"No signs so far."

She gave him a sympathetic smile and headed down the street to her house. Kelly brushed the grit off the seat of his jeans and wondered how slowly he could walk back.

Not slowly enough to beat LA traffic.

It was an hour of stiff conversation, jangled bells, and a heavy, sick anger in his gut that roiled back to life every time he thought it was gone. And there was half an hour of silently worried looks from Aggie before she got called back to the morgue.

"...just need to wait for the manifold to get here," Jim said as he popped the tab pointedly on a ginger beer. He looked sweaty, his scalp pink through his cropped hair, and he'd scabbed his knuckles on the engine. "Some bloke in Idaho I found online."

Kelly grabbed a handful of chips. "You going to actually get that old Jeep running?"

"Eh, don't know. I've had a few offers. No point in fixing it up if I'm just gonna hand it on. Besides, you buy an old car like that, you want to get your hands stuck into the engine." He leaned back on the chair, balanced his weight on the creaky back legs, and gave Maxie a fond look. "Maybe get some new project. Something I can get this one and the girls to work on with me. Something they'd like."

Kathleen sniffed as she poured bourbon over a bucket of split ribs. "Betty and Lou don't have the time to spend their weekends getting dirty, Jim," she said. "You know Trisha has them signed up for all sorts of classes. They have no time to do anything, even with Trisha's mother to ferry them around."

"Well, if she and Wilde get divorced"—Jim shrugged—"he'll have custody some days."

Kathleen hissed at him. "Don't say things like that," she said. "Father Peters will be here tomorrow. What if he heard you saying something like that? They're not getting divorced, and if they do, we're not telling the Father."

Even Maxie looked skeptical, and most of his attention was on whether or not he could put his foot in his mouth. Before Kelly had to think of something to say, his phone buzzed briskly and someone rapped on the front door.

"Are you expecting anyone?" Kathleen asked as she shook globs of barbecue sauce off her fingers. She reached for a dish towel to wipe her hands, and worry pinched her lips together as they rapped the door again. "Do you think they've found something out about Byron's accident?"

Kelly scooped his phone up off the table as Clayton's name scrolled over the screen. He slid it into his back pocket and pushed the chair back. The legs were loud as they scraped over the tiles as he stood up.

"I'll get it," he said. "It's for me."

He dodged the immediate questions and went to let Clayton in.

"Jesus," he said when he opened the door. Shock flattened his voice. "Are you all right?"

There were dark circles under Clayton's eyes, bruised in as though someone had dug their thumbs into the soft skin, and his arm was tucked into a bleach-white sling that sliced across the front of his shirt. It was yesterday's shirt—yesterday's suit—with the collar tugged loose and stains on the cuffs.

Clayton looked surprised for a second, and then he glanced down at his bandaged hand. He moved his fingers stiffly.

"Last night some of your brother's friends wanted to express their opinion on his… situation." Clayton glanced past Kelly as he paused and then settled on that last word. "It's just bruises."

Kelly gingerly touched his hand. The skin was hot under the rough bandages, and he reached up to cup Clayton's face. He grazed his thumb along the stubble-rough edge of Clayton's jaw and slid his hand back to grip the nape of his neck.

"You should have called me."

"I was at the hospital," Clayton said. "And I had to deal with the police. There was nothing you could have done."

Maybe not, but Kelly wished he'd been there anyway. He supposed that was Clayton's call to make, though, so he swallowed the bitter taste of rejection.

"What happened?"

Clayton reached up to grip Kelly's wrist and pulled it down from his face. "I'll tell you later."

From behind Kelly, he heard Jim clear his throat.

"This the friend you were talking about?" he asked. "You might want to ask him in off the doorstep."

Kelly felt a jolt of anger—like electricity under his skin—but he wasn't sure why. It wasn't as though Jim wanted to kick Clayton out, but something still rubbed him wrong about the way Jim said it. Maybe it was the carefully unweighted *friend*. It wasn't the time to deal with him. Kelly ignored the frustrated growl in the back of his mind that wondered if it ever would be time.

"Clayton," he said as he finally got around to letting go of him. He stepped back and gestured. "My dad, Jim. Jim, this is Clayton."

Jim scratched the side of his nose, cleared his throat, and gave a stiff incline of his chin.

"Clayton." He glanced briefly at Kelly, rubbed his hand briskly on the thigh of his jeans, and then thrust it out. "Nice to meet you. I've heard a lot about you."

There was a pause. It dragged out long enough to be awkward, and then the flinty hardness of Clayton's face softened. He gripped Jim's hand for a brisk no-nonsense shake.

"You too," he said. "Sorry, but I'm actually here to speak to your other son Byron. If that's all right with you."

Jim looked confused, but when he was halfway through a shrug, Kathleen butted in from the kitchen. "Why?" she asked sharply as she stalked out. "He's not well. I don't know if he wants to see anyone."

"It's all right, Mom," Kelly said. "Clayton's a lawyer. He's just here to see if Byron has a case."

Kathleen put her hands on her hips and gave Clayton a once-over. "He doesn't look like a lawyer."

"You son works for me," Clayton said. There was nothing overtly chilly in his voice, but there was nothing warm either. Room-temperature detachment. "I agreed to do this as a favor, so if you object to my appearance, I'll do as the ER nurse suggested—go home and get over the mugging."

Before Kathleen could say anything, Jim put his hand on her shoulder.

"You work for ADA Baker? Former, that is," he asked. When Clayton nodded, Jim looked approving. "He was a good lawyer and a better man. Always thought what happened was shit. Let them be, Kath. Byron will probably be glad for a visit that's not you fussing over him. He's in the guest room."

He turned and nudged Kathleen back into the kitchen. Kelly raised his eyebrows briefly. It wasn't a surprise that Jim knew Baker—that was one reason Kelly had landed the firm's investigative contract—but he'd never seen his dad endorse anyone that wholeheartedly, especially not a lawyer.

Clayton nudged him. "Guest room?"

Kelly hesitated.

"Second thoughts?" Clayton asked. He reached up and tugged at the knot in the sling where it rubbed against his throat. "Bit late."

"I thought Baker wanted us to hold off until the investigation was over," Kelly said quietly. He cast a cautious look toward the kitchen in case anyone overheard them. "That was just yesterday."

A muscle clenched in Clayton's jaw, hard enough to make Kelly's ache in sympathy.

"I'm not Baker's lawyer, I'm Nadine's," Clayton said. "My job is to represent her best interests, to get her away from your brother, not clean house for the LAPD. Guest room?"

In the end Kelly supposed that if his loyalty lay anywhere right then, it was with Clayton. He pointed down the hall.

"Just… don't let him get to you," he said. "Byron's good at pushing buttons."

A smile appeared briefly on Clayton's face, and then it was gone again. "I'm good at not being pushed."

Kelly wondered if he looked as dubious as he felt. He just shrugged in the end and waved his hand for Clayton to precede him.

The hinge in the door creaked as it opened. Byron looked up as they stepped into the room, and he grinned a sharp, white-toothed smile.

"So, I guess you're Nadine's lawyer," Byron said as he pushed himself up into a sitting position. His leg was propped up precariously on a pile of pillows, the halo-cast sharp and painful-looking where it drilled down into his skin. "You know, you got my little brother beat to hell?"

"Fuck you, Byron." Kelly closed the door behind him.

Clayton didn't say anything. He circled the bed, adjusted the angle of the fiddleback kitchen chair, and sat down. Byron's smile tightened at the corners. There was something ugly under the sharp charm.

"What? Nothing to say?" he asked. "Or you just wear yourself out sucking cock?"

"I thought you were good at pushing buttons," Clayton said as he pulled his phone clumsily out of his pocket. He swiped and tapped at the screen one-handed. "Saying a gay man gives enthusiastic head is more of a compliment."

"It's like anything else," Byron said pleasantly. "You have to season to taste, calibrate to the individual. I need your baseline before I can really get to work."

"Shut up," Kelly told him.

"Fuck off. The big boys are talking."

It was a stupid thing to be the last straw—after everything that Byron had done the last few days and all these years—but the jibe slid under Kelly's guard. He grabbed a handful of Byron's T-shirt, crumpled the police academy logo in his fist, and yanked him off the pillows. The weight of him pulled at Kelly's shoulder. Heavy and loose with surprise, Byron smelled of iodine, sweat, and blood. A heavy hospital stink sweated out of him.

"Shut up and listen to him," Kelly told him flatly. "Or I'll—"

"What? Punch me?" Byron jibed back. He grabbed a handful of Kelly's hair and wrenched back on it. Kelly clenched his jaw and ignored the sharp pain in his scalp as he refused to move his head. "How long have you wanted to do that? Only took you until I'd already been run down by a car to work up the balls for it."

Kelly had just enough presence of mind to be worried about what he might do, but not enough to make himself let go of Byron. He was just... sick to his stomach of all of it. Not just Nadine—the loans, the lies, the late-night calls to bail him out of whatever Byron had fucked up now.

It must have shown on his face. Alarm flickered through Byron's eyes, and he flipped his mood the way some people would flip a coin. He rearranged his sneer into an expression that made a stab at both regretful and injured.

"I didn't know you were the PI sniffing around," he said. "If I had I'd have called Lepson off. We're brothers. We stick together."

Next to the bed, Clayton shifted in the chair. "Punching him won't help Nadine. And it's not your style."

"See, listen to your boyfriend," Byron coaxed. "He's right. This won't help anyone."

Kelly grinned. It felt like the same hard mockery of a smile that Byron had greeted them with.

"It'll make me feel better," he said. It was how true that was that finally convinced him to let go of Byron's T-shirt. He shoved his brother back into the cushions with a disgusted grunt. "Fine. Talk to Clayton, you asshole."

He stalked over to the wide window and stared at the street outside, his hands shoved into his pockets to keep them out of trouble.

"You know I'm your wife's lawyer," Clayton said.

"Well, Jimmy's wife's lawyer." Byron shifted in the bed, and the old mattress groaned under his weight. "I'm not sure where we'd stand legally."

"Well, if I took it to court, I'd argue it was rape," Clayton said. "There's enough precedent that I could make a strong case."

Silence, and then Byron gave a dry, unamused chuckle. "She's never complained."

"Shut up," Clayton said. "IA knows what you've done. They can make that case against you. I just want to get Nadine home safe. Someone took her from the safe house where she was staying. They've threatened her. They've threatened your son's life. Where is she?"

Kelly turned sharply to stare at the back of Clayton's head. He had known they were going off Baker's script when they came in, but not that Clayton planned to put a spoke in Internal Affair's wheel.

"Well, I don't have her," Byron said. "You can look under the bed if you want."

"Jesus Christ, Byron," Kelly blurted out. "She's your wife. The mother of your kid. Don't you care about them at all?"

Byron mugged a thoughtful face. "They left me, remember."

"You broke her arm," Clayton said. "Locked her in a closet."

"She fell over. I never touched her," Byron spat defensively. "The closet was for her own good. If the kid hadn't gone and let her out, I'd have sorted all this out by now. If she told you I hit her, the bitch is lying."

Clayton leaned forward. "You owe someone a lot of money, Detective Kelly," he said. "That's what they want. So you know whose money you've taken."

Byron stayed silent and glowered sullenly at Clayton. He fiddled with the sheet over his lap as he rolled the edge between finger and thumb and then smoothed it out again.

"That's the money you wanted from Cole?" Kelly asked. "You wanted to pay them off, get Nadine back?"

Those were Kathleen's words in Kelly's mouth. He recognized them the minute he spat them out—the ready-made excuse that cast Byron in the best light. It left a bad taste in his mouth. But it wasn't a good enough excuse for Byron, because he stayed mum.

Kelly listened with half an ear as Clayton tried, with clipped logic and a pro forma appeal to his better nature, to convince Byron to tell them what he knew. Even a few minutes in, Clayton could tell that wasn't the most profitable avenue to pursue. Neither was logic.

"No harm to Nadine. She's a sweet girl," Byron said. "Not really sure it's in my interest to find her right now."

Kelly rubbed his eye and pressed the heel of his hand down hard against the cool round of glass under his eyelid. It was weird, but he could still "see" the smeared blur of phosphenes sometimes. The doctors said it was similar to phantom limbs, his visual cortex's best effort at a translation of a misfired nerve.

"Either you help us find Nadine," he said, his voice rough as he cut through Clayton's, "or I'll tell, Byron."

"You already told, you idiot," Byron said with contempt. "You can't use it as a threat when your boy toy here has already run crying to IA. Catch up."

"Not IA."

"Who, then? Mom?" Byron shrugged that idea off and laid his head back on the pillows. "She'd be pissed, but she'll come around. She always does. I mean, she'll have a new grandkid. That always cheers her up."

"No," Kelly said. "I'll tell Dad."

Byron had the gall to look affronted. Clayton looked... exasperated, as though Kelly were being childish. But he didn't get it—this was family.

They never told Jim. It had practically been Kathleen's catchphrase. Jim would just get into a fight with the neighbor whose window was broken, and he didn't need to know that Worth had dented Kathleen's car because they'd fixed it already, and as for Byron getting caught peeping on a neighbor's daughter? He'd just be embarrassed.

Don't tell your Dad. No need to upset him.

"What makes you think he doesn't know?" Byron blustered. "Me and Dad, we're both cops. We get what needs to be done."

"He knows about Jimmy," Kelly admitted. "Maybe he knows about Nadine. I bet he doesn't know about Harry. Dad loves the kids. He wouldn't have ignored that."

It felt true, but Byron's glare confirmed it.

"You'll kill him," Byron said. "He's still recovering. You get him involved in this…."

Kelly walked over to the bed, leaned down, and braced one arm against the headboard. "Not just about this," he said. "About everything. I'll tell him about all the times Cole has bailed you out over the years, that drunk-driving case that just went away, and that you tried to sell your son."

"That was to family," Byron said. "Hardly counts."

It did. There was no point in trying to explain that to Byron, though. Kelly reached up and flicked his eye with his finger. It made a satisfying, brittle ping.

"I'll tell him what really happened to my eye that day," Kelly said. "That you took the sucker off the arrow, that you sharpened it with the knife you'd stolen from the kitchen, and that you told me to run."

He'd always thought it would feel good to finally say it out loud, to get the truth out from where he'd stuck it behind Kathleen's injunction of "you don't remember." It would be cathartic. Instead, his throat just hurt, and he felt that same sick pop of fear he'd felt when Byron had said, "Run." Byron wasn't that much older than Kelly, but there'd been something eager in his voice that felt older.

The unshaven line of Byron's throat moved as he swallowed and looked away from Kelly. He licked his lips.

"Jesus," he groused. "You going to dredge up all our ancient history?"

Kelly pushed himself back from the bed. "Yeah," he said. "Every single shitty thing you've ever done, for everyone I meet. My eye, that poor fucking French girl you abandoned in Mexico that time and Worth had to drive down and get her. Until nobody in the family—not even Cole, not even Dad—will give you the time of day. They'll never bail you out again. Or you can help us and play the martyr for Mom when IA comes calling. Tell her I snitched on you again."

On the bed Byron thought about it. He rolled the edge of the sheet back and forth in his fingers. The starched white was already grubby from handling. When Kelly turned around, Clayton had an odd expression on his face.

Probably the expression someone wore when they'd dodged the dysfunctional family bullet. Aggie would sympathize. She'd missed her chance.

"I do this," Byron finally said, "then we're square, right?"

Kelly missed the anger. At some point during his conversation with Byron, it had just drained out of him. All that was left was a sort of aching weariness, like the emotional equivalent of that moment in the ring when, flat on your back on the canvas, you just couldn't see the point in getting up.

"Yeah," he said. "Why not. You help us find Nadine, and we're square."

That made Byron grin, and his cheerful, easy gleam of charm made you wonder if this time he'd actually gotten rid of his demons.

"Cool," he said. "Because you aren't going to like this."

CHAPTER SEVENTEEN

"I THOUGHT you might be thirsty. You've been in here talking for so long."

Mrs. Kelly—"Call me Kathleen"—handed out cold glasses of lemonade with added bright-eyed, saucy-old-lady charm. Clayton recognized it. His mom used to greet social workers with the same glassy cheer when the stink of freshly applied bleach wasn't enough to hide the wear on the seats and holes in the walls.

Nothing to see here, just a normal, loving family.

Clayton drank the lemonade and smiled an unreadable social-worker's smile back at her.

"Hey, maybe this one will stick around," Byron cracked. He winked at Clayton. "Mr. Reynolds here could be my brother-in-law. Gotta make sure he's up to it."

"Stop teasing your brother," Kathleen chided him as she tugged the sheet straight on the bed. "He doesn't get the joke."

"That's because it's not funny," Kelly said.

"You have to learn to laugh at yourself." Kathleen ruffled Kelly's hair with an affectionate hand on the way past. The sharp urge to push her hand away caught Clayton by surprise, and he tightened his fingers on the frosted glass. It didn't seem to bother Kelly, who just brushed his hair back when she was done, but the casual affection didn't sit right with Clayton.

I don't really remember. That was the sort of lie a parent taught you.

"We're nearly done, Mrs. Kelly," Clayton said. "If we could just have a few more minutes."

She glanced at Byron and raised her eyebrows in a mute question. He nodded impatiently and waved her out of the room.

"Okay, then," she said. "I'll go. And call me Kathleen, Clayton. If you want some ice for that poor hand of yours, just let me know."

She tucked the tray under her arm and let herself out.

"She still hasn't asked about my eye," Kelly muttered as he leaned back to set his lemonade on the windowsill.

"Oh, I told her you'd been fucking some guy and his wife decked you," Byron said. He took a drink of lemonade and wiped his mouth on his arm. "Figured you wouldn't want to worry her."

"Great," Kelly said dryly. "Thanks."

Byron shrugged and turned back to Clayton. "So, what you want to know?"

"Who have you pissed off enough that they'd kidnap your wife and threaten your child."

"Might need to narrow that down," Byron said. "I've fucked over a lot of people who trusted me. Some of them were real assholes too. Any of the guys I sent down as Jimmy, if they found out I'm really a cop, they aren't going to give me a 'good job' trophy."

"Who currently wants to kill you?"

Byron rubbed his jaw. His fingers rasped through the stubble. It had gone gray quicker than his hair and was almost silver already.

"That's the thing. Nobody," he said. "Jimmy is doing okay. He's impressed the right people, got his foot in the door of the drug ring we're after, and I've been playing it safe. No reason for anyone to suspect anything. I mean, my neighbors wouldn't piss on me if I were on fire, but none of them have the guts to actually start the fire."

"I bet Mrs. Sirkasian would," Kelly said.

Byron chuckled. "That old bag," he said, almost fondly. "She would too. Got a set of brass ones on her, but she liked Nadine. Was fond of the kid."

"Harry," Clayton said.

"Yeah, him."

"Nadine said you knew the men that came to the house that night," Clayton said. "That you owed them money."

"Then she either lied or she got it wrong," Byron said. "I don't know what happened that night. We had a fight. I called her a stupid cow, and then she started crying like it was news to her. The kid was yelling 'Don't you talk to my mom that way,' and it was starting to do my head in. So I fucked off and left them to it. When I got back, she's a bloody mess on the couch, and the kid won't say anything. She tried to call the police, but that's not exactly workable in my line of work, you know. So I got the phone off her and went to call Lepson. When I got back, she'd run off to you. Never told me she knew the guys who did it. Doesn't make sense. I owe money. Jimmy doesn't."

"You tried to get Cole to mortgage his house," Kelly pointed out. "You offered to sell Aggie your son for a couple of grand. Why'd you need the money?"

"Because my ex drove her car into a wall and then didn't die until she got to the hospital," Byron said. He shifted on the bed, grimaced, and rubbed his knuckles into the meat of his thigh. Clayton wasn't about to waste any sympathy on him, but a glance down at the raw, bruised pulp of Byron's lower leg made him glad it wasn't his. The torn tendons in his hand hurt enough. "I had to pay some bills, settle her debts, put Mom up in a hotel, and all the baby crap with Max. I needed quick cash to pay off some bills and, well, I'm not good with money."

Kelly sighed. "But Jimmy is, with help from the LAPD."

Byron made a gun with his finger and pointed it at Kelly.

"I had access to operational money to rent a warehouse, the buy-in to the dealer's business, and to flash the cash when I needed. If they checked me out, I had to look the part on paper, didn't I?" Byron rubbed his thigh again. "Money was there. I needed it. I figured I could slot it back in later—move some funds around—no harm done. Except you idiots froze Jimmy's accounts, and I had to try and scramble to cover my ass. So unless you think the LAPD have employed leg breakers to collect on debts... nothing to do with me."

Clayton rubbed his eyes. His head ached with a sick pulse in time with his hand. It hurt more since they bandaged it, and the pressure of the dressing against tender bones made it throb harder. He could taste failure in the back of his throat, like Utah dust and cheap beer. It had been a mistake to come here today, to make a decision while he was angry and still twitchy with adrenaline. All he'd done was give Byron a heads-up that he was under investigation.

"I told you that you wouldn't like it," Byron said smugly. "I don't know who took Nadine or how they even knew she left Jimmy. It's not exactly something I was boasting about—"

"Shit."

Clayton twisted around to look at Kelly. Guilt hung on his face like a weight. Clayton knew the feeling. "What?"

Kelly hesitated for a second and then grimaced.

"What about Kevoian," he asked. "There's bad blood there, right?"

Confusion creased Byron's face. "Gregor?" He snorted. "Naw, he's Jimmy's business partner. They're tight. We've been working him for years. He was Jimmy's 'in' to Glendale. Low-level carjacker, but he's got aspirations to power, and that makes him useful. No reason to burn him yet."

"You tell him that?" Kelly asked. "Because when I talked to him, he said Jimmy had double-crossed him. Then he implied you double-crossed your new partners as well, and they weren't happy about it."

Byron swore viciously under his breath and threw the half-drunk glass of lemonade at Kelly's head. Pink liquid and lumps of strawberry splattered over Kelly and the wall behind him an instant after Kelly got his arms up to block the tumbler's impact with his face. It smashed against his forearms and scattered over the ground.

"Five years," Byron yelled. He grabbed for the plate on the bedside table next to him. "Five fucking years of pretending I liked that greasy dickhole, and you mess it up in five minutes. Fucked up my life when you were born. Fucked it up now."

Clayton bolted to his feet. He yanked his arm out of the sling and shoved Byron down onto the bed before he could chuck the plate.

"It sounds like you already did that," Clayton snapped. Despite his injuries, Byron had muscle, and it wasn't easy to hold him down. It certainly didn't shut up the rant of curse words and insults that spilled out of him. The injured tendons in Clayton's hand stretched as he tightened his grip. It felt like they were about to snap. The backwash of pain and anger slipped his control, and he shook Byron with a short vicious terrier snap just to shut him up. "Why would this business partner turn on you?"

Byron spat at him. It hit Clayton's shoulder, wet and more disgusting than it should be as it soaked through his shirt.

Down the hall an anxious voice called, "Is everything all right in there? What's going on?"

Glass crunched behind Clayton as Kelly walked to the door. He opened it and leaned out.

"Everything's fine, Mom. Byron just dropped his glass." He closed the door and turned around to brace his back against it. His face was cold as he looked at Byron. "If anything happens to Nadine, to that boy, we're done."

The temper went out of Byron like someone had turned off a tap. For a second, when the angry body went still under him, Clayton thought he'd killed him. He pushed himself off Byron's shoulders and stepped back.

"You don't mean that. We're family." The man who'd just thrown a glass at his brother's face had the temerity to sound affronted. "Don't be all butthurt about the glass. If I meant to hit you, I'd have waited till I was in your blind spot."

Kelly snorted out a strangled laugh. "Yeah, I remember playing baseball with you," he said. Blood dripped down his forearms where broken glass had nicked him. "And I mean it. If you don't help us, you're not my brother."

Calculation flashed through Byron's pale eyes as he tried to work out how serious Kelly was. He glanced at Clayton finally and spat the words out.

"Some of the money I moved might not have been Jimmy's," he said. "Technically. I might just have been... warehousing it for Gregor and our business partners. If Gregor checked and found it gone? He'd pull this sort of stupid *Godfather* shit instead of just finding out what was going on. Moron."

The door behind Kelly rattled as Kathleen tried to open it. He pushed his shoulders back against it. "Not yet, Mom."

"What about the new gang you were working with?" Clayton asked. He pulled the phone out of his pocket and dialed half a number. Then he deleted it and sent a text to Nadine instead. Sometimes you just had to commit to your mistakes. *Need you to sign Motion to Dismiss for restraining order and bank accounts released*, he typed out as he asked, "Could they be behind this?"

Byron grimaced. "They'd have called me and threatened to hurt Nadine if I didn't get it back to them," he said. "Gregor knows that wouldn't work."

"Why'd you even marry her?" Kelly asked as he stepped away from the door and let Kathleen and Jim in. "Did you love her? At all?"

Byron snarled and shrugged off Kathleen's attempt to fuss over him.

"About as much as I loved that French girl," he said. "A whole lot, until I got bored and left her in Mexico. Now if you'll all fuck off, and that means you too, Mom, I need to let Lepson know the shit hit the fan when he wasn't looking."

CLAYTON HELD the baby while Jim Kelly patched his son's bloody arms up with *Monster High* Band-Aids and impatience. Somewhere in the house, Kathleen cried messily while she begged Byron to explain himself.

"That temper will be the death of him," Jim muttered as he swiped iodine with one hand and slapped the plaster on with the other. "He's like a kid when it goes off, just can't control himself."

"He calmed down quickly enough when throwing things didn't get him what he wanted," Clayton said coolly. "Maybe you should try that."

Jim didn't acknowledge the suggestion—unless the clenched jaw under his cropped beard counted—but he shut up. That was good enough. In the crook of Clayton's good arm, Maxie squirmed, croaked, and reached demandingly for someone he knew better. It probably wasn't good childrearing practice, but Clayton dipped a finger into a glass of lemonade and popped it into Maxie's mouth.

He'd never cared much about kids—one way or the other—but he was good enough with them. Some of the foster families he'd lived with had farmed kids like they were rabbits, three beds to a room and the money straight into their pocket. Others meant well, but an overtaxed system still squeezed more kids into their houses than they could care about individually. Babies didn't expect much, and Clayton had been old enough and sane enough to be trusted with them.

The taste of sugar and lemon made Maxie screw up his face in confusion, but it distracted him from squirming.

"There," Jim said. He slapped the last plaster on and stood up. Then he gathered all the bits of paper and cotton wool and tossed it in the garbage. "Go grab a clean T-shirt from my room. You've got blood on that."

Kelly plucked his T-shirt out from his body to check. The splatter of blood over the worn gray Pogues logo made him grimace.

"Thanks." He stood up and then hesitated. "Can you tell Mom I'm sorry? I didn't do this to spite Byron."

"You still did it," Jim said tiredly. "No matter how he fucked up, he's still your brother. You should have come to us first. Not—"

He gave Clayton a sour look. Even an association with Baker could only get you so far, apparently. Still, it was better that he blamed Clayton than Kelly.

"He's married a woman under false pretenses," Kelly said with an edge of exasperation to his voice. "I'm pretty sure he's a bigamist. He has a son. What were you going to do?"

He pulled his T-shirt off and used the stained fabric to scrub his lemonade-sticky hair. Apparently, Clayton noted to himself, the habit of walking around half-dressed wasn't just for Clayton's benefit after all.

Not that that stopped him appreciating the view. The bruises were still livid against Kelly's tanned skin, fading out to a swamp-murky green around the edges, but it didn't disguise the hard lines of his body or the honed muscles.

The memory of that heavy, solid body under Clayton—and its easy surrender to him—made Clayton's throat go dry. He dragged his attention away and caught Jim's scowl as it darkened. It was bleakly satisfying to make the man's day worse, even if it was only a bit.

"We could have managed it," Jim said. "Got ahead of it. Protected him."

"And her?" Clayton asked.

Kelly gave him a hard look. The cat might be out of the bag where Byron's bigamy was concerned, but Kelly had kept his word and not told anything else.

"We'd have done what we could," Jim said. "As much as she wanted."

"Well, it's done now," Kelly said. "I'll go get your T-shirt. Then we'll get out of your hair."

He tossed his T-shirt into the bin on the way out of the kitchen. Clayton shifted Max on his arm. His elbow ached from the awkward weight, and he moved his hand so he could flex his fingers. They felt stiff, and the bones pinched when he moved.

Jim walked to the garbage can and jabbed the tail end of the T-shirt in through the lid. "I have no bone to pick with you. You were just doing your job," he said. "But Kathleen, she has no patience with anyone who's hurt her boys. So I think you're done with my family."

Probably. Clayton didn't fool himself about that. Maybe the Kellys weren't quite the perfect family he always imagined, but they were tight-knit. He *could* ask Kelly to choose between him and his family, but he wouldn't.

He looked down at Maxie. In one foster family, there'd been five different babies in and out before he got sent somewhere new. All of them were sent back to one home or another, to parents who swore they'd sorted themselves out.

"Do you know why I'm Nadine's lawyer?" he asked.

"Money?"

"Because she came to the women's shelter I work with sometimes and begged me," Clayton said. The words made Jim flinch. "He'd worn her self-confidence down so far that she thought she deserved the way he treated her. But she wanted to protect their son."

Clayton hadn't promised Byron anything.

"He'd not raise a hand to a woman," Jim said. He tried to bluster, but he didn't sound confident. "He knows better. There's no coming back for a man who hurts a woman or a child."

"Maybe. Maybe not," Clayton said. He heard a door close with a creak of hinges that could use some oil. "But you know as well as I do, abuse doesn't just come with a black eye."

Jim might have been able to come up with something to counter that, but Kelly returned into the kitchen before he could. Old cotton stretched over his shoulders and bagged around his lean waist. The fit was off just enough and in all the wrong places that Clayton slanted a look sideways at Jim just in time to see him suck in his stomach.

It was a petty thing to take satisfaction in, but Clayton did anyway.

"Dad—"

"Enough," Jim snapped. "You've upset your mother, and whatever Byron's done, or not done, he's just out of hospital. Just let it lie."

Clayton's phone finally chimed the arrival of an incoming. It was Nadine's name on the screen, but he doubted she'd written the terse message that scrolled along next to it.

Safe house. Tonight at seven.

His stomach twisted grimly, but he ignored it as he tapped out a quick confirmation. Hopefully it wouldn't be necessary to keep that appointment. He just wanted them to need Nadine in good health a while longer and to think they were going to get what they wanted.

"We need to go," he said.

Kelly gave him a quick apologetic look, and Clayton hated himself for the second of surprise that hit him. People disappointed you. He already knew that. So he braced himself for Kelly to beg off. It wasn't as though he hadn't already more than fulfilled the original favor.

"I'm still taking Maxie," he said.

Jim scowled. "The hell you will," he said. "Your mother can take care of him."

He took a step toward Clayton, arms out as he reached for the baby. Kelly blocked him. "Dad, I'm not leaving the kid with Byron. Not right now. I don't trust him."

"Why not?" Jim blustered. "What do you think he's going to do? That's his own flesh and blood, boy."

"Do you really want me to tell you?" Kelly asked after a moment. There was a hard note in his voice. "Because I will, Dad."

The lawyer in Clayton appreciated the neat trap the question laid out. Either Jim heard something he didn't want to about Byron, or he admitted that he knew there was something about his son that he'd turned a blind eye to. Whatever door you opened was going to hurt.

"What will I tell your mom," Jim asked as he looked away. "She'll be round at your house before you get back."

Clayton cleared his throat. "I wouldn't recommend that," he said. "If this gets forced into the legal arena, it isn't going to end well for Byron."

It took a second, but finally Jim backed down. He crossed his arms over his chest and glared at Kelly. "I'm disappointed in you," he said. "We raised you better than this."

"Yeah, well," Kelly said roughly as he grabbed a bag from under the table. "I'm disappointed in you too, Dad."

Kelly stalked out of the kitchen without looking back. So he didn't see the stricken look on Jim Kelly's face.

CHAPTER EIGHTEEN

"SORRY," KELLY rasped out.

The word sounded like it had been stuck in his throat for a while. It had taken twenty minutes on the I-10 from the Kelly house to the roadworks at the Sacramento off-ramp for him to spit them out. After Maxie dozed off in the back, drugged into sleep by the groan of the engine, it had been a quiet drive.

Clayton rubbed the back of his neck. Despite the air-conditioning, his fingers came away sweaty. He hadn't minded the silence, but he was relieved that it was broken. The stillness hadn't felt like Kelly.

"They're your family, not your fault," Clayton said. He checked his phone again. The quick swipe and scan for new messages was driven by nerves—mindless and not that reassuring. Still nothing. He closed the screen down with a determined press of his thumb. In a minute he'd swipe and check again, but he tried to pull his attention back to the slow crawl of Kelly's truck. "I should have believed you when you said you didn't know Byron was Jimmy. I had no reason to think you were a liar."

Kelly shrugged. He drove with one hand on the wheel, the sun bright on his tanned arm. It burnished the fine hairs on his skin down to gilt.

"I can't blame you for that. If it hadn't been Byron," he said. "If it had been Cole or Wilde? I might have covered for them. Or at least let them in on things sooner. I knew what Byron was like. I just didn't think he was like this. And I'm sorry you got hurt."

It was still a bad idea. Clayton was still going to do it. He couldn't seem to resist.

"Me too." Clayton reached out and brushed his thumb over Kelly's bruised cheekbone. He felt the warmth of the bruise and the startled twitch that ran through Kelly. "How old were you?"

"Three," Kelly said. "Byron was… either just turned six or nearly six… and I think he wanted to see what happened if he hurt someone. It was, like he said, he needed to calibrate his behavior."

"See how far he could go."

"Nothing personal," Kelly said. The dry smile that curved his mouth brushed against Clayton's palm. "To be honest I think the fact that I got so much attention was more of a deterrent than the trouble he got into. There you go. That's my story. So what happened last night?"

The cars ahead of Kelly's pickup crawled forward a car length, and Kelly rolled forward to close the distance again. It didn't look as though the traffic was going to clear up and miraculously give Clayton an out.

He didn't know why he wanted one. It hadn't been the highlight of his week, but he'd been mugged and come out worse.

"They brought Nadine to the office last night. They must have been outside for hours. I worked late." Clayton provided the Cliffs Notes for the evening, from the scuffle on the road to the antiseptic visit to the hospital to get his hand X-rayed. It was actually, although he didn't mention that, the first sick day he'd had in five years. It was appendicitis last time. He finished the story and felt the hard fist of regret in his gut again. "Nadine could have gotten away from them if the security guard had gone out sooner, but she didn't trust me to keep her and Harry safe."

"Us. We both promised her," Kelly corrected him. "And if it weren't for me, Kevoian wouldn't have known they split."

The car ahead moved again, a bit farther this time. Clayton missed his bike. He flexed his fingers, and the pain reminded him why it was still parked at work.

"I was the one who was there. It was… when I was a kid, I was in foster care," he said abruptly. Out of the corner of his eye, he saw Kelly twist around to look at him, his blue eyes intent on him for a second until he turned back to the road. Whatever he'd seen on Clayton's face… he didn't say anything. He just waited.

The whole confession scrolled out in Clayton's head—that his mother might have loved him but not as much as she loved the asshole she'd either met or was about to meet in a bar, about the beatings, the blood, the assholes who got worse every year she got older, or that one time he tried to fight off the guy who laid into her, but a slap and a flat, dead-eyed threat had sent him off to cower in his locked room.

When he saw his mother the next day, she looked at him with her bruised eyes the way Nadine had.

It was too much, too messy. Clayton wasn't even sure why he wanted to tell it. He never did. It was the past. So he took a knife to the tangled string of the narrative and cut it down to the bone.

"My mother fell in love with a lot of frogs," he said with a deliberate flash of black humor. "They only ever turned into losers when she kissed them. It never changed for her. I thought it might for Nadine."

He thought he could change it *for* her. His mother hadn't wanted him to save her—the next frog was supposed to do that—and he thought he'd come to terms with it. Maybe not.

It was his turn to be surprised as Kelly reached out and scruffed the back of his neck. He slid his warm, callused fingers under the collar of Clayton's shirt and brushed his collarbone. It was barely intimate, but it still plucked Clayton like a string. He was tall enough that the only people who touched his neck other than himself were people he was in bed with.

"It doesn't matter if Nadine trusts us. We're still going to help her," Kelly said. "Then maybe she can change things for herself."

Clayton mocked out a groan. "An optimist and a romantic," he said. "What do I see in you again?"

And just like that, the grin was back, wide and easy and warm. Kelly laughed as he braked to let an angry man in a Beetle cut in front of him. "Well, you seemed to like my ass."

"That's true," Clayton said. "It is a nice ass."

There was more. A ridiculous, sappy amount more, but Clayton wasn't an optimist or a romantic. So he held his tongue.

"I should call Aggie," Kelly said. He glanced back into the back where Clayton had rather forgotten Maxie was. "Get her to babysit. Although Cole... if Mom puts pressure on, he'll fold."

Clayton smiled. "Actually," he said. "I have that covered."

"FIRST THINGS first. There are rules regarding babies in this office," Baker said sternly as he got up from behind Clayton's desk. He held out his expensively sleeved arms. "Give him to me."

Kelly obediently handed Maxie over. Awake and alert after the long car nap, Maxie squawked and waved sticky fists in either triumph or alarm. Baker looked delighted.

"Aren't you a cutie," he crooned as he cuddled Maxie into the fold of his arm. One big hand almost covered Maxie entirely, from knee to shoulder, as he rocked him. "So much trouble going on around you, and you have no clue what it's all about, hmm?"

"It is a lot of trouble," Clayton admitted. "I'm sorry I got you into—"

Baker shook his head and freed his hand from Maxie's fingers so he could point at Clayton. "Not this time. If this goes wrong, it's all on you. You should have talked to me before you did this."

Deserved or not, Clayton still winced as he thought about what it would do to his career. It would have been nice to say that he didn't care, that the only thing that mattered was Nadine, but he did care.

Failure meant he'd hang his shingle in some miserable little town—not the same one he started in, not in Utah if he could help it, but still the same—and have to charge bruise-eyed women to chase their exes for child support. If he was lucky.

"That's fair," he said. "Does that mean you aren't going to help us?"

Baker gave him a wry look. "That depends entirely on what you want," Baker said. "And if I can do it without my peachy fresh ass getting hauled over the coals."

"We don't want you to get in trouble," Kelly said. "We can—"

Baker shushed him. "Considering how many favors I burned so you could screw the pooch with the Internal Affairs investigation? You don't get to turn me down. Either you accept my help gratefully or I tell you to stick what you need where the grass doesn't grow, but either way it's my choice. So?"

"Take care of Maxie?"

"Oh, that I'll do," Baker said. He looked down at Maxie, who was chewing on a custom-carved resin button, and said, "I'll teach you about the importance of a watertight contract for marital happiness. What else?"

"First, I need to talk to Harry. Maureen said that the police took him into protective custody?"

Baker didn't look up from Maxie as he nodded, but his voice stayed crisply businesslike. "Some people might not call it the nanny state, but when one of our lawyers gets attacked on the street outside, the police are informed. And since I didn't know you decided to go off course on this, I informed my contact in IA. They were concerned enough to want Harry under their watchful eye for a bit. Why?"

"I need to talk to him."

Baker looked up and considered Clayton for a second. "I always liked how hard you work, how far you'd go for a client. Your commitment," he said. "Liked, past tense."

"I will owe you. Everything."

"Yes, you will," Baker said. He thought about it as he jiggled Maxie competently in his arms. "I'll see what I can do. It shouldn't take long. The answer will either be yes or laughter. If that's first, what's second?"

"Just another call," Clayton said. "It shouldn't take more than a few minutes."

"HI." HARRY'S voice was tight and small. In the background a dog barked, and an irritated man muttered something about never working with dogs or children.

"Harry, have you spoken to your mom since the night at the safe house?" Clayton asked. In the guilty pause that followed, he listened to Heather and Kelly talk quietly outside.

"She called the place," Harry muttered.

"I need you to trust me. It might be hard, but I promise I want to help," Clayton said. "The men that came to your house the night your mother got hurt. You saw them, didn't you?"

"No."

It wasn't just loyalty that stuffed Harry's nose and made his voice crack like that. It was guilt, the guilt of a kid who would never forget that he hid while someone hurt his mother, although hopefully, one day he would understand that it wasn't his fault.

"You couldn't have stopped them. They were grown men, bad men."

"Dad said... when he came back... he said he'd trade me in for a dog. Least a dog'd bark."

Clayton wished he'd let Kelly punch his brother.

"Did Maureen let you take one of her puppies to keep you company?" He could feel the pressure of time on the back of his neck, but it wouldn't help. When Harry mumbled a yes on the other end, he asked, "If the dog had been with you the other night, would you have sent it to stop the men?"

"No!" Harry said with a sharp jolt of distress in his voice. "They'd hurt Giz. She's just a puppy."

"They'd have hurt you too, and still hurt your mom," Clayton said. "Instead you stayed out of their way and you were able to get help. You didn't do what your dad said. That was brave."

"I don't know."

"Was Gregor Kevoian there that night? Was he one of the men who hurt your mom?"

"No."

Shit. Clayton scrubbed his hand over his face as though he could wipe away the cobwebby feeling of defeat as it settled. Had they been wrong about Kevoian, or had he just not gotten through to Harry?

"But I saw him outside," Harry admitted, sounding nervous as he quickly spat them out. "Outside in a big car. It wasn't his car, but he has lots of cars he uses. Dad gets mad at him because they aren't their cars. Uncle Gregor told him to lighten up. I thought it was nice."

Clayton thought about the big blue SUV, an oddly suburban choice of vehicle for violent gangsters. "Have you seen these cars?"

"I wasn't supposed to," Harry said. "But sometimes Dad left me with Uncle Gregor, and he'd take me out for a drive in one. They were all locked up in a big garage…. Mr. Reynolds, when Mom called, she said that Uncle Gregor had hurt Dad. I… is he okay?"

No matter how much they deserved it, sometimes it was hard to hate family.

"He just hurt his ankle," Clayton said. He tugged a drawer open and rifled through the files he had tucked in there for quick consultation—the Tates' financial report, a stack of past and paid-out prenups, but not what he was looking for. He shoved the drawer shut and stood up. "Harry, you've been a real help. You know that?"

"Really?"

"Your mom will be very proud of you, and your dad should be too."

"He won't," Harry said sadly. "That's okay."

Clayton hesitated. It felt like there should be something to say, but there wasn't—nothing that he could cover in a phone call.

"That's his problem," Clayton said. "I have to go, Harry. Okay?"

"Okay."

Harry hung up. Kids—no time for adult sentimentality or drawn-out goodbyes. Clayton put the phone in his pocket and walked around the desk. He stuck his head out around the door.

"…he just sounds so stern." Heather was midsentence. "I like to imagine he's a knight and I'm his lady wife, and he tells me to be chaste while he's gone to the Crusades. Then I bang the maidservant."

"Before you do, where did you put Jimmy Graham's background report?"

Heather turned in her chair. It was a sign of the stress of the last few days that she had the same hairstyle as yesterday. She reached up and rubbed her hand over the fuzz.

"I thought that, since the police were involved, we were done with that client," she said. "I filed the supplementary material in the archives, but after what happened last night, I told them to pull it. It hasn't come back yet, but it might be in the mailroom."

"Could you check?"

Heather nodded and popped up out of her chair. "Give me five minutes. I might need to flirt to get Bets to dig into the unsorted mail."

She trotted off down the hall, and Clayton glanced at Kelly. "What exactly were you talking about?"

"That I had no idea why Baker wanted Maxie," Kelly said. He was perched on the end of the desk and twisted around to look at Clayton. "I still just handed him over. He could have thrown him out a window."

"The windows don't open."

"Still," Kelly said. He rubbed one finger between his eyebrows. "You make a big deal to your family about how your brother can't be trusted, then just hand the baby over to the first big suited man who asks."

The frustration in Kelly's voice made Clayton laugh—not much, but enough to cut through some of the old pain and fresh guilt that clotted in his chest.

"The rule is that if you bring a baby to the office, Baker gets a hold," he said. "He loves babies more than he loves cufflinks and expensive tea."

"That's a lot."

"Yeah." Clayton reached out and gave Kelly's shoulder a reassuring squeeze. "You made the right call not to leave him there. People in corners don't make good choices, and even at his best, your brother shouldn't be in charge of fleas."

"I guess," Kelly said. He dipped his chin and brushed a soft-lipped kiss over Clayton's bruised knuckles. "Thanks."

Clayton felt a flush try to crawl up from under his cheekbones. He pulled his hand back and glanced around to see if anyone had seen the gesture. No one had, and he was slightly disappointed.

He rolled his eyes at himself. The sooner he got over this "little bit in love" thing the better, before it made him sentimental.

"Do you want to sit this out?" he asked. "It's going to involve interfering further in an IA investigation."

Kelly scratched his jaw. "Why aren't we just handing this over to the cops?" he asked. "This is what they do."

It was a fair question. Clayton pulled the loose sling off over his head and tossed it onto Heather's desk. His hand ached the same no matter what he did to it. If he wasn't going to use it, there was no point in hanging the sling around his neck like a sad attempt at a hipster scarf.

"I don't trust them," he admitted. "The police were happy enough to let Byron—or Jimmy—get away with mistreating Nadine when it suited them. Internal Affairs was happy to let her case wait while they tried to work out what to do about Jimmy, or Detective Byron Kelly, if that's your pick. I want her free of this—all of it—and the best way to do that is to make this messy and public."

"Okay."

"Okay, what?"

"You're right," Kelly said. "Whatever sanctions land on Byron's lap, the LAPD will still want to keep this quiet if they can. It's embarrassing. It could be expensive. The best outcome for Nadine and Harry will be that they get paid to disappear, not just swept under a rug. Besides, I've already interfered in an Internal Affairs investigation. I might as well make it count."

Clayton snorted.

"What did you want with my report anyhow?" Kelly asked.

"You had a list of properties owned by Jimmy Graham, either by himself or in Nadine's name, in the report," Clayton said. "I need to find a warehouse big enough to store a large number of probably stolen cars."

Kelly bit his lower lip and frowned. "There were a couple of nonresidential properties. I remember that," he said. "Not sure if I drilled down deep enough to get their measurements, though."

"We can find it out," Clayton said.

At the other end of the hall, the elevator doors opened, and Heather waved a heavy file triumphantly at him as she stepped out.

"You could have gotten that yourself," Kelly pointed out as he slid off the desk.

"I'm not actually confident what floor the mailroom is on," Clayton admitted. "I'm absolutely confident that Bets in the mailroom isn't my type, or vice versa."

Kelly chuckled. "Don't worry," he said as they walked toward Heather. "You've still got me."

Yeah, but not for long.

CHAPTER NINETEEN

THE WAREHOUSE turned out to be a stripped-out factory a few miles outside of Glendale. Records said it had been closed down a few years before for using trafficked immigrants as their workforce. After that it was sold at auction by the police... except apparently not.

Kelly parked on the street opposite. Thick sandy dust layered the windshield of his pickup, but he didn't bother to turn on the wipers. In some parts of town, dirty cars drew less attention than clean ones.

"Last chance," he said to Clayton. "You sure you want to do this?"

Clayton gave him a withering sidelong look and otherwise ignored the question. He nodded toward the large blue SUV parked in the shadow of the building. A man in dirty blue overalls crouched at the back of it and worked at the bumper.

"That's the car they brought Nadine to the office in," he said.

As they watched, the man popped off the license plate and started to screw another into place. His sleeves were rolled back to his elbows, a few inches farther than usual from the flash of pale skin as he worked.

Kelly turned the engine off. The air-conditioning cut off with it, and the heavy heat of the day started to soak through the metal of the car.

"Looks like they want to use it again," he said. "Are you ready?"

Clayton grimaced. "This is ridiculous, dangerous, and probably going to end my career," he said. "So I'm as ready as I'm likely to get."

He got out of the car. The sun picked out gilt and sand in his short curls and painted harsh shadows down his lean cheeks. Kelly knew he should focus, but his stomach detoured his brain with a rough clench of awareness. He knew how a smile could soften the thin line of Clayton's mouth, and how an unexpected kiss could surprise the sternness away from his face.

Or it had once. Kelly wanted to know if it would again, if he could coax that low laugh out of Clayton with a joke and a rude pass of his hands. He wanted... more than Clayton wanted to give probably. Definitely more than Kelly could afford right then.

His life was too complicated to invite someone else and expect them to stay, and it was only going to get worse. He wasn't sure he even liked his family much, but they were still his family. Even if the IA investigation never took root, there'd been an awful lot of truth thrown about for people who weren't used to it.

People were like fish. Introduce something new into their environment, and, if they could get away with it, they'd rather die of shock.

He still *wanted* it, though. Usually his heart was pretty good about logic—breakups still hurt, but once you accepted it was necessary, if you'd always known it was necessary—but this time it just wouldn't let go.

Kelly leaned down and groped under the driver's seat for the old wrecking bar stashed under there. He scrambled out of the car and reached around to tuck the heavy metal bar down the back of his jeans.

"Do you really think that's going to help if this goes wrong?" Clayton asked.

"Probably not," Kelly admitted. He tugged his T-shirt down over the tool. The rough edge of it scraped against his back as he breathed in. "It just makes me feel better—like I didn't walk in unprepared."

"I think a gun would be better."

"My aim's not what you'd call great."

That startled a laugh out of Clayton. It wasn't exactly how Kelly had imagined it—there should be more skin, less hot industrial air—but it still felt good. Stupid, but good.

"If this doesn't work," Clayton said as they walked across the road, "you really do have a wonderful ass."

Kelly snorted.

The factory gates were open. A chain and padlock dangled from one side of the frame. Clayton squeezed Kelly's shoulder quickly, wished him luck and veered off. Kelly waited until he was out of sight and then walked through gates. As he crossed the forecourt, the grubby man who'd been at work on the SUV jogged to intercept him. Kelly thought he recognized him as one of the mechanics who'd lurked behind Kevoian at the garage. But he couldn't be sure.

"Hey," he said through bruised, split lips. "This is private property. Get the fuck off."

"I'm here to see Gregor," Kelly said.

"You are, are you?" the man sneered. The expression split the scabs on his lips, and Kelly remembered the bruised knuckles on Clayton's unbroken hand. He clenched his jaw against the quick burst of temper. It wasn't helpful. Not yet. But he did make a note of the man's face. A childhood with Byron had taught him that grudges took up a lot of your time and were rarely satisfied. Still, he wouldn't miss a chance to split this guy's mouth open again if he got it. "What the hell makes you think he wants to see you?"

"I've got a message for him from Clayton Reynolds," Kelly said. "The lawyer. He'll want to hear it. It's about his money."

The man licked blood from his lips, spat on the tarmac, and looked around. He searched the scrubby lots around them and found nothing. "You better hope he does," he said as he pulled a phone out his pocket and dialed. "If not, it'll be your funeral."

ONE OF Kevoian's men frisked Kelly briskly from ankles to balls and on up. It didn't take him long to find the crowbar and take it. He bounced it in his hand to check the weight of it and then tossed it. It hit the ground with a thud and skidded under one of the cars.

Kelly winced. It might not have done much good, but it had made him feel better.

The other day in Glendale, with greasy hands at Frank's Body Shop, Kevoian had looked like a wannabe gangster neighborhood thug with a bit of cash and delusions of his own toughness. In the gutted old factory, surrounded by half-stripped cars and sacks of plastic-film-covered white powder, he still looked like a wannabe gangster, just a more dangerous one.

"It's nothing personal," Kevoian said as he wiped his hands on a torn T-shirt. "Jimmy thought he could rob me, cut me out of the deal, and take all the credit for himself. Now. Other way round. Or it will be soon."

Nadine huddled on a torn leather car seat, her hands tucked nervously under her thighs. Her grubby T-shirt was stuck to her stomach and sides with sweat. "I told you, Gregor," she said. "I don't know what happened to your money. I've never known anything about James's business."

He gripped her chin between his fingers and tilted her head back, leaving oily fingerprints stark against her skin. "And I believe you. Now," he said. "Unfortunately, that doesn't change anything, does it? Whether you knew or not, your husband still has my money. And I want it back."

Nadine pulled her chin out of his grip. "I don't care about the money. You can have it," she said. Her eyes flicked toward Kelly hopefully. "Right? Mr. Reynolds is going to do that? He'll make it happen?"

"Of course," Kelly said. "By morning the accounts will be unfrozen. All you need to do is sign this."

He pulled a folded rectangle of paper out of his pocket and took a step forward with it held out in front of him. Before he could take another step, Kevoian "ah ah'd" him and gestured for one of his men to snatch it from between Kelly's fingers.

"No offense," Kevoian said. "But weren't we meant to meet tonight, at that sad little safe house of yours? Why the change in plan?"

He took the paper and opened it. His fingers left dirty marks on the thick, good-quality paper as he thumbed through the sheets as though he knew what he was looking for. The dense legalese made him frown, but at least he didn't have to mouth the words as he read them.

"That didn't work for Mr. Reynolds," Kelly said. "Your last meeting with him didn't exactly go off smoothly. He thought it would be better to meet at your place of business."

Kevoian laughed, and Kelly felt the sour burn of anger in his stomach. He bit down on the inside of his cheek to stop from saying anything that would push Kevoian into violence. The plan needed a bit more time to work, and he needed to keep his teeth.

"The string bean and the shortass," Kevoian said. He glanced at the man with bruised lips and jerked his head toward Kelly. "The two of them should have a double act, eh, Vic? Fucking jokers trying to intimidate me. Well, Shortass, I've got nothing to worry about. The police aren't going to do shit to me. Never do, never will."

Kelly hooked his thumbs in the pockets of his jeans and grinned at Kevoian.

"You mean Jimmy did," he said. "It was Jimmy who was the big man, right? He was the one with the track record. He was the one who had the cops in his pocket."

A muscle jumped under the unshaven skin of Kevoian's jaw. "So what? Jimmy Graham was this, he was that. Jimmy Graham might have been a whole lot of things. Now he's in the hospital and I've got his business, his wife, and—as soon as she signs this bit of paper—his money. A couple of stacks of green and that cute, bought-off red-haired cop he worked with will be in my pocket. Not his. So what exactly does Reynolds think he's got on me here?"

Kelly shrugged. "Last I heard, Jimmy was out of the hospital," he said. "He's got a few bumps and scrapes, and he's asking a lot of questions about what's going on. And you really think the only hold he had on those cops was money? Anything happens to me or Nadine, and Reynolds will tell Jimmy just who was responsible."

"You think he gives a crap about her?" Kevoian asked with a harsh laugh. He ruffled his hand roughly through Nadine's hair, and his fingers caught in the tangles. "She tried to leave him. Take his kid. You think he's going to give a flying fuck what happens to her now?"

"You tried to kill him," Kelly pointed out. He could feel the sweat itch in the small of his back. "You're going to steal from him. I bet he'll give a crap about that."

Kevoian snorted and looked around to enlist his men's help in scoffing at the idea. "Shortass here thinks I'm scared of Jimmy Graham. What the fuck, right?" He turned back to Kelly with a snarl. "You know what Jimmy Graham was before I met him? Nothing. I was the one with the contacts. I was the one with the business. You think Jimmy Graham is behind all of this? All he brought to the table was something on a few grubby cops and a prison record."

It would have been more convincing without the bluster. Kelly supposed he should have more sympathy. He knew better than most how disorienting it was to deal with the erratic, flash paper moods that took Byron from good humor to red-faced rage and back again.

Clayton had told him to keep Kevoian talking for ten minutes. It felt like he'd already done that. It felt more like half an hour, but he'd lost track of the count in his head.

"Then I guess you don't have anything to worry about," he said.

"And I guess that you're finally right about something, PI Shortass," Kevoian said with a forced laugh. He stalked over and stiff-armed the creased handful of papers against Kelly's chest. "Show her where she's gotta sign. Then we'll see who's scared of Jimmy Graham."

Kelly walked over to Nadine and crouched down next to her. He smoothed the crumpled sheets out roughly, the swipe of his hand smearing the gritty smudges of oil further over the heavy paper and pointed randomly at three blank spots in the text.

"Here, here, and initial here," he said.

Nadine nodded shakily. She flicked back to the beginning and started to read through the dense wall of text, one finger at a time as she marked her way down.

"You don't need to read it," Kevoian snapped. The harsh tone made Nadine jump and lose her place. "Just sign it. Someone give her a pen."

One of the men—not Vic—stepped forward with a well-chewed pen and pressed it into Nadine's stiff fingers. She stared at it for a second as it trembled and then scribbled a test in the empty margins of the paper to get the ink to run.

"James always said I shouldn't sign something without reading it," she said in a tight voice.

Kevoian yelled in frustration as he heard Jimmy's name one too many times. He grabbed an unanchored steering wheel from one of the cars and threw it in Nadine's direction. It missed her by a couple of feet and clattered off a sedan that was up on blocks. When she flinched and dropped the pen, Kelly slung a protective arm and pulled her head down. She smelled sour and faintly metallic as he hugged her close—of sweat and fear and the nervous energy that made her tremble under Kelly's hands.

Somewhere in the building, a fire alarm started to blare, the sound of the siren loud enough to make everyone flinch as it echoed off the high ceilings and bare walls. Kelly breathed a sigh of relief and gently squeezed Nadine's knee.

"It's all right," he muttered in her ear. "We'll get out of this. Harry's safe and sound. No one will get to him."

She grimaced. "Just give him the money," she begged in a breathy whisper. "I don't care what he does to me."

"Just sign the goddamn papers, Nadine," Kevoian yelled, his voice thick and his face red blotched up to his hairline. The anger was authentic. The explosion wasn't. Kevoian had taken a second to decide what to throw, and he'd thrown too wide to really sell that he'd tried to hit them. It was like he'd watched Byron—Jimmy, Kelly supposed—and hadn't quite practiced enough to pull the scene off.

"It'll be okay," Kelly told Nadine. He didn't know if she believed him or not. He supposed she didn't have much choice, but he picked up the pen from the floor and handed it to her. "Here, here, and here," he repeated.

She clutched the pen tightly, her knuckles white, and used her knee as a desk as she scrawled an unsteady, ragged-edged version of her name in the first space. Behind them Kevoian grabbed one of the men by the collar and growled at him to "go kill that fucking alarm."

"Not long now," Kelly told Nadine.

She gave him a worried look as she turned the page and jaggedly scrawled her name again. "Are you sure that Harry's safe?"

How much could you trust the police, Kelly wondered. They had their own motivation for the investigation, and it was to expose Byron, not protect Nadine. But doubts weren't what Nadine needed.

"I'm sure," he lied.

She closed her eyes with sharp relief. The final signature was the steadiest.

The alarm blared, stuttered, and then whined into silence.

"Finally," Kevoian groused. He stuck his finger in his ear and wriggled it as he turned around. "You signed it?"

Nadine mutely handed it over. Kevoian looked at it, grunted with satisfaction, and folded it up to tuck into his shirt. Then his pleased expression soured, and he grabbed Nadine's arm to yank her onto her feet.

"Now all I need you to do take the money out of the bank for me," he said as he shoved her roughly toward Vic. Once she was out of the way, he turned to look down at Kelly. There was something self-satisfied around his mouth when he said, "As for you, I don't need you at all, do I?"

He cocked his fist back and punched down at Kelly's face in a short, angled jab. Kelly caught the fist against his forearm and fell back onto his ass. The jolt of tailbone on concrete ran up to his skull.

"You know, I'm going to enjoy this," Kevoian said as he stepped forward to straddle Kelly's legs. "There's just something I don't like about you."

Someone hammered on the door outside, loudly enough to rattle it in the frame. "Open up!" they barked. "Police."

Apparently Kevoian's men were loyal enough to terrorize a woman and her kid, but not to stick around once the cops turned up. They scattered and ran for the back of the building.

"I probably remind you of my brother," Kelly said. He drew his knee back to his chest and drove his heel up into Kevoian's crotch. The air whooshed out of Kevoian on a pained groan, and the color drained from his face as he hunched over. "Asshole."

Kelly scrambled to his knees and drove a short, vicious uppercut into Kevoian's jaw. He felt the impact jar his knuckles and snap Kevoian's teeth together with the sound of a crack and a spray of blood.

Kevoian's eyes blurred over, and he staggered backward into one of the cars. He tried to catch himself against it but just broke the side mirror off and slid to the ground.

The police hit the door with something, and the wood cracked. Kelly shook the feeling back into his hand and took a step forward.

"Who's the shortass now?" he jibed.

Nadine's voice cut through the noise. "Watch out!"

He had forgotten about Vic. Kelly turned just in time to see Vic drop a hammer and clutch at his neck. Blood poured out around the pen that Nadine had jammed into his throat.

"Bitch," he spluttered indignantly. "Look what the bitch did to me!"

He wrenched the pen out and threw it away. That was a mistake. A gout of fresh red blood poured down his chest, and his eyes rolled back in his head. He went down like a bloody tree.

"Is he...." Nadine wiped bloody hands on her dirty T-shirt with a fastidiousness that looked out of place. She licked her lips, and her voice went small and shocked. "Dead?"

"No," Kelly said.

Not yet.

The temptation to do nothing was far too strong. It wasn't as though it were even all Vic's fault, but Vic would have made an easy scapegoat.

A dead thug, however, would probably be more messy than they needed.

He pulled his T-shirt—his dad's T-shirt—over his head and limped over to Vic's prone, bloody body. How much blood did "too much blood to lose" look like, he wondered as he knelt down next to him. It looked like a lot, but maybe that was just because it was all over the ground. It couldn't be that easy to kill someone. He wadded up the T-shirt and pressed it down hard against Vic's throat.

"Let the police in, Nadine," he said.

She wiped her hands on her T-shirt again and limped over to the cracked blue door.

"I'm going to open the door," she yelled. "Let me open the door."

The hammering stopped for a second, and she stumbled forward to fumble the lock. Then she dragged the door open, and two policemen and three firemen burst into the room.

Messy, Clayton had said, and loud.

CHAPTER TWENTY

KELLY GAVE up his place to a paramedic and let a uniformed cop lead him outside. Kevoian was cuffed and in the back of a police car already, and, from the look of it, most of the men who'd scattered had been caught trying to leave the building.

A news van was already there. Well, when an ex-ADA called the station with a tip, it would be a dumb anchor who didn't at least send one crew to investigate.

"Shit," the cop muttered as he turned Kelly away from the cameras. "Keep your head down."

He gave Kelly a shove toward one of the empty cars.

"Wait. He works with me," Clayton said as he cut across the pockmarked parking lot toward them. He had ash on his hands and dirt on his shirt where he'd crawled through a gap into the warehouse. "I'm the one who called in what I saw."

The cop shifted his body between Kelly and Clayton, one hand pointedly on his gun.

"Sir, I'll need you to step back. Until we've finished our interviews—"

"Let him go." Kelly recognized the voice before Claire pulled the ballistic helmet off. Her red hair was plastered down against her cheeks and curled with sweat. "He's Captain Kelly's son."

The cop glanced dubiously at Kelly. "I thought Cole was taller."

"Captain Kelly has more than one son," Claire said impatiently. "Let him be. He has nothing to do with this. Get back in there and help clear out the factory."

The uniform hesitated—torn between duty and orders—but finally did as he was told.

"Thanks," Kelly said.

He slumped back against the side of the patrol car, the metal hot through his jeans. Clayton brushed a hand over the nape of his neck and then settled on his shoulder.

"Don't thank me yet," Claire said. She raked her bright hair back from her face with her fingers and stuck it behind her ears. Her face was pink with sweat, and there was a line dug into her forehead and over her eyebrows where the visor had rested. She glanced over to where Nadine was being questioned by two other officers. "She says she's Jimmy Graham's wife."

She tried to keep her voice professional, but there was a crack of pain under it.

"You knew him?" Kelly asked.

Claire wiped her forehead on her sleeve and grimaced sourly. She glanced around and said quietly, "I was his go-between with Lepson. Anytime Jimmy needed a message, we'd have a run-in. That's how I got to know Byron. I knew he was separated, but I thought she died. Your mom said that's why he had Maxie."

Kelly hesitated. "You should talk to Byron," he said. "It's his business."

"You should talk to Internal Affairs," Clayton corrected. "It's their business now."

Claire took a deep breath and pressed her lips together in a grim white line. "So, yeah," she muttered as she pulled the visor back down over her forehead. "She's telling the truth. What the hell was he thinking?"

Kelly shrugged. It wasn't the first time that someone had asked him that. He never knew the answer. Most of the time he doubted that Byron had even thought about whatever it was. He just did things and decided what he meant later.

"Do me a favor," Claire said briskly. She snapped the visor in place, her face stern behind the scuffed plastic. "Tell your mother that I won't be able to make the barbecue tomorrow."

She jogged away.

Kelly was pretty sure his mom wasn't going to take his calls anytime soon. He supposed he could pass the message on through Cole. His brother had always been able to turn bad news into something his mother would agree to hear.

"Stop it," Clayton said.

"What?"

Clayton tightened his fingers on the back of Kelly's neck and pulled him in close to press a kiss against his temple. His lips lingered for a second.

"Just this once, don't worry about your family," he said. "They can sort themselves out."

Kelly thought about what that would be like. It felt strange. "Easier said than done," he admitted wearily. Especially now that *family* included Maxie, and his brother's traumatized new—old?—wife. "It's what I've always done."

"It's what I've always tried not to do," Clayton said. He let his hand slide down Kelly's back, from his shoulders to the dip just above his jeans. Then he took it away and stepped back from the car. "Anyhow, I should go and check in with Nadine. She's still my client, unless she's changed her mind."

There was something in the tone of Clayton's voice—a resigned edge to it—that made Kelly look up at him.

"That sounds final," he said.

Clayton brushed his hair back from his face with one hand. "I told you I wasn't anyone's Prince Charming," he said regretfully. "Not even for you. Maybe we could have drawn it out a bit longer before it went wrong—"

"My record is a year," Kelly joked through the stupid ache in his chest. He hadn't put in the time to have earned the right to hurt over this, but it still did. Apparently his heart just wasn't ready to accept reality.

"Not quite that for me," Clayton said. "I'm Nadine's lawyer. You're Byron's brother. There's a conflict of interest there, and now I know it."

"I'm not that fond of Byron right now," Kelly offered without much hope it would work.

"Still."

Still. It would have been easier to argue if Clayton weren't right. They might both want it to work—at least, work a bit longer—but it wouldn't. That had never been in the cards.

Kelly couldn't resist one last mistake, though. He hooked his fingers in Clayton's waistband and pulled him back in for a kiss. There was dust on Clayton's lips and adrenaline sour on Kelly's tongue. The kiss still curled sweetness all the way down into Kelly's thigh with a dully eager ache.

"I still think you're a good man, Clayton," he said against warm lips.

Clayton cupped Kelly's face in his hands. He brushed over the curve of Kelly's lower lip with the soft pads of his thumbs—a brief caress that prickled all the way down his nerves.

"I still think you're wrong," he said. Kelly waited for a kiss, but Clayton seemed to have conquered the need to make bad decisions. "But I hope you find one. You deserve it."

Kelly swallowed the dry itch of regret in his throat and dragged a smile up out of his boots while Clayton stepped back.

"I've had worse breakups," he said. "But the whole dramatic goodbye is going to seem a bit odd next time I'm at the office."

The twist of Clayton's lips acknowledged the truth of that. "I'm sure we can be civilized."

He walked away, and Kelly crossed his fingers and waited for the usual guilty pang of relief. However much he cared about someone, it was usually easier to have broken up than to be breaking up. Besides, it took away one layer of tension between him and his family.

Not this time. This time, as he watched Clayton's knife-lean form walk away, he just felt like shit.

IT TURNED out that when Clayton said "civilized" he meant "avoid each other as much as possible." In the two weeks since they rescued Nadine—or since Nadine rescued Kelly—they'd seen each other three times and spoken once.

Even that had involved Kelly shamelessly taking every excuse to put himself in Clayton's way.

It was pathetic, Kelly thought sourly to himself as he got onto the elevator. He'd always been cheerfully, hopelessly romantic but never pathetic. Or at least he never thought he was.

Not that that realization seemed likely to stop him anytime soon.

Kelly slouched back against the mirrored glass wall of the elevator and watched the floors count up. It stopped once to let an overcaffeinated student—three pens twisted in his hair and a dusty streak on the sleeve of his jacket—push his cart of files onto the car.

The top layer of files wobbled and spilled as he stopped, and Kelly caught them before they hit the ground.

"Sorry," the student said. "Thank you. Are you looking for someone? Representation, I mean."

The eagerness in his voice made Kelly wonder if the young man hoped to recruit his first client between floors.

"No, thanks," Kelly said. He thought of the last few conversations he'd had with his family—accusations of treachery mixed with appeals to his family loyalty, all seasoned with the unspoken reminder that it was all *his* fault—made him grimace. "Not just yet."

The student looked confused, but Kelly got off on the next floor before he had to explain. His feet squeaked on the polished wooden floor as he headed through the office. Half of him scrambled to come up with an excuse to detour past Clayton's office—luckily he'd already used up the best ones on other days, so he had to struggle—but he squashed it and walked on past.

He was there to see Baker. He just *wanted* to see Clayton.

The one person he didn't expect to see was Nadine in Baker's reception, her hair chopped into a pixie bob and her plaster cast a rainbow of Sharpie doodles and names. He hesitated in the doorway, his stomach tight with a mixture of curiosity and guilt.

Not that he'd done anything to her... not directly. On the other hand, since she'd found out who Byron really was, Kelly hadn't done anything to help her either. He knew he should, but... it had just been easier not to. His family was angry enough with him.

"Kelly," Nadine said as she looked up and saw him. She stood up abruptly and then froze uncomfortably in place. "I mean—"

He quickly held up his hand. "Kelly," he said. "That's what everyone calls me."

Nadine nodded. She shifted her weight awkwardly from one foot to the other as she looked down at the paperwork she'd been absorbed in. "I'm sorry," she blurted suddenly. "I didn't know you were going to be here. I know it has to be awkward."

"It isn't," Kelly said. It was entirely true, but he corrected himself. "Or, if it is, it's not your fault."

She smiled tiredly. "That's not what James... Byron... said last time we spoke. Apparently it's all my fault. If only I'd have been a better wife, he could have introduced me to his—to your—family."

There Kelly felt like he was on solid ground. "Byron's never taken responsibility for anything in his life," he said. "I don't think he ever will. How are you?"

"I'm okay," Nadine said. "So's Harry. He wants to meet your family, but I don't know if it's a good idea?"

She didn't put him on the spot with a direct question, but the uncertainty in her voice suggested one. Kelly thought about what would happen if Harry met his family. They would love the boy—as much as they frustrated him, his family weren't monsters—but they'd also pressure him. Or Mom would push at him to forgive his father, to make his mother back down from what she was doing to poor, misunderstood Byron. And everyone would let them.

"Not yet," he said. "They'd mean well, but my mom is the one who taught Byron to dodge responsibility. Once everything with Byron is done and dusted."

She sat down and waited until he gingerly did the same. "Do you think I'm doing the right thing?" she asked. "Mr. Baker says I am—"

"Baker?" Kelly asked.

She nodded. "He's my lawyer now. Clayton said it would be more efficient, since Mr. Baker could handle my divorce and the suit against the LAPD. He's an... odd man, but Harry and the puppy love him. Dogs never liked Byron."

Old habit poked at Kelly to defend his brother. It was what you did for family—made excuses and overlooked warning signs. Kelly was trying to stop that. He just admitted they never did.

It was a careful conversation, one that skirted the edges of anything too raw and skimmed over conflict, but it was a conversation. The ice was broken, and maybe that would make it easier for Kelly to do the right thing next time.

Or now.

"Would you like to meet him?" he asked. "Maxie. I mean, would Harry like to?"

For a moment Nadine looked blank. Then her eyes widened. "You mean the baby?" she said. "Byron's son. The one he wanted."

"The one he had," Kelly corrected.

Nadine frowned for a second and then shook her head. "No. I mean, I don't think so," she said. "It's too much. Maybe if it were just that my husband had another family, but they were his real family. We were.... Not yet."

"It's up to you," Kelly said. "I get that it can't be easy."

She looked like she doubted that, but she nodded. "I'll ask Harry once things are more settled," she said. "If he wants to see Maxie, then we can do that. Just… he's gone through too much for now, I don't want to put any more pressure on him."

"You have my number."

The door to Baker's office opened, and he stepped outside. His eyebrows rose when he saw they were talking. "Mr. Kelly. Do you and Mrs. Kelly need a minute?"

They glanced at each other and mutely acknowledged that they'd run out of things to talk about.

"I think we're done," Kelly said. He stood up and extended his hand to Nadine. She shook it clumsily, wrong-handed by her cast. "If you need anything, call me."

"I will," Nadine said. She smiled faintly. "I trust you."

He left her to her paperwork and followed Baker into the office.

"Are you sure about this?" Baker asked as Kelly closed the door. He sat down behind his long, glossy black desk and steepled his fingers under his chin. "It won't be easy."

Kelly knew that. It was nothing new. It was never easy to do the right thing—to go against the peacemaking flow with his family—but sometimes, when you couldn't see any other option, you just had to do it.

"I'm sure."

It was six hours later that someone knocked on Kelly's door. He had a pretty good idea of who it was, but he couldn't quite let go of the hope it might be Clayton. That would make him loitering around Clayton's office a bit less sad, a bit more hopeful. He put the paintbrush down, wiped purple on his jeans, and headed down the hall to answer the door.

It was Jim, with a beer and a scowl. Kelly wasn't sure which of the two had annoyed him.

"Dad?"

"What the hell are you doing?"

"Someone has to do it," Kelly said. "You know what Byron is like—he isn't up to parenting a child. You'd never even let him have a dog."

"He's not your son."

Kelly shrugged. "I love him. He needs me. Who else is going to do it?"

It was the sort of answer that usually made Jim bristle and bluster. Tonight it just made him slump, as though heavy weights had suddenly settled over his shoulders.

"I don't know," Jim said tiredly. "It should be me. Byron's my son, my responsibility, but your mom…. She thinks if she loves Byron enough, he'll become someone worth loving."

"I know. Do you want to come in?" Kelly asked. He stepped back from the door and waved a hand at the living-room door. "I've not got a car to work on, but you can help me paint the wall."

In his entire life, even when he'd been in the hospital and everyone was crying, Kelly had never seen his dad cry. He didn't want to see it either. For an instant, as Jim pressed his lips together and took a deep breath through his nose, he thought he was about to. Instead Jim shoved the cans into Kelly's chest and strode past him into the main room.

It turned out that Kelly had done it wrong. He wasn't sure how, but when he went upstairs to give Maxie his dinner, Jim started to paint over what he'd already done.

"Your granddad was a painter," Jim said after a while, as he crouched to drag the paintbrush along the taped-off skirting. "Well, painted, decorated, did odd jobs. Did I ever tell you that?"

"No," Kelly said. He slapped paint over the square foot of wall he'd been directed to work on. "You never talked about my granddad on your side much."

"That's because he was a bastard." Jim straightened up with a wince. He braced his knuckles in the small of his back and stretched until something popped loudly enough for Kelly to hear. "He looked a bit like Byron. Had a temper like Byron too when he had a skinful. I always wondered if maybe I was too hard on Byron because of that. If I wasn't being fair."

"Did Byron ever do anything bad?" Kelly asked. It was a question he'd wondered for a long time, ever since he realized how often they'd moved before they settled in LA, how Byron always started with his new doctor before the rest of them even had a new school. As a little kid, he always wondered why his pediatrician didn't need to see him once a week, and why they didn't have puppets. "Anything really bad."

"Other than what he did to you?" Jim asked. He didn't look around at Kelly, just at the wall as he stepped back and ran his eye along where he'd cut in.

"You knew?" Kelly asked. He supposed he should be angry. Or something. It was just too much of a surprise to feel anything past that.

That Jim didn't know, that he couldn't know, had always just been something he assumed was true.

"Yes. No. Not really," Jim said. "Your friend Clayton... your boyfriend... he told me, but I wasn't surprised when he did. So I suppose, on some level, I always suspected it."

He put the paint down and picked at the paint on the back of his hands. Kelly still didn't know what he should feel. He never expected to hear Jim had called someone, anyone, his boyfriend.

"I don't think he meant to blind me," Kelly said. It was too unprecedented a conversation to avoid the lure of old habits. "Just hurt me."

Jim winced. "That's not any better."

"No, I suppose not," Kelly admitted. "I just don't know what to say."

Jim sat down on the couch and dangled his paint-splattered hands between his knees. "Me neither," he said. His shoulders rose and fell as he sighed deeply. "I spent my whole life proud of one thing—that I was a better dad than your grandad was. None of my kids ever went cold or hungry. They never wanted for new clothes. Yet I never stopped this. I let your mom convince me that the doctors were all wrong, that Byron was just hyperactive or something or... anything but what the doctors wanted to say he was. I let Cole spend his life covering for Byron. I told you that you should hide who you are to stop gossip, instead of just telling the gossips to shut up. All my life I was so proud of myself, and I failed you all. I failed Maxie. I failed that little boy I might never get to meet."

"Harry."

Jim nodded and rubbed his hand over the back of his neck. "I was so scared that I wouldn't be able to protect you from things, I just ignored them instead of at least *trying* to protect you."

"What does that mean?" Kelly asked.

"It means that you shouldn't have to raise your brother's son, but I'm proud that you stepped up to do it. It means... that if anyone says anything when you bring Clayton to the next barbecue, I'll flatten them." Jim looked up at Kelly with an almost-pleading expression. "It means that I should have done better, but I can't fix that. All I can do is try and do better in the future."

Kelly swallowed hard.

"Dad, could you mind Maxie for the night?" he asked.

Jim looked as though that weren't quite the response he'd hoped for. "Why?"

"I need to do something."

"Something you just remembered?"

Kelly scratched at his jaw and picked a lump of paint from the stubble. "Something I just worked out," he said. "Look, I don't know if what you just said changes anything. I didn't even know I was mad at you until recently. So, I don't know. If you want to do better, though, I need to do this."

After a puzzled second, Jim shook his head and spread his hands helplessly. "I suppose," he said. "If it's important."

Kelly considered that for a moment. "It is, and I didn't want to admit that... any more than you wanted to deal with Byron. So I guess we're both doing the right thing tonight."

CLAYTON OPENED the door to his apartment with a tumbler of whiskey in one hand and silk trousers low around his hips. He looked surprised to see Kelly on his doorstep, although it was hard to tell whether it was a good or a bad surprise.

"I want to marry you," Kelly blurted out. He'd worked out a whole speech on the way over. It hadn't been eloquent, but it had been clear. He thought it explained his feelings pretty well. But it had dissolved like cotton candy, and the only words he could find were insane. "I want to go to France on our honeymoon. I want you to worry about me getting hurt at work and not understand when I worry that some mad ex is going to try and kill you. And you should be careful, because we might have kids. I don't really know that, not yet. I'm going to adopt Maxie, but it won't be easy. I want it, though. And you. I want you."

He only stopped because he ran out of breath.

"What?" Clayton said.

Kelly rubbed his hands over his face and shoved them up into his hair. His fingers caught in the dense mat of it.

"There's more," he said. "First, do you have someone else with you? That would be really awkward right now."

Clayton stepped back and let the door swing open. He invited Kelly in with a slightly sloppy wave of the glass of whiskey.

"I might not be a romantic," Clayton rasped as Kelly walked past him. "But it still hurts to end something."

"So why end it?" Kelly asked.

"Because I told you—"

"You're no one's Prince Charming," Kelly interrupted. He stalked across the apartment, too full of nervous energy to stay still. It was all caffeine and bluster, enough to keep him just ahead of the urge to play it safe and chicken out. The apartment was good for pacing, all long stretches of wood with no baby toys or unfinished DIY to get in the way. "Well, maybe that's good. I've spent my whole life on the heels of a fairy-tale romance. I've been swept off my feet. I've been promised the moon and stars. None of it was real. It felt real at the time, maybe we both wanted it to be real, but there's no 'The End' when it's real."

Clayton laughed. It caught between sardonic and wistful—not convinced but willing to admit it wished it was.

"You think this is real?" he asked as he went over and sprawled out on the leather couch. He took a sullen gulp of whiskey, and Kelly wondered if he knew how beautiful he looked, all pale hair and cream skin against the dark grain of the leather. "That if we got married after fucking twice, that's real?"

It would have been easy to laugh and back out—to call it a joke and blame it on the drink he hadn't had. Except his dad's example had gotten him that far. It had literally never helped to just try and ignore something you knew was true.

Kelly crawled onto the couch and straddled Clayton's lean thighs. His knees dug into the cushions, buried his fingers in Clayton's loose, product-free curls, and tugged his head back until the line of his freshly shaven neck was taut and kissable. Fresh aftershave had a sharp burn against Kelly's jaw as he kissed his way from collarbone to the corner of his mouth.

"I don't know what this is," he admitted against Clayton's soft lips. "All I know is what I want it be, that I want it be okay to want that. Maybe the marriage thing is crazy, but... I don't mean tomorrow. Or even next year. I just don't see why it couldn't happen one day."

"What if I don't want to."

Kelly kissed him—deeply, sweetly, eagerly. It might well be the last time ever did, and if it was the end, he wanted something better to remember it by than their tepid, cautious public kiss under the eyes of the cops.

"Then this is even more awkward than if you had someone else in here," Kelly said with a nervous laugh. "Then I'm the romantic idiot you always said I was. If I'm not, though, if we could do this, then *you're* the idiot if you don't try."

Clayton snorted and ran his hands up Kelly's thigh to cup his ass. "I don't believe that love will last, Kelly," he said. "Every relationship I've ever had ended. Every relationship I've ever seen ended."

"Me too." Kelly reached down between their bodies and cupped Clayton's cock. It was heavy and thick through the silk. He rubbed his thumb along the length of it, from the tight base to the wet smear at the head. Lust wasn't a commitment to anything, but it wasn't indifference either. Clayton swore softly and tilted his head back against the couch as Kelly nuzzled his throat. "I still want to try. I mean, every happy couple out there had a string of failed relationships before they met the right person. And even if we're one of the relationships that fail, I still want that. I want that much of you."

"Why?" Clayton asked.

"Because…." Kelly hesitated. He could wrap it up. He could talk about it as some future aspiration. Except he intended to be honest. "I think I'm in love with you. No, I am. Maybe it won't last forever—I'm not sure it will—but right now? I love you, and I want it to stick."

Clayton snarled with a sharp, angry sound and twisted under Kelly. His narrow hips ground against Kelly's erection and sent a sharp jolt of overstimulation that left him breathless and boneless. Clayton took advantage of Kelly's distraction to tumble them off the low couch and onto the floor. He wrapped his fingers around Kelly's wrists and pinned him down.

"You can't do that," he said, his voice rough and almost desperate. He stripped Kelly's T-shirt off as he talked, his hands and his body and his cock convinced how real it was, even if his brain had balked. Clayton kissed a bruise under Kelly's collarbone. It was a rough possessive kiss with tongue and teeth. "You can't just… you can't just say you love me, for fuck's sake. It's not fair, Kelly."

The jeans took a minute more to get out of—a crumpled packet of lube dragged out of his pocket—and kick away as his sneakers tangled up in the legs.

"I do, though," Kelly said cockily. "I love you. Maybe it's stupid, but it's mine, and you can't stop me."

Clayton kissed him. The force of it made Kelly's jaw ache as Clayton tried to absorb him before he had to break for real.

"I don't want to stop you," Clayton groaned finally. He rested his forehead against Kelly's and closed his eyes, his jaw tight as he struggled for control. "I just don't think I can do this. I couldn't let you go if you loved me."

"My name's Shelley."

It was the first time that Kelly had willingly said that out loud since he was four. Clayton stared at him, nonplussed by either the shift in topic or the terrible name.

"Shelley Kelly?" He didn't quite laugh, but something wicked danced in his eyes as he took the lube from Kelly and ripped it open. Pale gel slicked his fingers as he roughly squeezed it out. "You're lying."

Kelly whimpered and lifted his hips off the ground as Clayton pushed his long fingers inside him. The chill of the gel flushed expectant heat through his body and tightened his cock. It pressed hard and eager against his body.

"I wish I were," he panted raggedly. He gripped Clayton's shoulders and tried to make sense. "I've never told that to anyone I slept with. Some of them knew, some of them found out. You're the only one I've ever actually told, because I wanted you to have that. I want you to know I love you. You don't have to love me back. You don't even have to try."

Clayton snorted and hooked his arms under Kelly's thighs to lift them up. His cock pressed against Kelly with a blunt pressure that made him squirm for more as Clayton dragged a hard kiss across his mouth.

"You're an idiot," he said as he rolled his hips forward. The hot thickness of him filled Kelly with a hard, impatient thrust. "I already love you. I loved you first."

They made love on the floor—wet and messy and eager. Kelly's ass stuck to the polished wood, and Clayton caught his elbow on the edge of the couch. It wasn't perfect. It wasn't a fairy tale. But it was definitely real.

Kelly groaned against Clayton's shoulder as each thrust pulsed hunger and pleasure through him. It caught in the electric tangle of embarrassment and nerves that had driven him that far and knotted in and around him until he felt like he couldn't breathe. He reached down and wrapped his hand around his cock. The pace of his strokes was quick and eager, a race to the finish line.

This time.

Next time, maybe they'd go slowly.

He came first, the wet pulse of pleasure squeezed into the heart of his hand. Clayton caught his wrist and pulled his arm so he could kiss sticky fingers and a wet palm. He licked come off his lips and came with a rough thrust that buried him so deeply in Kelly that it almost hurt.

They sprawled on top of each other. Kelly felt loose and spent, a warm, pleasant feeling that filled him from ears to midthigh. All the frenetic energy that had powered his desperate, over-the-top confession was gone.

Without it, he felt a bit self-conscious and a lot stupid.

Still in love, just embarrassed.

"I hate France," Clayton murmured as he finally pulled out of Kelly and sprawled out on the floor next to him. "I'd rather go to Hawaii."

"France has culture," Kelly said. "I only picked it because I thought you'd like it."

Clayton kissed him. It was sticky and metallic—there was come and whiskey on his breath. "I know. You'd love Hawaii, and if we wait until Maxie is old enough, so will he." He shuddered and laughed as he buried his face in Kelly's hair. "I was going to let you go. I didn't want to come between you and your family. I know how much you love them. But if we do this… I don't know if I can let go of you loving me."

Kelly laughed and tucked himself along the length of Clayton's body. He didn't fit at all, but it still felt perfect.

"So don't let go," he said. "And I knew there was a romantic under there somewhere."

Clayton snorted skeptically against his shoulder.

EPILOGUE

THE SOUND of his phone as it rattled to life… somewhere… jolted Clayton awake. He rolled over, cotton sheets tangled around his legs, and stretched out in the bed until his fingers touched the headboard and his toes brushed wood. A glance at the clock showed the minute hand just shy of five o'clock.

"Hell," he muttered. No one ever called about anything good at five in the morning.

He carefully untangled the sheets from his legs and crawled out of bed. His phone was in a tangle of silk, cotton, and denim they'd discarded on the floor the night before. He plucked it out and swiped to answer.

"Yeah?" he said.

He turned back to the bed to check that Kelly was asleep. He was flat on his stomach, the line of his back distracting, and the taut curve of his ass hard to resist.

"Is it too early?" Nadine asked.

"I'm up," Clayton said. He switched the phone from one ear to the other and dragged himself away from the bed. It was too tempting to think he could roll Kelly over to kiss his throat, down his chest to the taut bud of his nipple, and Nadine wouldn't realize. He picked his way carefully down the hall, along the memorized route of safe, unsqueaky boards. "Is this about the case?"

"Not the case," Nadine said. She sighed down the phone and admitted, "It's a favor. I know it's a lot to ask. You guys are just married and barely home, but…."

She paused. *Aw shit.*

Clayton nudged open the door to the nursery and went in to check on Max. The toddler lay on his back and blew wet spit bubbles as he snored gently. Clayton reached into the cot and brushed dark curls out of Max's face. He looked older than three, all long, gangly limbs and thick, sun-roughened hair.

"What is it?" he asked. He mentally juggled his schedule for the day to see if he could fit her in if he needed to. The meeting with Declan Tate hung by a thread—unless Declan came up with something convincing, Clayton was going to refuse to represent him. The man had been bad enough on the other side of the table, and he'd given his lawyer a gray streak. He waited for Nadine to answer.

"Can Harry come and stay the weekend?" she asked. "He wants to see Max, and his grandpa has promised to show him how to change a tire."

So Declan got to get rejected in person, after all.

"That should be fine," he said. "I'll check with Kelly in the morning."

"Thanks," Nadine said. "Sorry for calling so late. I've been doing so many late nights I think I've lost track of time completely. Congratulations again, by the way."

She hung up.

"Check with me about what?" Kelly asked. He wrapped his arms around Clayton's waist from behind and kissed his shoulder. "Should I be worried?"

"Just Nadine," Clayton said. "Go back to bed."

"How about come back to bed?" Kelly suggested.

Clayton laughed and let Kelly pull him out of the room and down the hall. He should get some sleep. It would be a busy day at the firm tomorrow, even if he hadn't had to slot in another consultation, and he needed to be sharp. He was the youngest partner now, and he had a lot to prove. First, though, he wanted to prove to himself that it was all still real.

As they fell onto the bed in a tangle of long limbs and fingers, reality tasted like his come in Kelly's mouth and felt like a too-short, too-muscular man who was still the hottest thing Clayton had ever seen.

TA MOORE genuinely believed that she was a Cabbage Patch Kid when she was a small child. That was the start of a lifelong attachment to the weird and fantastic. These days she lives in a market town on the Northern Irish coast and her friends have a rule that she can only send them three weird and disturbing links a month—although she still holds that a DIY penis bifurcation guide is interesting, not disturbing. She believes that adding 'in space!' to anything makes it at least 40 percent cooler, will try to pet pretty much any animal she meets—this includes snakes, excludes bugs—and once lied to her friend that she had climbed all the way up to Tintagel Castle in Cornwall, when actually she'd only gotten to the beach, realized it was really high, and chickened out.

She aspires to be a cynical misanthrope but is unfortunately held back by a sunny disposition and an inability to be mean to strangers. If TA Moore is mean to you, that means you're friends now.

Website: www.nevertobetold.co.uk
Facebook: www.facebook.com/TA.Moores
Twitter: @tammy_moore

BONE
TO PICK

TA MOORE

Cloister Witte is a man with a dark past and a cute dog. He's happy to talk about the dog all day, but after growing up in the shadow of a missing brother, a deadbeat dad, and a criminal stepfather, he'd rather leave the past back in Montana. These days he's a K-9 officer in the San Diego County Sheriff's Department and pays a tithe to his ghosts by doing what no one was able to do for his brother—find the missing and bring them home.

He's good at solving difficult mysteries. The dog is even better.

This time the missing person is a ten-year-old boy who walked into the woods in the middle of the night and didn't come back. With the antagonistic help of distractingly handsome FBI agent Javi Merlo, it quickly becomes clear that Drew Hartley didn't run away. He was taken, and the evidence implies he's not the kidnapper's first victim. As the search intensifies, old grudges and tragedies are pulled into the light of day. But with each clue they uncover, it looks less and less likely that Drew will be found alive.

www.dreamspinnerpress.com

LIAR, LIAR

TA MOORE

Just another day at the office.

For some people that means spreadsheets, and for others it's stitching endless hems. For Jacob Archer a day at the office is stealing proprietary information from a bioengineering firm for a paranoid software billionaire. He's a liar and a thief, parlaying a glib tongue and a facile conscience into a lucrative career. He just has one rule—never get involved with a mark.

Well, had one rule. To be fair, though, Simon Ramsey is dark, dangerous, and has shoulders like a Greek statue. Besides, it's not as though Jacob's even really stealing from Simon… just his boss and his brother-in-law. Simon didn't buy that excuse either after he caught Jacob breaking into the company's computer network.

That would have been that—one messy breakup, one ticket to Bali booked—but it turns out that the stolen information is worth more than Jacob thought. With his life—and his ribs—threatened, Jacob needs Simon to help him out. Or maybe he just needs Simon.

www.dreamspinnerpress.com

Wanted -
BAD BOYFRIEND
WANTED
REAL ESTATE
BUSINESS
CAREERS
TA MOORE

His mother. His best friend. The barmaid at the local pub. Everyone is determined to find Nathan Moffatt a boyfriend. It's the last thing Nathan wants. After spending every day making sure his clients experience nothing but romantic magic, the Granshire Hotel's wedding organiser just wants to go home, binge watch crime dramas, and eat pizza in his underwear.

Unfortunately, no one believes him, and he's stuck with lectures about dying alone. Then inspiration strikes. He needs the people in his life to want him to stay single as much as he does. He needs a bad boyfriend.

There's only one man for the job.

Flynn Delaney is used to people on the island of Ceremony thinking the worst of him. But he isn't sure he wants the dubious honor of worst boyfriend on the entire island. On the other hand, if he plays along, he gets to hang out with the gorgeous Nathan and piss off the owners of the Granshire Hotel. It's a win-win.

There's only one problem—Flynn's actually quite a good boyfriend, and now Nathan's wondering if getting off the sofa occasionally is really the worst thing in the world.

www.dreamspinnerpress.com

TA MOORE

DOG DAYS

A Wolf Winter Novel

The world ends not with a bang, but with a downpour. Tornadoes spin through the heart of London, New York cooks in a heat wave that melts tarmac, and Russia freezes under an ever-thickening layer of permafrost. People rally at first—organizing aid drops and evacuating populations—but the weather is only getting worse.

In Durham, mild-mannered academic Danny Fennick has battened down to sit out the storm. He grew up in the Scottish Highlands, so he's seen harsh winters before. Besides, he has an advantage. He's a werewolf. Or, to be precise, a weredog. Less impressive, but still useful.

Except the other werewolves don't believe this is any ordinary winter, and they're coming down over the Wall to mark their new territory. Including Danny's ex, Jack—the Crown Prince Pup of the Numitor's pack—and the prince's brother, who wants to kill him.

A wolf winter isn't white. It's red as blood.

www.dreamspinnerpress.com

TA MOORE

STONE THE CROWS

Sequel to *Dog Days*
A Wolf Winter Novel

When the Winter arrives, the Wolves will come down over the walls and eat little boys in their beds.

Doctor Nicholas Blake might still be afraid of the dark, but the monsters his grandmother tormented him with as a child aren't real.

Or so he thought…until the sea freezes, the country grinds to a halt under the snow, and he finds a half-dead man bleeding out while a dead woman watches. Now his nightmares impinge on his waking life, and the only one who knows what's going on is his unexpected patient.

For Gregor it's simple. The treacherous prophets mutilated him and stole his brother Jack, and he's going to kill them for it. Without his wolf, it might be difficult, but he'll be damned if anyone else gets to kill Jack—even if he has to enlist the help of his distractingly attractive, but very human, doctor.

Except maybe the prophets want something worse than death, and maybe Nick is less human than Gregor believes. As the dead gather and the old stories come true, the two men will need each other if they're going to rescue Jack and stop the prophets' plan to loose something more terrible than the wolf winter.